I0555541

The Storm Knight III: Howling Winds

by Zachary Watson

1

For more information, address: z.watson.author@gmail.com.

Website: https://zachwatsonauthor.com/

Edited by Dana Morck, John Watson, Jordan Perona, & Samantha Watson

Cover Art by Ed Bourelle

ISBN 979-8-9860285-7-6 (Kindle ebook)
ISBN 979-8-9860285-8-3 (Paperback)

For my family, friends, and everyone who told me I could do this.

Semper Victoria

Other Stories by Zach Watson

The Knights of the Compact

The Lost Knight
Awakening
Fealty
Ronin
Huntsman
Vengeance
Einherjar

The Storm Knight
Dark Skies
Falling Mist
Howling Winds

Warblades of Saerda Novellas
The Amethyst Blade

Other Stories in the Knights of the Compact Universe

Welcome to Nowhere by Keven Karaki

Glossary of Terms

Ark Fleet; An unified collection of Kelthi and Humans descended from refugees after the loss of their homeworlds. Usually operating in isolated flotillas across the Near Reaches, the Ark Fleet relies on a mixture of temporary colonies, the strip mining of dead worlds, and piracy in order to sustain itself.

Caranat; Literally meaning 'The Language', Caranat is the primary spoken word of the Trahcon people and the Empire in particular.

Humanity; The newest addition to the Empire after Earth was conquered roughly a century in the past. Not particularly well regarded by most other species, they are increasingly being forced off of Earth and scattered across various colonial regions. An Imperial Human's term of conscription begins at the age of 15 Imperial (roughly 17 Terran), and lasts until they're 27 (roughly 30 Terran).

Imperial Intelligence; While its official main purpose is espionage and counter-espionage against foreign powers, the sheer size of the Empire ensures that most of its agents are dedicated to internal security and investigations.

Index; The record of an Imperial Citizen's life, used to determine both military promotions as well as to evaluate their progress through the technocratic civilian government.

Naule; A four armed, simian species counted among the five Humanoid races. Universally covered by long strands of hair, their small interstellar nations were overwhelmed and conquered by the Empire several centuries ago.

Sorcery; A range of telekinetic and pyrokinetic abilities focused on manipulating the same sub-reality that allows for FTL travel. Organized as 'spells', the difficulties in learning the more complicated spells ensures few Trahcon learn more than basics in the modern era.

Trahcon; The founding species of the Empire, and the only Humanoid species naturally capable of manipulating energy without cybernetic enhancement. On average shorter than Humans, they have uniformly gray skin but extremely bright eyes. Unique in possessing a nearly three to one gender imbalance between females to males, and for having a five century long lifespan.

5

Prologue
Rerth'riah

Date: Day 19, Month 15, 2163 Imperial
Location: Trinity Base Seven, Trinity Fortress, Near Reaches

Some things were inevitable in this universe. You couldn't escape them, couldn't alter them. Even trying to do so only begged for higher powers to push back, to punish you for making the attempt.

All things died, in the end. No one would ever truly understand the mechanics of hyperspace. Citizens of the Empire paid their taxes, willingly or not. The Homeworld would be an eternally storm-wrecked mess of a planet.

And Ashe'lori would always have the worst luck of any soul in existence.

"Two hours, Jet." I growled into my comms, tapping an impatient foot as the lift brought me back towards ground level. Hands tugged at the dress uniform I'd worn for my now aborted meeting with the Void Lord. "We left her alone for two hours and she found a way to start a riot."

My Naulian packmate chuckled without humor, his low voice replying, *"Closer to an hour and a half."*

I clenched my jaw, not in the mood for his brand of humor. "Is local security on site already?"

"They're cordoning off the area now." He replied.

"Good." I said, "Are you still with Holde? I doubt this is a targeted event, but I'm not making any presumptions given how our enemy has acted so far."

"I'm with him, no one's attempted to breach his room yet. Doctors have already put the floor on lock-down until the situation in the restaurant is resolved." His shrug was audible. *"We're secure with no signs of trouble on the horizon."*

I rolled my neck and shoulders, flexing my tarah a little to try and

6

ease the strain. A single glance let me see the lift numbers still falling.

"Remain there until I contact you again. I'm nearly to the ground. As soon as I get a hold of her we're returning to orbit."

"*Got it, boss.*" Jet acknowledged, closing the channel a moment later.

I was grateful for that. It let me curse under my breath without him hearing. Without anyone hearing.

Ashe was a wonderful, adorable packmate. She was earnest, kind, determined, curious... every trait I appreciated in a person. Even her constant discomfort with her own species tended to be more cute than annoying.

That being said, her luck was so abysmally bad I was increasingly convinced she really was cursed by Kahsh. Only that spectacularly vindictive Aspect could be responsible for the disasters she constantly stumbled into.

Today's stumble was a particularly egregious one, yanking me out of a direct report to one of the eight Void Lords, The confused reports that had come in, of a riot at a hospital of all places, had been enough to make him more curiously amused than angry, but it still was a potential black mark on our pack's collective Index.

"Ashahn's blood." I kept tapping my foot, growling at nothing. "Your explanation had better be a good one, Ashe."

The lift's chime on reaching ground level was far too cheerful for my current mood. I nearly threw a Strike at it out of sheer annoyance, only barely getting my not-inconsiderable temper under control before I could start smashing things to pieces with sorcery.

Stalking out into the open, I got my legs moving in a quick jog. Seeing an Intelligence Agent moving at speed got most of the local crowd clearing space, letting me make good time back to the building I'd left my packmates in.

Thankfully it was a short distance to begin with. Between that and my pace, it didn't take me long to get there. Or to run into far too few men and women in Security uniforms trying to enforce order on far too many people who seemed much more interested in beating one another senseless with whatever they could grab.

"Shift Leader!" My shout was lost in the chaos, the noise only getting worse when two women started hurling sorcery at each other with snarls on their faces. "Shift Leader!"

When my third shout brought no officer to tell me what in the Aspect's Holy Names was going on, I finished losing my temper.

The sound of my Thunderer booming out three rounds into the side of the building made everything go blessedly silent, several dozen stunned pairs of eyes all snapping around to find me pointing the heavy pistol at the mass of them.

"I," I shouted, tarah lifted in anger, "am Imperial Agent Rerth'riah! You will *all* keep your bloody mouths shut and line up for inspection and processing! Now!"

A few in the crowd, mostly those in the uniforms of junior officers, started to awkwardly straighten up. The rest mostly glared at me, at least until the Security officials got themselves free and began drawing their own sidearms.

The mob's mood slowly crashed onto the shore that was our bared firearms.

I let my gaze slide over the crowd as it broke apart, members obeying my orders. Now that they were spreading out I saw the reason for the vitriol; nearly half of the customers had the black-and-starfield uniforms of the Void Fleet, while most of the rest were in the dark blue of the Imperial Navy.

Even as they separated, they lined up next to their comrades, reserving their glares for those in the other lines rather than the people with guns. More than a few had to be helped by their companions. Even my cursory look made me think there were at least seven broken arms, two broken legs, and several men and women clutching badly bruised tarah.

The attendant hospital would be busy tonight, all because of inter-service stupidity. Provided that my initial theory was correct, and that Ashe hadn't been involved.

I would have hope... but managed hope. I knew better than to trust my first theory, especially when she was involved.

More security forces began arriving around then, all of them looking

8

relieved to find things already lashed to the docks. They spread out, some directing foot traffic away from the building, while others began to check on the most obviously wounded.

"Ashe!" I barked when my first pass didn't reveal my tall packmate. "Rifle-Experienced Ashe'lori! Out in front, now!"

She did not emerge.

I frowned, doing a second sweep, and tried a different set of names. "Pack Thun!"

No one stepped up.

"Pack Thun!" I snapped more loudly. "Conscripts, before me! Now!"

A woman in a Navy uniform, the rank insignia of a Deck Commander on her shoulder, glanced behind her, then waved me forward. "Agent! I've got a few conscripts back here, all unconscious!"

My boots clicked on the floor as I moved forward, holstering my gun now that things were calming down. Walking between the lines, I found the first of them right behind the Navy's formation.

I recognized her; the most blatant flirt of them. An impatient gesture had the line move back, letting me kneel down beside her.

"Conscript Uru'thun." I said, checking her throat. Her hearts were beating... but they were beating slowly. Dangerously slowly. "Medical team! Now! I need the rest of the conscripts found!"

Given a task, the lines of men and women found them fairly quickly; they were all on the ground, motionless.

All but one.

Ashe wasn't on the floor.

My pace quickened, hearts starting to thrum as fear crept its way into my mental ocean. I shoved it aside, as any good officer should, and instead focused on what was in front of me.

Uru'thun hadn't been touched by the brawl. Her gray skin had no bruises, her uniform was unblemished. The restaurant was too suffused with the smell of spilled booze to tell me how much she'd been drinking, but I couldn't imagine she'd drunk herself into collapsing so quickly. Not in less than two hours.

"Medics!" A man called. "Where are we needed?"

"Here!" I waved them over. "Send for more as well! There's at least seven more, possibly eight of them. All down and unconscious."

I was pushed back as two medics focused on the first Conscript I'd found, murmuring in low tones as they inspected her. One drew blood from her arm, quickly pushing the resulting vial into a scanner.

"...Thennet-Five." He reported to me. "That's an extremely strong tranquilizer... Ashahn's blood, she was drinking something strong on top of that. We need to get her into a care unit immediately."

Clenching my jaw, I waved for them to get her out of there. They did, barking for still arriving security officers to assist with the others.

I did a second count as they were hauled out, confirming that not a single one of them was Human. Another wave of fear crested a bit higher inside of my soul.

"You!' I snapped at the officer who'd pointed me to the conscript. "Where's the Human who was with them?"

The other woman shrank a little at my tone, "Uh... brown skin, dark fur?"

When I nodded, she rolled a shoulder in a tiny shrug. "I remember seeing her drinking at a table with that one, but that was the last I saw her before some Voider hit me."

My tarah twitched sharply, the muscles tugging at my cheeks. When I spoke again it was with my voice raised, directing it to everyone still waiting to be processed by the authorities. "I am looking for the Human who was here with the Conscripts! Who remembers seeing her last?"

Men and women glanced at one another, then a young man in a bartender's uniform raised a hand. "I saw her going for the bathroom, with that first girl they just took out I think. Their third was trying to order more

10

drinks from me when he just... fell over."

I was up and in front of the employee at once, abusing my height to loom over him. "How many drinks did they have?"

"J-just one each, Agent." His hands shook, "Uh, their bill should still be in the system."

"And you made their drinks/" I demanded.

His head shook at once. "N-no, I just do the orders. Gera did them, she handled all of the drinks tonight."

"Where is she?"

"She's..." He turned, blinking, then turned the other way. "I... I don't see her."

"...staff members!" I barked, making him jump. "Who last saw the one named Gera?"

An older Guide stepped up from where she'd been in line with the Void Fleet Officers. Her tarah were starting to droop with age, but she stood straight when she nodded to me. "She went on break a few minutes before it all started, Agent. Said she needed to relieve herself."

A woman in Security armor stepped up before I could order it, "I'll check, sir!"

I jerked my head, and she ran for the bathrooms, clearly excited to be in an actual investigation for once. The others began quietly processing the rank badges of everyone still inside, registering them for the fines and potential judicial appointments that would come soon enough.

"No one!" My newest assistant reported when she returned. "It's entirely empty. No other ways in or out, sir."

My packmate was missing. Fear rose, creeping ever closer to my chin.

Swearing under my breath, I jammed my fingers down on my wrist-comp. A few quick flicks got me connected once more, "Jet! Ashe is missing. I need all of the security camera footage for the hospital's exterior, and I need it now."

11

Jet had been my packmate long enough to know when he needed to shut up and obey. *"On it, five minutes."*

"Faster." I snapped, cutting the line and changing to another. "This is Agent Rerth'riah! I have a priority three situation!"

"Intelligence Dispatch." A woman replied at once. *"Priority three, go ahead."*

"I have eight poisoned conscripts, one missing, presumed abducted. I need a full security sweep of East Hospital and the nearest starport."

"Confirmed poisoned?"

"Medics confirmed, Thennet-Five, probably mixed into their drinks. No other victims, the bartender who mixed the drinks is absent."

"Confirmed, Dispatch is authorizing an emergency sweep. Additional Agents are on the way. Do you require combat assets?"

I didn't hesitate. "Yes. Full coverage for the Hospital, and I'll need holding cells for at least fifty witnesses."

Everyone nearby grimaced, shifting their weight in discomfort or irritation, but none of them was stupid enough to complain.

"Combat teams alerted and prepared for prisoner transfer. Dispatch will contact you with further information."

"Agent out." I muttered, ending that call.

Fear ascended, threatening to spill out of control. Reminded me that I had yet to ever pay Ashe the debt that I owed her. That I had never made up for the foolish mistakes I had made, mistakes that had hurt her soul in a way I didn't know would ever heal.

I spun on a heel, stalking to the next staff member I could get to. He didn't know anything.

Neither did the next.

Or the one after that.

12

My-wrist comp chimed to alert me I had a new file transfer. A glance proved it to be from Jet, and I opened it without hesitation.

A clear video feed opened, letting me see the entrance to the restaurant I was standing within. People were already pushing and shoving in the background, punches were striking home, sorcery being used to hurl furniture at one another. The staff manning the door moved in, arms waving, trying to calm things down... and two figures emerged from the chaos, helping a woozy third between them.

Ashe was stumbling, shaking, clearly holding none of her weight on her own feet.

Two Trahcon in Navy uniforms carried her, their movements swift and purposeful.

That was all I could tell, because their faces had been blurred out.

And five long strides from the door, the feed cut, flickered, and then changed to a calm scene of people coming and going from a completely peaceful building.

Jet had sent a message with it.

They reset all of the other cameras at that time. It was deliberate, leaving that section of them pulling her out. They wanted us to know. They must have hacked and manipulated that feed nearly in real time, boss.

They had her. I didn't even know who they were. A shadowy cabal of Trahcon supremacists that we'd been chasing halfway across the Reaches. People with access to resources far beyond what they should have had. Informants and members in places they should not have had them. People whose plans we'd ended, despite the fact that I only had the most limited theories of what those plans may have been.

We'd clearly done enough.

We'd angered them.

And they'd taken my packmate.

They'd taken her.

13

"Dispatch.... confirmed abduction. Shut down all spaceports." My voice sounded thin, far away. "Terrorists have seized a member of Imperial Intelligence."

Dispatch hesitated, "*Starport closure requires Void Lord approval.*"

"Then get it!" Something tore in my throat at my shout. "They have my packmate!"

"*Confirmed! Sending priority request now!*"

Please, Ashahn, Aspect of Dreams and Storms... do not take her from me like this. Not like this.

Not like this.

I
Ashe'lori

You're supposed to stay calm when you're captured. That was really the only lesson I remembered on the subject.

There'd been more, of course. What I should try to do, not do, what to say, what rights I had under the rules of the Compact. There'd been several days worth of that kind of dry material during my early training as a Conscript.

I hadn't paid much attention, to be honest. I'd never seriously thought I'd be sent to a combat zone to begin with, never mind actually run the risk of being captured. I'd been far more invested in memorizing other things. Like what I was allowed and not allowed to do during my free time.

Staying calm though... that bit I remembered.

It was easier than it should have been. Mostly because I felt too miserable to panic, and I ached too much to let the fear take control of me.

My stomach was that painful mixture of churning and empty. A feeling not at all helped by how badly my head was pounding, or by how dry my mouth was. There was a deep ache in my back that told me that I'd been sleeping with terrible posture, and my neck wasn't feeling much better.

I couldn't stop myself from groaning in pain, or stop from wincing at how much that quiet sound hurt my throat.

"Du bist wach!" A woman practically shouted into my ear. "Gott sei Dank!"

Flinching from the noise let me feel the cold tiles below my cheek. They contrasted with the warm touch of skin on my jaw. Someone gently cupped my face, fingers trailing up to rub just below my eyes.

I didn't quite get why they were doing that until I tried to open them only to find them practically sealed shut with crust and grime.

"Vorsichtig. Langsam."

"...don't understand you." I muttered before trying once again. I got them open a little, and promptly flinched from the bright light above me.

"Caranat? Scheisse." There was a long pause before she tried again. "Sprechen sie Englisch?"

That didn't clarify anything for me, though I thought I recognized the name of one of the Human languages in there. "...I only speak Caranat."

"Was?"

Swallowing, I forced my eyes to open one more time. It took a few more pained blinks, but I finally managed to get a proper look.

A pale skinned Human woman was kneeling beside me, hovering over me. Her black fur was cut raggedly short, exposing her ears. Pale green eyes were staring down at me with worry, though the fading bruise covering her right cheek made the expression look pained.

She was wearing a bright green shirt and pants, both of which were far too large for her. A quick glance down at my own limbs revealed that I was wearing the same outfit. It didn't fit me any better than it did her.

"...prison uniforms." I mumbled.

"Ich verstehe nicht. Sprechen sie Spanisch? Französisch?"

Looking past her, I saw exactly what I feared; a heavy security door. Some kind of armored glass was set in the top third of it, probably to let any guards easily see inside.

Another groan came as I pushed myself up a little, my new companion gently wrapping an arm around my shoulders to help.

The rest of the cell wasn't much to look at. It was a rectangle, probably... five yards deep by three or so wide. If I was being very generous, at least. It was probably smaller than that. There were no beds, no cots. Just the relatively soft tiles I was sitting on

Well, that and what looked like a small hole in the floor in the back

16

corner. I could guess the purpose of that one easily enough.

"Windows in the walls..." Another groan as I got myself into a kneeling position, bracing myself in preparation for standing. "...faucet on the back wall. Water. I hope it's not drugged."

"...ich verstehe nicht."

I met her eyes, staring blankly at her.

She stared right back at me, lips turned down a little.

Ashahn's blood. Communication was going to be a problem if we were stuck in here for a while.

No. I had to focus. Being able to speak with my cellmate could wait. I had to... stay calm, then ensure I had shelter, water, and food. That was the next thing to concentrate on.

I closed my eyes, focusing on my hearing. My too-quick breathing, my cellmate's quiet shifting of her weight. There was a fan somewhere above us, circulating the air. More distantly... a deep rumble that I'd almost reflexively tuned out.

A ship's engines. We were in a ship that was underway.

My heart clenched somewhere inside me, a bit of panic rising to the surface. If we were in a ship, a moving ship, then... then the odds of Rerth rescuing me were decreasing every minute it traveled farther from Trinity.

Focus. I had to focus. I was in a ship, so I had shelter. That left water and food. Water being the biggest priority, especially with how dry my throat felt.

"Water?"

My cellmate kept staring at me, expression becoming a little more annoyed.

"...right. Uh..." Shaking my head, I got one of my hands up to mime drinking something.

"Wasser."

17

Licking my lips, I repeated the word. She nodded once, then gave my shoulders a little tug.

Actually standing up wasn't nearly as bad as I thought it would be. I was a little dizzy, but I'd felt worse just from a night out at a bar. Or even after a couple of nights alone with too many drinks if I was being honest with myself.

I still felt terrible in general, but I didn't have problems letting her guide me over to the little faucet.

There wasn't a straw or tube attached. It was, quite literally, just a tiny pipe that started spewing out cold water the moment she pushed the small button next to it. Drinking from it without splashing it everywhere was practically impossible.

It must have run on a timer. By the time I figured out how to avoid getting sprayed, I only managed about three decent gulps before it abruptly cut off. Enough for now, but not a good sign of how we were going to be treated in the future.

After that... after that I stumbled around the cell, trying to see if there was anything I'd missed in my first look.

The answer was a hard no.

I had a decent view into the cells on either side thanks to the windows. Both held a pair of Humans just like ours, though everyone else was apparently trying to sleep... or maybe they were still drugged.

"Assuming they were drugged at all. They could have been..." I bit down on my lip, exhaling sharply to cut off the rambling. My hands were starting to shake as well. Bad signs. Very bad signs.

A few more steps brought me to the cell door. The armored glass let me see a plain hallway, another cell across from us, and more stretching out in both directions.

Everything was a nearly uniform gray, the lights were dull, and apart from that there was... absolutely nothing at all to look at.

There was nothing.

I was trapped in a tiny cell. I had no tools, weapons, assets. My only company was a woman who I couldn't understand, and who couldn't understand me in return.

I had no idea where I was. Where this ship was taking me. Not a clue as how long I'd been unconscious. If they'd done anything to me while I was out.

Inhaling sharply, I focused on that last fear. I could at least try to figure that one out. A necessary distraction.

I started with my hands, holding them up and checking them over. My brown skin looked as healthy as it ever did. No marks. No bumps. I could flex each finger just fine. Good. My arms were next, which was a problem with the long sleeves of the shirt.

My cellmate's skin reddened considerably when I yanked it off. She whipped around so quickly I thought she nearly fell, keeping her back to me while muttering nonstop under her breath.

"Well that's weird." I muttered in return, focusing on my forearms first. "No cuts, or new scars... I can bend them just fine. No obvious bumps or insertions. Probably didn't keep us under with drugs then."

Nothing on my upper arms, shoulders, or chest either. My breasts felt the same, no lumps or objects in them. A few quick flexes made me think I hadn't lost any muscle mass either, so I definitely hadn't been unconscious for weeks or months.

Stripping my pants off didn't reveal anything on my legs or feet, and I pulled them back on to try and help the other Human calm down a little. That just left my head and my back. The first one I could do on my own; gentle touching didn't reveal anything besides my scars on my face, nothing at all my neck, and the fact that my shoulder-length fur needed a wash.

I doubted I'd be getting one anytime soon. That was going to be... unpleasant.

Still, with that done, there was only my back left.

"I need you to... right. This is going to be awkward." I blew out a breath, eyeing her. Up close and upright she proved to be quite a bit shorter than me, her eyes level with my shoulder. It was hard to tell with the baggy clothing, but I didn't think she had much muscle or fat on her frame.

A longer term prisoner, maybe? Had they been so good they could store prisoners on Trinity, right under our noses? Or had she been some kind of refugee, arriving on Trinity only to get abducted before she could be helped?

Ugh. I could leave those paranoid considerations for later. I'd probably have the time.

"So... how do I mime this?"

Tapping her shoulder had her glance over, see that I was still topless, and quickly jerk her head back around. "Nein! Du bist nackt!"

"What is it with other Humans?" I groaned in frustration. "All right, let's see if my naked back is too much to handle as well."

Getting turned around after a moment, I reached back and tapped her shoulder again. Then a few more times as insistently as I could.

It took several more tries before she risked another glance, blinking when she realized I was only baring my back. That was apparently fine, because she turned slightly and finally met my gaze.

Humans. Ugh. So weird.

"Right, um..." I brought a hand up to point at my eyes, then tried to indicate my back. When she merely frowned I repeated the gesture, then held my left arm up.

She kept frowning as I tried to pretend like I was making an incision on my arm with an invisible knife. After a moment she shook her head, clearly not getting it, so I tried a different approach.

I did the same look-at-my-back thing, but when I held my arm up I grabbed my skin, then tried to act like I was peeling it back. Then I pretended to push something inside, then pull the skin closed again.

Her frown deepened, but her own hand rose to gently trail a finger along my skin. She paused, pulled her finger back, then jammed it down once. She followed that by carefully acting like she was pinching my skin along the same line she touched.

".,.cutting, inserting, suturing." I muttered, thinking that I got it. "Yes!"

When I nodded, and gestured sharply at my back again, she gave me a hesitant smile and stepped directly behind me.

Finger tips began gently poking and prodding. I closed my eyes, exhaling as I waited for her to finish. She went up and down my spine, checked my ribs, then my neck and shoulders.

The sharp poke on the back of my left shoulder was worrying even before she began feeling all around that area.

"...Ashahn's blood." I closed my eyes when I felt her tap that spot three times in a clear message. "Dammit."

I turned around to find her already standing with her back to me, her own shirt coming up and off.

"Bitte?"

"I don't know if that means, 'Me too', 'look', or 'please'." I said, though I still stepped closer to look over her pale skin.

My first thought was that I'd been right; she was extremely slender. Not quite bad enough that I could count all of her ribs or the bumps on her spine, but she looked like she was only a couple of skipped meals away from that point.

I started on the same shoulder she'd found mine, and within a few seconds my fingers found something rigid on her shoulder-blade. A perfect circle under what might have been a faded red line.

It was too large to be a simple tracking device. They could have, probably had, inserted something far smaller for that job. Something we couldn't easily feel or find.

An object that big was meant to be found. Meant for us to know it was there. Explosives, maybe? Or something to release drugs into our system. Or electrocute us.

21

The options were as endless as they were unpleasant.

My fingers tapped there three times, just as she had.

"Scheisse."

"Hope that's a curse." I muttered, stepping back so that she could fix her shirt. After a moment I sighed and grabbed my own, pulling the baggy thing back on.

Then I... was back to having nothing to do. Nothing to focus on.

Nothing beyond the fact that I had no idea where I was. Where we were going. Where Rerth was. Where Hold was. Where Jet was. Safe on Trinity? Chasing after this ship even as I stood here?

I had no idea... had no idea how... *if* they could find me...

"Johanna."

I blinked, turning to properly face my cellmate again. "I'm sorry?"

Her pale throat worked as she swallowed, one hand rising to her chest. "Johanna. Ich bin Johanna."

Oh.

"Ashe." I mimicked her motion, "My name is Ashe. Uh, ich... bin Ashe."

Lips tugged in a smile, then she tried to mimic my words. "My... nahm is.. Johanna."

A bit more miming later, and we were sitting down, repeating phrases to each other until the louder rumble of a ship entering FTL made us both go quiet and still.

That... was it then. Unless Rerth knew what ship I was on, unless she had a tracking beacon on it...

She'd managed that before. Quickly isolating and tracking the people who'd tried to beat me to death in the hotel. Leading us to Nueva Genova. She'd done it once. She could have done it again.

I had to believe that, because if I didn't...

If I didn't... it was a big galaxy. Most of it unexplored. They could be taking us anywhere, and she would have no way of ever finding me.

Johanna sniffled, tears welling up in her eyes. She'd probably been doing the same math as me. Knew that, unless someone had already acted, we were lost. Doomed to whatever fate our captors felt like visiting upon us.

Aspects save us.

She started crying first. I pulled her against me, hugging her as my own cheeks became wet.

We wept together until sleep took us.

II

The people who had taken me had called me a beast, and it seemed that they'd meant it.

My lips parted in disgust, staring down at the... gruel was the only word that seemed close to describe the nauseating slop in front of me. It was more of a gray sludge than anything else. No meat, no vegetables, just... gray slime.

An automation had delivered it through a small hatch in the door, the machine sliding two trays through before lumbering on to the next cell.

Trays. We had trays, and no utensils to eat with.

I looked over to Johanna to find her giving me a helpless shrug. She sat down, carefully bringing a corner of her tray up to her lips. A gentle angle had the slop slowly, painfully slowly, slide down into her mouth.

"...Ashahn's blood." I seriously debated not eating at all, but a cramp in my belly told me that I'd have to try it sooner or later. "...fine."

I imitated her, sitting down and getting the tray settled in front of my face. The sludge smelt vaguely like oats, which wasn't exactly appetizing, but at least it smelled like food. It could have been worse.

Bracing myself, I slowly angled it up and back, letting the first mouthful slide in.

It... wasn't good. It didn't make me want to throw it back up, but that was the extent of my praise. The consistency was awful, and it tasted like it smelled. I felt like I was eating food meant for a beast of burden on a primitive backwater.

Choking it down, I forced myself to keep going. I managed to get about two thirds of it into my stomach before I couldn't do it any more, doing my best not to spill any of it when I lowered the tray.

Johanna had already finished hers. She hadn't gone so far as to lick the tray or scoop it up with her fingers, but she'd clearly eaten as much as she could without going that far.

"Here." I pushed what was left of mine over to her. "Yours."

She gave me an almost shy smile, taking it, "Danke."

"You're welcome." I guessed at the word before pushing myself to my feet, stretching out my back and arms. Leaving her to the leftovers from my tray, I padded over to check on our neighbors.

The people on our right were eating as well, both of the women inside completely ignoring my inquisitive glance through the window. The same wasn't true for the two men on the other side. One of them was still finishing his own 'food', but the other was leaning against the back wall, and glanced up at me when my face appeared in the glass.

Taking a gamble, I gave him a hesitant wave through the window. When he didn't react, I tried calling through it. "Can you hear me?"

He was pale, like Johanna, but his hair was a dusty brown instead of black. He also shared the same look of half-starvation as her; his slightly gaunt features making me think he'd lost a good bit of weight recently.

At my words he turned a little, nodding once.

"And you understand me?" I asked.

"Unfortunately." His voice was quiet, but audible. The window must have been thin, or maybe filled with micro-perforations for airflow. "Not a fan of speaking Gray, but I've got nothing else to do. Name's Michael. Yours?"

"Ashe." I bit my lip, taking a guess based on his slur. "Ark Fleet?"

"Yeah, mining colony." He replied before asking, "Empire or Cathia for you?"

"Empire. They took me from Trinity, I think that's where we just left."

He grunted. "Figures the Impies wouldn't even notice a ship full of Human prisoners. Arrogant gray bastards."

A spark of anger drew a glare from me, which he completely ignored. Instead he went on to give me a few details, "Whoever has us wiped out our

25

colony. Killed all the Kelthi living with us, even after we surrendered. The rest of us got drugs in our rations. Woke in these pens when they wore off."

"How long ago?" I asked.

His shoulder went up and down in that Human way of shrugging. "Hard to say. They dumped you in here three meals ago, but that's about as well as we can track time."

That made me frown. "Can't you just correlate meals to days?"

I think he snorted, from how his nose flexed, but I didn't actually hear it. "They're too smart for that. They vary up how long it is between meals. Sometimes we get three in what feels like a day, sometimes we get two. They don't ever turn off the lights either. Makes it practically impossible to keep track of time."

Well. Damn.

"How'd they get you?" He asked when I fell silent.

"...I was celebrating with friends in a bar. They drugged us all, just like you." I turned a little, leaning a shoulder on the wall. That let me see my cellmate finishing off her second meal. "I think they shot me up with something else just to make sure when I didn't have enough to drink."

Another of the odd shrugs. "Probably. Johanna spent most of yesterday trying to wake you up, but you didn't budge."

I perked up at that. "You can speak her language?"

"We're from the same colony. Of course I do." He shook his head, "I'm not going to be a translator for you. You want to communicate with her? Learn a proper language. And be quick about it."

"I..." I stopped myself from complaining. "...guess I don't have anything else to do."

His smile didn't reach his eyes. "That's the spirit."

"Do you mind if I ask you about the people who attacked your colony?"

26

That non-smile faded at once. "I mind, and I don't think it really matters. We haven't seen a living soul since they shut us in these cells. Just the automations bringing food and hauling out the odd corpse."

I couldn't stop a little flinch. "Corpse?"

"Not all of the people they put in cells together got along." He replied grimly. "Even if you do, it's still real easy to get on each other's nerves in here. No way to escape, no way to get some time alone."

His own cellmate proved that by tossing his tray aside, growling something that didn't sound pleased. Michael waved a hand at him, then ended our conversation.

"He doesn't want to hear any more words in gray. Try again tomorrow."

By his own words, how would I even know when it was tomorrow? I half considered asking that, but some instinct had me hold the question in.

He pushed off from the wall, walking past the window to sit down next to the other man. I watched for a minute longer as they started talking quietly in their own language, then forced myself to walk away as well.

Johanna watched as I checked the other window to find the two women glaring at me when I glanced through.

"Verpiss dich, Schwein." The shorter of the two snapped before I could try to ask if they could understand me as well.

I had no idea what that meant, but the insulting tone was enough to make me back off.

Left with nothing else to do, I walked back to Johanna and let myself sink down to the floor. She gave me a sympathetic look, turning a little so that we were facing each other.

"Speak?" She asked.

"Sprechen." I replied tiredly. I really wasn't in the mood for more language lessons, but... the other Human had been right. There wasn't anything else to do in here. I'd hoped he'd be able to give me a little bit of information. Something, *anything*, that might help me make sense of what

27

was going on here.

Just why they'd taken us, and what our fate might be.

"Essen?" Johanna mimed putting something into her mouth and chewing.

"Eating."

I don't know how long we spent in our second language session. Miming requests for words worked for some things, but we started to feel our lack of good examples pretty fast.

Learning each other's words for clothes or body parts was pretty easy. Same for food, water, floor, walls, stuff like that.

More complicated concepts were... well, more complicated. It took us a while to figure out 'please' and 'thank you' for example. She'd kept miming something that looked like vaguely like a religious gesture, thoroughly confusing us both until she'd tried to use it in a broken sentence.

That little breakthrough led to us simply inserting what few words we'd memorized into our own language, and relying on context.

It sounded incredibly stupid at times... well, most of the time. I'd have been embarrassed in any other circumstance. But in here? Well, it passed the time, and helped us make progress.

We took a break when the automations came back with our next meals. My encroaching depression wasn't helped by the fact that it was the same gruel as before, and once again I wasn't able to finish it.

Johanna did, though she didn't look any more enamored of the sludge. The pair of us slid our trays through the tiny flap in the door when we were done.

After that 'meal' I was done for the day. I didn't actually know if the corner was more comfortable than any other place in the cell, but it seemed like the best place to lay down. Johanna followed my lead, settling down with her back to mine.

And that pretty much set our routine.

I would wake up first, and do what limited exercises and stretches that I could in the confined space. Johanna would mimic me if we'd had three meals recently, or would try to keep sleeping if we hadn't.

After that we practiced our numbers by keeping track of how many meals we'd had; it was the only way to track time that we had.

Michael continued to refuse to answer any questions about our captors. Instead he'd allow me one language clarification every meal or so. His cellmate, who had the name of Wolfgang, started contributing once in a while as well.

Mostly to tell me how loathsome of a language Caranat was, but he still helped Johanna figure out past tense. I think because he was bored, and tired of not being involved in our conversations with Michael.

Meals passed. Time passed.

Our fur grew longer. Our routine expanded, the two of us sitting down and using our fingers to untangle each other's after we slept. I finally got her to stop being so weird about clothing so that we could use some water from the faucet to wash our clothes.

Michael and Wolfgang didn't help with that; both got too interested in the view through the window, their comments annoying us to the point where we both sat out of their view while we waited for our shirts and pants to dry.

Someone in a different cell came up with a game where you added a single sentence to a story, then passed it along to the next cell in line. I could barely follow any of it, but it made Johanna break down in laughter. That was really the only bright moment in those first... weeks? Months?

It had to be months.

I saw my first body at sixty-five meals. A tiny woman had been strangled by her cellmate. The automations hauled the limp body down the hall, followed closely by the kicking and screaming form of her murderer.

They never brought her back.

By one hundred meals I realized that I was as lean and gaunt as everyone else. My exercise regimen sank to the depths, replaced by the light stretching I actually had the energy for. I kept clinging to that routine, to our

29

language lessons.

To my silent prayers that Rerth was somewhere behind us. Chasing us. Coming in the *Posa'vilt* to rescue me. To free everyone on board.

We were one hundred and fifty-five meals into my stay aboard when the monotony finally broke.

When our captors found a new way to torture us.

III

Muffled shouting made me snap awake, shoving myself into a crouch as I looked around wildly.

Well, as I *tried* to look around. As I blinked rapidly, a tide of panic rising inside of my chest when I realized that I... that I couldn't *see* anything.

They'd turned the lights off.

Ashahn's blood.

"Ashe!" Johanna's gasp from the other side of the cell told me she was awake as well. She sounded breathy, but not totally panicked. Calm enough to remember that 'today' was a Caranat day. "Light!"

"I know!" I called back, "Stay there, I'm coming over!"

"Stay!" She repeated the part she'd actually understood. "I stay!"

Good. Feeling around me didn't reveal anything besides the usual soft panels of the floor and wall. I forced myself to take deep breaths, staying calm as I pictured just where I was in the cell.

I'd been sleeping in my back corner, near Michael and Wolfgang's cell. If I went straight across to my cellmate's corner there was every chance I'd shove my foot into the hole for our waste. That sounded like a great way to break my ankle and be thrown out an airlock, or else be stuck with a foot covered in something unpleasant until the lights came back.

I'd need to work my way around that.

"Stand up." I whispered, suiting action to word. "Back to wall. Follow it to the front. Then straight across. Pause at the door, see if I can see anything. Then to the wall. Then right until I find Johanna."

Turning slowly, I kept my shoulder pressed against the wall before I took slow, careful strides with one arm held out in front of me. I stopped the moment it touched the front wall, turned, then slowly walked until I felt the cold metal of the door instead of the cushions of the wall.

31

I felt around until my fingertips found the window. I got as close to it as I could, trying to see any glimmer of light...

Nothing. No emergency lights. No running markers on an automation. Just more perfect darkness.

A tiny wave of anger swept around, breaking through some of the panic and fear. They finally broke the monotony we'd been suffering through by doing this? Making us panic and suffer even more? Bastards...

"They call us beasts. Torture us with fire for fun." I murmured, shaking my head. I really shouldn't have been surprised. "Now they torture us with the night."

Biting my lip, I turned my head and pressed an ear to the window. I was hoping to hear any sounds of movement. Voices speaking Caranat. Distant alarms if the ship was damaged.

All it did was let me hear the cursing and shouting from my fellow prisoners a bit better.

Damn. It had been worth a try, I supposed.

Turning away from the sightless dark, I resumed walking until I got to the next wall. A quick turn, and I was heading for where I'd last seen Johanna. I slowed my pace a lot on that last wall, shuffling far more slowly to make sure I didn't step on her. Or kick her.

She must have gotten up to a crouch like I had, because a searching hand grabbed my hip when I got close enough.

Reaching down, I found her fingers with mine, her grip tight. I quickly got back down, kneeling beside her as we used our free hands to figure out where the other was actually sitting. After a bit of awkward fumbling we managed to sit side by side, shoulders touching, fingers still entwined.

"It's dark outside too." I told her. "I couldn't hear anything. Just people shouting."

"People... afraid." She replied. "I afraid am."

32

"I am afraid." I corrected.

"I am afraid." Johanna amended, giving my hand a gentle squeeze. "Danke."

"Bitte."

"Automations feed us in dark?" She asked.

I grimaced at the very thought. "I hope not."

"I hope not." She echoed. "Mess."

"Very messy." I agreed. "Do you need to relieve yourself?"

"Nein. Ashe?"

"Nein." Thank the Aspects for that. It had been unpleasant enough, having to do that into just a hole in the floor, it would be even more so without the lights on to see exactly where the stupid hole even was. "Did you sleep all right?"

"Yes. You?"

"Not especially." I admitted. "It's getting worse."

Her weight leaned into me a little more, her fingers tightening in another little show of support. "I am sorry."

"It's not your fault." It was the confinement. The plain walls. The disgusting food. Even the distant hum of the FTL engines had stopped being something I could take comfort in, instead just becoming another thing I was utterly sick of hearing.

It was the unrelenting boredom of having nothing to do besides stretch, practice a language, and sleep.

It had gotten to the point where I'd considered trying to flirt with Johanna, just to break up the monotony. I wasn't especially attracted to her, but it would have been something else to do once in a while.

That had lasted until the relay of messages between the cells had informed us that someone at the far end of the block had started raping their cellmate to pass the time. Ida had broken her usual reticence about speaking Caranat to make sure I knew it wasn't consensual.

Sex had rather lost its appeal after that.

"It's my day to tell a story. Do you want me to?" I asked.

She shifted around a little, until I felt the side of her head resting against mine. "Yes. Good one. Not... Aspects."

"No religion." I agreed, thinking on what I could tell her instead.

I'd already told her about most of my prior packs. Prior assignments. How much she'd actually understood, I really wasn't sure. I certainly hadn't followed very much of her stories about her own past... or maybe they'd been about the Ark Fleet in general.

We'd probably made a mistake in telling those tales when we didn't have a firm grasp of each other's languages yet.

I wasn't really in the mood to repeat one of the tales I'd already shared, so... history then. I knew a few decent stories there.

"Torlah Madel'nixte'honsha was the greatest leader of the Empire." I began, "She led us during the final battles of the Airalon wars. Most historians love her for helping win that war, for reforming the Imperial government, creating the Void Fleets, and a dozen other serious things. Everyone else loves her for being a Huntress at heart."

"When the other leaders refused to show up for a Great Conclave that she was hosting, she had all of the ambassadors thrown out. The only one who did show up was the leader of the Vekki, the Enlightened One. She took him to the Homeworld, to talk to him about how she feared the First Compact was failing."

I smiled into the dark, remembering the first time my teachers had told us these stories. "She thought he would want to hide away in the old palaces. To talk seriously. Instead he dragged her out into the streets, demanded to know where every bar and tavern was in the capital. And so began the Three Months. For seventy-seven days the leaders of two nations did nothing but race from bar to bar, drinking, singing, acting like wild children rather than leaders."

34

A quiet laugh came out. "Even when the hurricanes crashed against the shore they didn't stop. Just used sorcery to keep themselves dry as they crossed streets, raised glasses. As they talked politics with the people who'd never seen their Torlah in person. Who'd never seen a Vekki before. She laughed in the faces of Elders who tried to berate her for acting like a child."

"It's said that it was during that trip that Nixte'honsha determined what needed to be done within both the Empire and the Compact. That she decided on the reforms that would make the modern state." My head shook a little, tangling our fur a little. "More importantly, after that she started making routine trips out into the cities of the Homeworld and the Capital. On every world she visited she ran through practice drills with conscript packs, then took them drinking. Learned what kind of reforms that the lower ranks actually wanted, needed."

I wasn't sure how much of the story Johanna was actually following, but she seemed to be doing better than the last time. "Nixte'honsha... what happened?"

A sad little sigh. "She was assassinated by the Union of Tribes, the Ovoolur. That started the First Compact War, and ended the great peace that followed the defeat of the Airalon. The day of her death is a huge holiday in the Empire."

"Holiday... sad holiday?"

"No." I chuckled. "Well, yes. But we remember her by trying to recreate her seventy-seven days in seven hours. Everyone who can, who's off duty or not busy, gets incredibly drunk, running from bar to bar."

Her giggle told me she grasped that much. "Big Empire has drinking holiday?"

"Drinking is very serious business in the Empire." I told her. "It gets even more so when an Enlightened One visits. They say that each one tries to make one trip to the Homeworld during their reign, to keep the alliance between our peoples."

"More drinking?" She guessed.

"Drinking is serious business in the Empire, but it's an art to the Vekki." I said.

35

"You holiday story?"

I had a few of those too. How Huvu and her pack had dragged me out on that day, all of us sprinting from bar to bar in the city we'd been garrisoned in. Trying to get one drink from every single tavern in the city. How six other packs had realized our game, and tried to do the same. The sheer revelry and laughter that filled the air.

Johanna's weight slowly shifted, and I realized she'd fallen back asleep about halfway through the story.

I still finished it, only letting my head fully rest against hers once I was done remembering better times. By then the shouting and calls between the other cells had tapered off. Everyone quieting as they got used to the lights being off.

Sleep was a fitful thing. Twice I jerked awake when someone yelled in the distance, drawing irritated shouts from others who were trying to sleep as well.

I finally woke with a painfully full bladder. Gently getting myself free from Johanna, I shushed her mumbled protest and helped her lay down before crawling away.

Finding the hole in the floor took longer than I'd have liked. Getting myself properly aligned wasn't any more pleasant, even if I felt a bit better in the aftermath.

A quiet voice from a window drew my attention just as I got my pants settled in place again. "Ashe? Johanna?"

"Michael." I called back. "What is it?"

"Automations were through. Food's here." He said.

"Thanks. Any news from the relay?" I asked.

"Nothing." He replied. "Better check with the girls past you, but everyone's still present this way. Annoyed, but present."

I nodded, belatedly realized he couldn't see me, and spoke instead. "I will."

Getting up carefully, I padded back over to where I'd left my cellmate. Doing my best to avoid stepping on her, I found the window in that wall and brought my lips close to the glass.

That time I spoke in my fractured Deutsch. They'd ignore me otherwise. "Emma? Ida? Are you awake?"

"...am now." Ida replied sullenly. "What is it?"

"Food." I said. "Michael says here."

"...thanks. Everyone alive?"

"Think so." I hesitated, then asked. "Check other side?"

"Ja, ja. After food."

"Danke." I eased back, "Johanna?"

My cellmate's groan was audible. "I heard. Help?"

Between us we managed to crawl over toward the door, eventually finding our trays in their usual place beside it. Eating the sludge in the darkness wasn't any more fun than eating in the light. I felt myself spill it on my shirt at least twice, and from Johanna's quiet swearing she'd done the same.

"I clean shirts." She offered when we finished. "And relieve me. Stay?"

"I'll stay here." I promised, taking her tray with only a bit of fumbling. Putting them down beside me, I stripped off my wet shirt and passed that over. "Thank you."

"Welcome."

I heard her cautiously padding away, tuning out everything she had to do. Focusing on getting the trays back through the door took up plenty of my time, and left me with plenty of residual 'food' on my fingers.

A hundred meals ago I'd have washed it off. In that moment I licked it off my fingers instead. It wasn't any less humiliating, but I knew I needed the fuel with how little we were being fed. Plus, well, at least the darkness hid what I was doing.

Wiping my damp hands on my pants when I was done, I'd just sat back down when a glimmer of light jerked my eyes up... and my entire body clenched in fear.

Two red orbs were hovering in the window of the door.

Two eyes were staring down at me.

"A-Ashe?" Johanna's voice shook from behind me. "See?"

"...yeah." I swallowed, unable to look away. "I see."

Those eyes blinked once... and then vanished as if they'd never been.

We didn't exercise or tell more stories after that. Johanna frantically finished cleaning, then we both moved to lurk in the corner nearest the door, where we'd be out of sight of whatever was out there.

I don't know if that was the right thing to do or not.

All I knew is that the lights came back on three meals later.

And a message quickly ran down our side of the cell-block; the two men who'd occupied the one at the far end were missing...

And their cell was filled with blood.

IV

Our captors deigned to give us a new routine in the aftermath of that first dark-cycle.

Every twenty meals the lights would go out for another four, and when they came back on a cell would be empty. Worse, they made sure that everyone remaining saw the eyes moving up and down the hall. Made sure all of us knew that we were being judged, and that to be found wanting was to be...

Well. Whatever was happening in perfect silence in those cells found empty.

It began affecting everyone immediately. The few little games of passing messages and stories along had stopped. Talking between the cells had similarly come to an almost complete stop. Michael and Wolfgang had been ignoring us for the last five meals, and Emma and Ida has stopped responding to even Johanna three dark cycles ago.

That left us with nothing to do but talk in circles, speaking only rarely about our pasts, trying to drag those stories as much as we could.

"Kelthi have eyes like that." Johanna murmured after the meal after the fifth dark cycle. "They glow just like that. I liked those eyes, when I was a little girl. Seeing them made me feel safe."

I shook my head, slowly stretching my arms above my head. "What would Kelthi or Xenthans be doing helping Trahcon supremacists?"

We were each speaking our own language by that point. Trusting the other would understand enough of what was being said to follow along. It made it easier, and... well, quite frankly neither one of us was doing all that well mentally.

No one was, by then.

"Besides," I went on, "Michael said our captors killed all of the Kelthi with you. I don't think they'd work with people who did that."

"True." She admitted. "Unless they weren't told what happened. Or they're true-born Xenthans."

"Maybe..." It didn't sound right though. "I still think it's just more automations with lights set up as eyes."

Johanna pursed her lips before nodding slowly, "That would explain some of it."

By which she meant the complete lack of communication with our captors.

Based on my math, I'd been aboard for two hundred and fifty-five meals. My rough guess, which Johanna agreed with, was that we were getting five meals spread across two days. On average, eat least.

I didn't have much to base that on, besides the quantity of the food we were getting and the fact that we were obviously still alive. We were thin, sure, but we all still had some muscles. It wasn't a starvation diet. Not yet, at least.

Using those numbers, that told me I'd been aboard for a hundred and two standard days, give or take a week.

Four months.

I'd been trapped in this cell for four months.

"No supremacist I've ever met has been able to resist gloating." I muttered, "Throwing dirty water in my face for my inferiority. There's no way they could have held off for four months. This ship has *got* to be entirely automated."

Johanna let her head fall back, her wild mane of dark fur cushioning it against the wall. "I think I agree with you, Ashe, but so what? We can't beg an automation to open our cell and look the other way."

"I have to figure this out." I said.

"Why?"

"Because it's the only thing keeping me sane right now." I bit my lip, taking a deep breath through my nose. "Am I bothering you?"

"I... yes, but no." She let out her own frustrated breath. "You are but you shouldn't be. It's getting to me."

Yeah. She'd been here at least a month longer than me. Pretty sure everyone else had been as well.

I did my best to reassure her. "It can't last forever. We've been at FTL for four months. I doubt we're in a Void-Ship, and I've never heard of any other kind of ships that can last this long without refueling. We just have to hold on a little longer."

Johanna seemed ready to argue anyway... then deflated tiredly. "I... yeah. All right. Wash my hair? Talk all you want while you do it."

I nodded an easy agreement, and we migrated to the back of our cell. She got settled again, kneeling on the floor next to the water faucet. I waited for her to wave for me to get started, then tapped the button.

She braced herself the moment before the icy water splashed over her scalp. I quickly reached over, getting my own hands wet, running them up to make sure the front was cleaned as well.

"Fifteen cells on each side of this hallway." I spoke as I worked, trying to rub as much of the oil and grime out of her hair as I could while the water ran. "That's sixty people to start with. That's a lot of food and water to keep us alive this long."

"...not much food." She countered.

"True." They could probably store a whole lot of that gray sludge, but it had to have a high water content too. That meant a lot of mass. "Still takes up space and weight, and I don't think we're the only cell-block on this ship. It would be too wasteful to just have thirty cells."

The water sputtered to a stop, and Johanna quickly scooted away from the wet spot on the floor. I followed, kneeling behind her to really get to work untangling the fur.

Hers was still far shorter than mine was, but it still needed more attention than we could really give it.

"Unless we really are in some kind of Void-Ship, there shouldn't be

41

much fuel left. Maybe a few more weeks at the most." I gently pulled a few sections of black fur apart, trying not to tug too hard on her scalp. "Maybe one more light cycle."

"One more chance to die in silence." She muttered.

I grimaced, then I *did* give her fur a bit of a yank. "No pessimism. We're not going to end up like Emma and Ida. Just laying there silently, waiting for the end."

She was quiet until I resumed my work, "...you really think we just need to hold out a little longer?"

"To get off this ship? I think so." I didn't say that they could always just refuel and replenish it, then get us moving without ever letting us off. I didn't want to consider that as a possibility.

I couldn't consider it, or I might sink into the depths just as our neighbors had.

"Just a bit longer." I told her, silently praying that I was right about that.

Her weight shifted, back straightening a little. "...all right. All right. Then some kind of camp or prison maybe. Something different, somewhere we might have a chance to escape."

"Yeah."

"Yeah... wait." She turned a little, frowning. "Didn't we just have this conversation a few meals ago?"

We'd had it twice already. At least that I could remember. "Who knows. At least talking in circles keeps us busy. It's your turn for stories, by the way."

"Right, it is. Um... did I ever tell you about my family?"

"No." I said at once. She really hadn't. We'd talked a lot about nothing, but she'd never once brought up her blood-pack. Only vague references when she told me about friends she'd had. "You don't have to. I don't think you got much when I was telling you about my packs."

42

"I got enough-ow! How bad is that one?"

I leaned in, frowning at the tangled bit of fur right behind her ear. "Not great. How did you manage this one?"

"You've been grabbing it in your sleep." She said.

That made me blink. "I have been? Since when?"

Her weight shifted. "At least a dark cycle. Maybe two. I didn't want to say anything, not when I was the one that asked you to start sleeping next to me to begin with."

"If you hadn't, I would have." I admitted, trying to untie the mess I'd apparently turned her fur into. "I.. really missed not sleeping alone. Let me know if I'm too rough."

"I will." Another deep breath. "You really don't know your parents?"

"Nope."

There was a long pause, then she asked. "And that doesn't bother you?"

"Nope." I repeated. "I still don't get the appeal of blood-family, to be honest."

"...sometimes I don't either." She muttered. "I was the third child in my family, we're from the *Friedrich Hecker*. It's one of the smaller ships in our flotilla, not much space, even less privacy. My mother was a steward for the upper class decks, and my father was a Kommissar."

"A what?"

Johanna seemed to struggle for a silent moment, picking out words that I would recognize. "An... officer that watches other officers. Makes sure they obey the Fleet's orders."

I frowned, shaking my head just as I finally got the knot mostly undone. "That doesn't make any sense, but all right. He's a military officer."

"More or less. All of the Human ones are paired with Kelthi, called Watchers. My father's was named Ren'lhun. He was... family too. We named him Onkel. We were very close. Spent lots of time together."

Something in her tone made me guess this story wasn't going to be a particularly happy one.

"What happened?" I asked.

"Mother was caught stealing from first deck. Ohrringe." A hand rose to touch her ear then dropped to her neck. "Halskette. She was sent to mining colony as punishment."

That seemed pretty minor. I was about to say as much when she went on, almost growling. "Father could have stayed in fleet. Waited for her. Instead moved us there without asking. Stopped Onkel Ren from keeping us in the Fleet."

"...he took you to a penal colony?"

I don't think she got the word 'penal', but she definitely got the context. "Yes. Lost own rooms. Lived in bunks. Lost money, ate food not much better than the gruel. Hated it. Hated him. Hated mother. So did brother and sister. Left when they turned eighteen."

"That's when you become huntresses?"

"Adults." She corrected. "I was one month from leaving when they took us."

Ashahn's holy blood. Here I'd been assuming that Johanna was at least my age. I supposed by Imperial standards she'd have been a Huntress for several years already, but apparently she'd only just become one by her own people's view of it.

"You came of age in here?" I asked, unable to keep the disgust out of my voice.

Her posture drooped once more. "Must have. Eighteen is important. Supposed to be big parties. Celebration. Onkel Ren was going to come and get me."

I let my hands slide down, resting them on her shoulders, gently rubbing them. She relaxed, leaning back into me.

44

"My packmates will come for me." I told her. "When they do, we'll help you get back to the Ark Fleet. To your Onkel. I promise by every Aspect of Aysh that there is."

"...thank you." A quiet hiccup. "No more stories. Rest."

"Want me to hold you?" I asked.

"...please."

V

Michael and Wolfgang vanished during the next dark cycle. I managed one look into their cell before I'd stumbled away, throwing up slop and bile.

Johanna had helped me clean it up as best she could. She didn't ask what I'd seen. Didn't ask me to describe the smears of blood that covered the floors and walls.

Neither of us went anywhere near the window on that side again.

Twenty meals later we huddled in the corner near the door, waiting for the lights to go out one more time. In that we weren't disappointed; they went black just as they had the last six times.

That wasn't what made me gasp.

The sudden absence of a rumble I'd long ago tuned out had that honor.

"The FTL engines just cut out." I sat up, practically trembling in excitement. "By Ashahn, I was right."

Johanna inhaled sharply, a hand clinging to my wrist. "Yeah. They did. They did. *Mein Gott*, you were right. You were right."

Now I just had to hope that I was right about this being our destination as well. That we weren't just stopping for fuel and provisions. That whatever was going to happen to us was finally going to happen.

Death. Torture. A prison camp. I didn't care. Anything to get out of this cell for even a minute.

They made us wait, which I could have expected.

We received one final meal of gruel an indefinite time later. My hands shook with nerves as I choked it down, praying constantly that this would be the *last* time I had to eat it. That we'd be getting something else when we landed or docked.

That Rerth was in a ship right behind us.

I'd just slid our empty trays back through the door when I heard the heavy clanks of a lock disengaging. My heart skipped a beat, than began hammering as I scrambled away. Hands grabbed my shoulders a moment later, Johanna pulling me against her as the door slammed open.

Loud cries of shock filling the air told me that they'd opened more than just ours.

I'd barely had time to realize that before something clamped down on my left ankle. My yelp was more startled than pained. A second cry was far more agonized when it started pulling. I kicked on pure reflex, and promptly convulsed in pain when my foot slammed into metal.

"Ashe!" Johanna slid her arms around my shoulders, holding as tightly as she could.

I tried to tell her it was an automation, but mechanical fingers snapped around my neck before I could speak or cry out again.

Johanna must have heard me choking because I felt her grip change, flesh hitting metal as she tried to free me.

All she managed to do was hurt herself just like I had. The thing ripped me away from her without any particular effort, letting go of my ankle a moment later. I didn't get to appreciate that; it hefted me up by my neck right after.

Fighting to breathe, I flailed until I got my legs under me, getting tiny bits of air through my nose once I was partially standing under my own weight. Fingers found its metal wrist, desperately trying to loosen the grip. To help take some of my weight.

I failed miserably, and the thing began pulling again within moments anyway. Its strength forced me to scramble on the tips of my toes out of the cell, into the hall.

Most of the shouting had cut out, and what was left was muffled. Behind me I heard Johanna cry my name one more time, then she abruptly cut off.

Grabbed like I was. I prayed that she was grabbed like I'd been, and

47

that they hadn't shut her away in the cell again.

My captor hauled me down the hall without slowing. I heard another door open, felt where it had slid aside with my bare toes. Another hall with muffled shouting and crying.

Another door.

Another hall.

Another door and light stabbed into my eyes.

I jerked in surprise a the bright luminescence, promptly choking once again when the automation's grip tightened.

The light at least let me see the thing, and I'd never seen one like it before. It was built in the clear mimicry of a Trahcon, but on the scale of a Thondian. Eight feet at least, covered in bronzed plating, and effortlessly walking backward as it pulled me deeper into the new space.

A final twist of its arm released me, sending me stumbling into another woman who caught me before I could fall.

"Breathe." She said in Deutsch. "Breathe."

I nodded, gasping for air as she rubbed my back. Once I could actually get air into my lungs again I did my best to look around.

We were in some kind of broad cargo hangar. The kind I'd been in a hundred times on various duties. It had the usual features; broad hangar doors, scaffolds high above, markers on the floor where things should be secured.

Several dozen ragged Humans, myself included, stood out against the gray deck and walls.

More were arriving even as I looked, being tossed in by more of the giant automations that promptly marched back out of the room. Another stood near the door; a silent guard that looked to have batted aside at least one man who'd gotten too close.

There were already at least forty of us, making me rethink just how many cell blocks the ship held. That math was interrupted by my cellmate's staggered arrival alongside one of the machines, making me push away from the crowd.

"Johanna!' I caught her stumbling form just as I'd just been helped, quickly wrapping my arms around her. "Breathe. Just breathe."

It took her a little while longer than it had taken me. She'd probably stumbled, putting more pressure on her neck. It made me wonder if the things killed anyone while they'd been dragging them here.

...even if they had, they probably wouldn't have cared.

Shuddering a little at the thought, I glanced at the woman who'd caught me, speaking her language. "Thank you."

"You're welcome." She was older, features just starting to wrinkle. An Elder, or close to one. "It seems we've finally arrived, after however long a trip."

"Four months, maybe closer to five." I provided. "Uh, probably six for the rest of you. I got here later."

"...you're sure?" The Elder asked.

"No." I admitted. "Best guess."

"...so long." She murmured. "We could be anywhere in the Reaches. Beyond the Reaches."

I didn't want to think about that. Mostly because she wasn't wrong.

If the ship had caught any of the major hyperspace currents, four to five months of travel from Trinity could have put us... well, practically anywhere this side of the Federation

And considering that the Reaches were poorly explored at the best of times...

If Rerth hadn't gotten a tracking beacon on this ship, there was... there was no chance she'd ever find me.

Johanna caught her breath, staying close as more people arrived. Men and women alike were simply shoved loose once they arrived, no matter how bad of shape they were in, and many were in very bad shape. The elder I'd

49

spoken with moved away a few minutes later, trying to help those who needed it.

Now and then there'd be a cry of relief; packmates or blood-family members racing out to embrace those thought lost.

I waited to see if Johanna's would be among them.

If they were, she didn't react, nervously holding on to my arm as the hangar filled up.

"Getting ready to offload us." I murmured, going back to Caranat. "Are you all right?"

"No." She admitted, speaking just as quietly. "I think we're just trading one cell for another."

She was probably right about that. "Keep hold of me. We'll stick together, all right? I'll keep you safe."

A step brought her closer, fingers tightening around my bicep and wrist. "Is the big, strong Imperial soldier going to protect me?"

"If I can." I admitted, "I'm not that strong right now."

Her laugh was a little manic. "It's a joke. Old Human joke."

"Oh." I swallowed, watching as the last automation exited the room, the door slamming shut behind it. "Sorry. Give me some context and I'll give you my version of it."

"Um, helpless little woman trades favor for a big man to protect her. Usually, um, sleeping favors. It's very klischee."

"...old fashioned?" I guessed at the word I missed.

"Stupid and stereotyp. Used in bad sex movies."

I nearly choked again. "Oh. Uh... is the strong woman going to help me lift things, I guess."

She blinked, "What do-oh. Trahcon women are bigger. Right. Wait. Empire has bad sex movies?"

A bit of heat rose to my cheeks. "Um, yes."

Johanna's second laugh wasn't any more stable sounding than her first.

It had just begun to trail off when the lights changed color from white to blue. "What is that?"

"Doors are opening." I answered, raising my voice and speaking in Deutsch. "Doors opening!"

My shout was quickly repeated by several people close to us, the words echoing as the crowd passed the message across the Hangar. Everyone scuttled a bit back, more than a hundred people waiting nervously.

The first thing I noticed was the air. Humid and heavy, so incredibly different than the dry air we'd been breathing that I groaned in almost lustful pleasure. I wasn't the only one; an eager moan ran around the room as the doors ponderously began to drop outwards.

Dark blue skies came next. Gray clouds in the far distance dropped hazy rain over a line of rolling hills, all of them shaded green. After four months of beige floors, walls, and ceilings, it was...

Beautiful.

I was on the verge of tears when the ramps finally crashed down, dragging my eyes back to see what kind of prison camp we were being thrown into.

It took me a few seconds to realize that there was no camp. Instead they were... well.

They were dropping us into a marshy swamp.

It was as dreary as the distant view had been lovely. Mist and fog clung to the ground, obscuring tall reeds and narrow strips of land. Here and there bits of color poked through, mostly some kind of yellow flower that seemed to grow above the fog. A couple of tall trees loomed in the distance, but mostly it was just... a bog.

A thoroughly unwelcoming looking bog.

51

Even after the cells no one seemed eager to march down into the stagnant water. I was definitely among them.

That changed when a synthesized voice came across overhead speakers, communicating in toneless Caranat. *"The Hangar will remain open to space when this ship takes off in ten minutes. Exit or breathe vacuum."*

A man translated before I could, his deep voice carrying across the hangar. "This is our stop, or they throw us into space. Come on."

Johanna and I had been close to the hangar doors, so we were among the first to descend the ramps. I let myself drop off the end, hissing in discomfort when the cold water came up above my knees. The feeling of my toes sinking into mud wasn't any better, but at least I wasn't swimming.

"Come on." I took my first step, grimacing at the effort I needed to yank my foot loose of the muck. "Let's get to dry land."

"...yeah." Johanna fell in with a quiet splashing, swearing quietly when the water's temperature made itself felt. "Scheisse! Cold!"

"Can you move?"

There was a sound of effort, her fingers grasping at my shoulder. "Yes. Slow down?"

I did, letting her keep pace as we waded towards the nearest bank of grassy soil.

All around us other people were groaning, cursing, and splashing as they got clear of the ship. Some didn't seem to want to get off even then, forcing others to pull or push them to get them moving.

From the outside our ride didn't look like much. A pretty standard Imperial barge, from what I could tell. Though no inter-system barge could have made a trip as long as the one we'd just taken.

It was certainly a good disguise though, at least if you were in an Imperial system. There had to be ten thousand of those things floating around.

"Warn Rerth about that for sure. It's clever." I added that observation to the list of things to tell her, if I ever... no. *When* I saw her again. When she came for me.

Pulling my legs free one last time, I planted my muddy feet on the little path of raised grass. It wasn't all that wide, a yard or two, but it stretched out in both directions enough to give me hope of avoiding another trip through the water.

Which, now that I could focus, smelled absolutely awful.

Or maybe that was us. I was months overdue for a real bath. So was Johanna.

I was trying to see how far the path actually went when I saw the first bit of movement in the distance. A dark shape in the mist, twisting one way than the other.

"You see that?" I asked, old training making me lower myself a little. "Right over there?"

Johanna finished pulling herself out of the water, frowning as she followed my gaze. After a moment she blinked. "Yes. That's... a Pferd?"

It emerged before I could ask the obvious question, the shadow revealing itself to tell me what a Pferd was; a large beast of burdon.

Four thin legs carried it forward, its dark... skin or fur, I couldn't tell, blending in well with the fog. A Human male was riding astride its back, his pale chest bare, one hand holding the beast's wild mane to direct it.

His other held a rifle, letting it rest on a shoulder... and behind him another pferd with a rider appeared. And another. And another.

The leader let out an excited yell in a tongue I didn't know, brought his gun down to aim at us, and kicked his beast in the side. It let out a high-pitched cry, legs beginning to churn as it rushed forward.

They were on us in moments.

VI

"Put your hands up." Johanna hissed, her own rising as the nearest local pointed their gun at us. "That's what they're shouting."

I mimicked her, doing my best to pay attention to everything.

This was *not* anything close to what I'd expected to see when we finally left the ship. I'd expected a sterile prison of some kind as a best case scenario, a quick execution in the middle case, and being transferred to another identical ship as the worst.

Being dumped into a swamp, to be attacked by wild looking Humans, riding strange animals... yeah. Nothing like that had entered my wildest dreams.

People were shouting all around us. Those who'd gotten away from the ship were raising their hands as ordered when guns were pointed at them, while those still struggling to help others through the bog shouted back what sounded like pleas.

I tuned out the shouting and focused on the closest man instead.

The gun came first. It was an old, *old* Kahdel model rifle. It didn't look like it was in very good shape either. Salvage? Given to them by our captors? Either way I would be impressed if it actually worked, but I wasn't really eager to test it either.

He was bare chested, revealing sparse fur covering tanned skin, and the fur on his face was absolutely wild. Below the waist he wore the same prison pants that we all did, though his were clearly old and frayed.

I must have been looking too closely because he barked something, Johanna quickly translating. "Stop looking at him like that."

I averted my eyes at once, raising my hands a little higher.

"What are they speaking?" I asked quietly. "Some of the words sound like Deutsch."

54

"Englisch." She murmured back. "They're telling everyone to group up on the grass."

"Collaborators." I guessed.

Her eyes blinked. "...that's a new word."

"People who help captors."

"Mitarbeiter." Her teeth worked at her bottom lip, "You think they're going to take us to the actual prison camp?"

I hoped so, because my new worry was that they'd dumped us on some kind of penal colony. Just one without any rules or guards watching from above to stop murder and abuse.

Well, at least there were only eight men on various pferd. Even with guns they'd be wary of angering the rough hundred of us slowly grouping up.

As if summoned by my attempt to reassure myself, more Humans began approaching from the same direction.

These weren't riding beasts, and they weren't armed with guns either. Instead they carried what looked like *spears* on their shoulders or in their hands, all of them forming up a rough mob behind the nearby leader.

"...thirty or forty of them." I grimaced, licking my lips nervously. "Uh. Is it just me or are all of them male?"

Johanna let out a quiet whimpering noise. "...I noticed too."

The leader ended our conversation by raising his voice, belting out some kind of speech. My cellmate started translating after a brief moment, "He says welcome to Last Stop. That we all have to start walking because the ship is leaving soon, and it won't wait for everyone to be away from it. That he'll explain how things work once we get to the nearest clearing."

He paused, pulling out a small canteen, sipping from it once before holding it up. "He says we're all safe now, and they have a camp in the plains. We'll have real food once we get there, and clean water at the clearing. There's a river we can bathe in too. There are a few dangerous animals in the bog, so stay on the path, and don't distract the men protecting us. He says it's time to move, the ship will be lifting off any time now."

55

I believed him about the ship, if nothing else. Everyone else did too, from the way they started shuffling in the direction he'd waved. Johanna started to walk, letting out a quiet sound of surprise when I held her back a moment.

"Don't be out in front." I murmured. "Let's let a few people get ahead of us. Stay near the middle so we have more options."

She nodded quickly, the pair of us letting twenty or thirty people form a rough line ahead before we got moving.

Those mounted on beasts trotted ahead, while the spear carriers started forming up on either side. None of them seemed to mind tromping through the water, keeping themselves out of grabbing range of anyone in line.

That, more than anything else, told me that we were in trouble.

These men expected us to want to get a hold of their weapons if we had the chance. You didn't do that if you were helping out fellow prisoners, just trying to make sure they didn't get incinerated when the barge took off again.

Johanna noticed without me having to say anything, whispering in Caranat as we walked. "We're their prisoners now, aren't we?"

"Yeah." I whispered back.

"What do we do?" She asked.

"What they say, for now." A deep breath, "Until we know where we are, what things are like here. If we can survive away from them or not."

She nodded jerkily, falling silent again.

We followed the trail for quite a while. An hour or two at least, from how much the sun moved. Fortunately it wasn't all that hot out, and our pace was pretty slow. Even the weaker people in the back of the line were able to keep up, thanks to help from others.

About halfway through the trip a roar of engines made us all stop, turning back to see the barge lifting off. Mud and water fell from its bottom as it slowly drifted back into the sky.

Everyone, escort and prisoners alike, watched until its main engines lit off, taking it into the clouds, and vaporizing a good stretch of swamp-water in the process.

We watched... and then we got moving again, well and truly trapped here. Wherever here was.

The path wound us in all kinds of directions, eventually leading us through a veritable wall of tall reeds and yellow flowers. On the far side was a long, low hill with a couple of old trees atop it. Our escort herded us to the top, where we finally got a glimpse of the promised river.

It was more of a creek, really, but the water was rushing quickly, and more importantly it looked clean. Just beyond it was the beginnings of a forest, thick with trees and undergrowth, already dark as the sun began to set behind it.

A few of the thirstier prisoners tried to head right for it, only to be held back by shouting and spear-pointing.

"Easy everyone," The leader shouted, Johanna murmuring his words into my ear. "We'll let you at the water in groups, to make sure you don't get it filthy for everyone else. Let's be old fashioned about this. Men group up around the tree to the right. Women and any kids to my left."

To my surprise there did turn out to be a few children. Not many, six or seven maybe, and they looked more skeletal than even the elders. They were also the first to quickly move to where they'd been told to go. Everyone else was more reluctant.

"The sooner you do it, the sooner you drink and get clean!" Johanna swallowed, then added her own words. "I don't like this."

"Me either." I muttered.

In the end we didn't have much choice. The crowd began to slowly break apart by gender as ordered, the pair of us reluctantly following along when we were among the last few who'd tried to stay put in the center.

The armed men quickly split up as well, forming a rough line between us, while the beast-riders slowly circled the hill. Only the leader stayed in

57

place, looking completely relaxed atop his pferd, rifle in his lap.

"First, the rules of Last Stop." He began yet another speech as soon as everyone was corralled once more. "This is where the grays dump everyone who they don't like. They let us live however we want. Those of us that obey them, who don't make a fuss, are exempt from the keulung that happens once a year."

He paused, apparently realizing that several people were translating for others, letting us catch up. "The keulung is when they come out of their fortress and take everyone they don't like to be processed. We never see them again, so it's best for you all to be obedient and loyal if you want to live comfortable lives."

Keulung. Probably meant culling. Ashahn's blood. They culled us like herd animals. Every time I thought they couldn't treat us any more like beasts than they already did, I was proven wrong.

"Men," He turned to face that group. "As new arrivals you'll start as farmers. Once you prove yourselves in trials of strength, you'll graduate to laborers, then to guards, and eventually to hunters. You'll be able to eat fish and meat as you like, perhaps own a pferd, and have your own homes."

The males shifted, murmuring to each other, but no one protested. Maybe out of shock and confusion, maybe they were just grateful to be off that cursed ship.

"Women," The leader turned, and I did not like his smile at all. "You get to act as nature intended. You'll clean homes, prepare food, and help take care of the few children. If you're exceptionally lucky a hunter will pick you for a wife."

Protests promptly rang out around me, at least until several men bellowed and brought their spears closer. A few similar shouts came from the men, and it was they who he addressed next.

"Easy, boys. If you're lucky enough that your wife came with, we'll respect that. We'll talk about the details once you're all cleaned up and have had your fill of water." He waved an expansive arm, "Come on down. Plenty for everyone to drink."

Some of the men still looked reluctant, but most were clearly too thirsty, too desperate to finally bathe, that they didn't hesitate to stroll down

58

the hill.

A few women tried to follow, and were pushed back by the spears once again.

"...we're slaves now. That's what he was really saying, right?" Johanna asked, staring as the male prisoners reached the water. Some quickly began drinking, others stripped down and threw themselves into the water with excited cries.

Their fears and concerns fading against their relief.

"Sounds it." I said, wishing I was anything close to relieved right now. "So are they, but I think they'll get a chance to not be. What is it with humans and genders?"

"...don't know. I wasn't a good history student. It's always been a problem, or something." She admitted.

I grimaced. I really needed to figure that out, but first I needed to find a way for us to get out of this. Cooking and cleaning didn't sound abominable, those were part and parcel of a conscript's duties even if they'd been dull.

The part that worried me was 'being picked as a wife'. That... I could guess what that meant.

And now that we were entirely cut off, I noticed that more of the spear armed guards had moved to encircle us, leaving only those with guns to watch over the men in the creek.

Said guards were eyeing us up, muttering and using their spears to point at various women. Grins and chuckles were swirling around the circle, along with gestures that even I could tell were suggestive in unpleasant ways.

"Picking their claims already." Another woman near me muttered, sounding exhausted, resigned. "It's almost night. They'll have us on our backs before we make their village."

A ripple of fear ran through the confined group of women, one that I felt crawl up my spine as well. Old fears, old nightmares, resurfacing for a moment before I shoved them back into the depths of my soul.

That wasn't going to happen. I just needed to think of a way out of

59

this.

I couldn't see a way to overpower them. Not easily at least. Maybe we could all rush the spearmen at once? Several of us would die, but we could probably overwhelm them. There were at least twice as many women as there were men with sharpened sticks.

But even if we did, the ones with guns would cut us down in a matter of seconds. Assuming their guns worked. Assuming I could convince all of the women to gamble their lives along with me.

Yeah. Force wasn't an option.

A quick look let me find the nearest mounted guard. I didn't know the first thing about riding an animal, but that was the only thing I could think of as far as getting away went. It wouldn't save everyone, but maybe Johanna and I could escape? We'd just have to overpower one guard rather than several, get atop his mount, and bolt for the trees.

Escape to what though? My wilderness survival training had been minimal, to say the least. It wasn't something a conscript was ever expected to actually need.

I doubted Johanna would be any better in that, having grown up on ships and then a mining colony.

I was trying to come up with a new plan when the mounted guard jerked his head around to one side, rifle coming up. He shouted something a moment before pulling the trigger, drawing startled screams at the tremendous noise.

None of that was as loud as the roar that came back from the bog.

Water exploded upwards as the titanic alien heaved itself forward, six limbs the size of tree trunks hauling it along almost faster than could be believed. Its head was something out of a nightmare; reptilian, too many sharp teeth, and the bright red glow of cybernetics where its eyes should have been.

My heart began hammering again, an eager trembling in my limbs as I realized what I was looking at.

"Regnon!" The man already shooting managed to make himself heard between bursts, frantically trying to keep his aim steady. "Regnon!"

The bullets didn't do much to the immense being. It had to have been at least forty feet long, no, far longer. Its scales were a dark green and black that had camouflaged it as it drew closer, until it had surged out of the water. Cybernetics dotted he entire body, whatever barriers were built into the alien easily repelling the gunfire.

Men and women were shouting. Some racing forward, more scattering in every direction. Johanna tried to run, yelping when I grabbed her arm, holding her steady, waiting for the right moment.

It was on top of the first guard within seconds, the man frantically trying to kick his mount into motion.

The pferd hardly needed the guidance; it was already panicking at the sight or smell of what was coming. It reared up, kicking its legs, and tried to spin around to bolt off. That proved to be too much for the soft ground. One of its legs sank in to the soil, twisting, making the animal cry in pain.

The Regnon swept over beast and rider before either could try to recover. One arm batted aside the guard like a toy, flinging him away, leaving it free to grab the pferd's neck with another hand. The beast's panicked bleating cut off when claws opened its neck.

More shouting. Men were waving for everyone to run into the woods, more guns were going off, sending up sparks as they bounced off invisible shields. The man who'd lost his mount scrambled away, rifle forgotten, running for his life with everyone else.

This was it. This was our moment!

"This way!" I hauled Johanna into motion.

"Wrong way!" She screamed, nearly ripping her wrist out of my grip when she tried to stop. "Wrong way!"

I pulled harder, not letting her get loose. "It's fine! It's fine! Come on! This is our way out of here!"

She kept yelling as I pulled her toward the Regnon, forcing her into a stumbling run.

It saw us coming, lips pulling back from sharp teeth as we came closer.

"Empire!" I shouted as loudly as I could. "We're Empire!"

Its mouth snapped shut, a deep rumble coming from its enormous throat. A synthetic male voice emerged from somewhere deep in his chest, producing an educated Icar accent. "You call the Compact?"

"Yes!" I called, trying not to sob in relief.

"A moment." He turned, glaring at the guards who were still shooting at him. His head lowered, revealing a heavy section of metal on his back. It unfolded within moments, a large rifle on a swivel tracking where he looked.

It boomed once; and the leader of the Humans collapsed with most of his chest missing. Those who hadn't already broke and ran at that, fleeing into the woods, the other prisoners scrambling along with them.

"Finally. Stupid little beasts." There was a pause, then he added as sheepishly as a fifty foot long alien could. "Present company excluded, Empire."

"Don't worry about it. I don't think they had good intentions for us." I said, finally letting go of Johanna.

She swayed, trembling badly. "A-Ashe... it's..."

"A Regnon, yeah." I beamed up at him. "They're big softies, and they don't eat people."

Said Regnon grunted irritably, which was a rather terrifying sound on its own. "Those stereotypes are incredibly frustrating to deal with. You have met my kind before then?"

"Once before, on Altair."

His mouth parted, revealing enormous fangs and a black tongue. "Altair. I have been there, a most hospitable world. Perhaps the most so within your quaint Empire. Come. We shall speak when we return to those who refuse to obey the Faithful."

I did my best to remember my limited interactions with his people, which had honestly mostly consisted of watching one drink beer out of a

62

carton the size of an aircar on New Years. Then riding on his back as he led a pub crawl that had resulted in a multi-day hangover after.

I tipped my head in a shallow bow, "We thank you. Do we have your permission?"

"You do." He turned, casually extending his middle limb. "Hold tightly, savannas. I shall take you home, so that you may understand the hell in which you now live."

Johanna needed several shoves to climb his arm, her face even paler than usual by the time she was sitting on his back. I climbed up after her, carefully holding her with one hand and some of the cybernetics riddling his back with the other.

Once we were settled he picked up the dead pferd in his mouth, turned, and plunged back into the swamp.

And for the first time in five months... I let myself truly relax as he carried us away.

Interlude
Rerth'riah

The tiny image of Fyvn'trell shook her head, hands on her hips as she spoke. "*Rerth. It's been six months. They could have taken her past the Reaches or into the Federation by now.*"

"What," I asked with a glare, "Is your point?"

"*My point is that I've gotten direct orders to stop assisting you, and to focus on my actual projects.*" She replied tiredly. "*I've sent you all of the data we've got, but I need to get two of my Agents searching for Pack Ythin. The rest are all overdue to help clean up Trinity with the Director still being questioned.*"

I upped my glare. "You're going to stop helping me find my packmate?"

Even in miniature, her own glare was a force. "*Of course not, but you know how bad things are here. Finding the Ythin has to be my focus, not analyzing the data you're sending me. If I can track them down we might get some answers.*"

She was right, as usual.

"...fine." I growled. "But you need to be careful. Sail away from Trinity if you can."

"*I know those dead fish are probably circling me, I'm an Operative, not stupid.*" My old pack-mate replied. "*I've already arranged for a Comet with a crew I trust to be brought in. My Agents and I will get back to you when we have any kind of lead on that analyst's death, or his missing packmates.*"

"Be quick about it."

Her scowl returned. "*Rerth. You are a former packmate, and I love you, but do not take that tone with a superior officer.*"

I was ready to reply when Holde's hands fell to my shoulders. My bond leaning over me to speak to her, "Forgive her, you know how she is. We appreciate everything you've been doing for us."

"...fine, but you'd best keep her storm contained before it lands you all on rocky shores. Trinity out."

"Altair out." He replied, reaching over me to close the channel. "Rerth, calm your waves, love."

I took a ragged breath, sinking back into the chair. "I cannot be calm. Not when I have spent every favor we were owed on this, when every current has led nowhere, every wind has died."

Holde sighed, fingers gently rubbing my tense muscles. "You didn't tell her that we were ordered to stop the search as well."

"No, because I have no intention of following that order." I paused, then amended. "Before you say anything, no, we will not be stupid about it. I am not that lost in the fog. Not yet."

"I did not believe that you were." He said mildly. "Nor was I going to suggest that we obey. Ashe is our packmate. All else is secondary."

"Agreed. Jet?" I asked.

"He is waiting outside with the latest information, and our... guest has arrived."

My tarah lifted at the last. "Finally. Her mood?"

"Brace yourself when you walk through the door." He advised. "She's a hurricane looking for a city to destroy, and we both know what she'll do when she sees you."

I let out a quiet huff, not surprised in the slightest. "We do. Let her, so long as she doesn't actually attempt to kill me."

There was another sigh. "It wasn't your fault, love. You did what you thought best."

"And my best has our packmate a prisoner of the same people who tortured her out of pure sadism. She would have been safer with Ithi on the bloody front lines in the Contested Region."

65

Holde pulled his hands back, though he flicked my right tarah in the process. "We both know that's a lie. She's never been a very good soldier."

"No," I admitted before countering, "but she would have been a content one with fewer demerits on her Index."

I pushed myself to my feet, rolling my shoulders and neck to prepare.

It also let me ignore the fact that my bond was probably right about her chances in combat, just as I'd probably been right to pull her out of Pack Ithi when they'd gotten their transfer to the front lines against the Concordat.

Taking a few final breaths, I strode over to the door of our bedroom, opening it with a gesture.

I made it three steps into our quarter's living area before a fist slammed into my face.

"You useless piece of fucking driftwood!" The battle-scarred woman snarled, crippled and scarred tarah hanging limply despite her fury. A second fist hit my stomach, driving me back a pace, the blow promptly followed by a savage backhand to my other cheek.

"Dual-Commander." I managed to gasp her rank before she put three more blows into my ribs, sending me staggering back into a wall.

I didn't make any attempt to fight back, though I could have easily brushed her aside with sorcery. Not when she had more than a few good reasons to vent her fury upon me.

She got two more hits in before my bond had enough. Ignoring my prior orders, Holde intervened when she wound up for another head-shot. He slipped behind her, his arms grabbing hers, holding her back.

"Enough!" He snapped. "That's enough! You have scored your point!"

She snarled, burned features twisting, her homeworld accent thickening in rage, "You lost Ashe! You failed her!"

My hearts slowed, my breathing following suit. "Yes. I did."

Dual-Commander Huvu'ithi, Ashe's first true mentor, first true

66

packmate, first true everything, glared death at me. "I should kill you, and damn the consequences."

"Easy there." Holde said quietly, "Don't say anything you can't take back, Ithi. We're all in pain, but we're all ranking members of the Empire."

"I'll say what I please." She shook him off without much effort, but didn't come at me again. "The only reason I'm not already becalmed in a jail cell for murdering you is because you're our best chance of getting her back."

"That is the plan." I straightened slowly, trying not to wince at the pain in my chest.

Huvu'ithi's sorcery had been crippled by the artillery that had maimed her, had killed her old pack, but there was nothing wrong with the strength of her arms. Nor her knowledge of just where to punch someone to make them hurt.

"Thank you for accepting the transfer." I went on, as if she hadn't just punched me a dozen times. "We'll need your pack's skills in this."

The other woman huffed, walking back down the short hallway without saying another word. Holde shook his head, giving me a questioning look that I waved off. I was fine.

He didn't look like he believed me, but stayed silent when we walked after her.

Jet was seated at our meeting table, a mess of tablets spread out before him. Two more were in his hands, his eyes flicking between them as he tapped away with cybernetic fingers on one, and scrolled through data on the other.

He glanced up, snorted, then returned his attention to his work. "How many punches did you let her get in?"

"Enough." Holde said flatly.

"Not enough." Ithi countered, taking a seat. "You've had six months to look for her. What do you have?"

"A mess." Jet supplied. "Which wind are we following first, boss?"

I grimaced as I sat down as well, already feeling the bruises forming. "With the context. How much did Ashe tell you of our projects, Ithi?"

"Next to nothing, besides that you were sailing in strange currents out in the Near Reaches."

A small trickle of pride rose within me. Ashe had known better than to reveal anything about an ongoing project, even to an old packmate that she trusted implicitly.

She'd been shaping up so well before...

"Jet, recap. From Oshflara to her capture." I ordered, shoving the mental pain back into the depths of my soul. "Holde? Drinks. The Vekki Dark."

Jet launched into the shortest version of what had happened to our pack over the past year and a half. From when I'd pulled Ashe into our pack, our few months sailing about trying to lure the Burned Hand into the open. How we had changed course when that hadn't worked.

Our tracking of the smuggled goods across the Near Reaches, the resulting mess on Trinity, and finally our successful operation on Nueva Genova. The fueling and reporting layover at Trinity after, when Ashe had been taken.

Ithi listened intently, sipping her alcohol when Holde provided it.

"All right." She growled when Jet finished. "And what have you found since? Did the prisoners you took on Genova give up anything?"

My jaw clenched, "No. At the same time as Ashe was taken, someone vented the air out of the ship they were being transported in. Half of the crew survived, but none of the prisoners did."

Ithi's green eyes blinked. "Ashahn's sacred blood. You've been infiltrated to that level?"

"Likely." Holde said quietly. "That was the excuse we used to arrange your team's transfer from the Contested Zone. The local Director is as concerned as we are."

Jet snorted, "Not that it does us much good now."

68

When Ithi glanced between us, I sighed and told her. "Altair's Director was recalled to the Capital last month for questioning in the wake of the Trinity Director's interrogation. My Operative wasn't happy that I was being given direct commands from those Directors, and thinks the situation under control. We've been ordered to focus on rooting out the remnants of the smuggling operation in this sector."

Ithi's fingers clenched into fists, her drawl worsening again. "They're ordering you to abandon Ashe?"

"Officially, no." Holde shook his head. "They think our best chance to find her is to run down the rest of the smuggling ring, because they think this entire thing is just part of a conspiracy of Near Reach colonies to acquire Imperial goods."

"Could it be?" She demanded.

"No." I said flatly. "But the reports out of Trinity are so inconsistent that we can't give hard evidence to say it isn't that. Not with no survivors left to interrogate, and virtually all of their equipment wiped."

Jet snorted, "And Trinity's entire Intelligence organization is collapsing into the waves as we speak. Everyone is blaming everyone else for failures that have apparently been happening for more than a decade. The few trustworthy Operatives are all getting away while they can."

The soldier scowled. "What do you have then?"

"Too much and not enough." I told her. "We can't disobey our orders, which means Holde and I are going to have to go back to chasing smugglers. We'll need one or two of your packmates to accompany us. You and the rest will stay here with Jet."

"Doing what?"

I flicked a tarah. "Protecting him, and providing firepower if his research ends up requiring it. There is every chance that the Burned Hand's agents will spot his masts while he searches, and come for him."

She nodded slowly. "And his research will help us find Ashe?"

Jet shifted, setting his last tablet down. "That's the objective. We don't

69

have a hope of finding her conventionally. We know she was moved to a shuttle, which docked with an automated shipment barge. A vessel matching its signature arrived briefly in the Alum system to refuel, but vanished after that."

His cybernetic hand reached out, tapping the table's controls to bring up a display. "We've got no hope of finding her in the Reaches, if that's even where they took her. Too many stars for a hundred lifetimes. Our only hope is to capture members of the conspiracy who took her, and interrogate them before they can be silenced."

"Or," Holde supplied, "Silence themselves."

"Or that." Jet agreed, tones grim. "None of us think that sailing after smugglers is going to end up with results. I may have to pretend to do some work there, but my focus is going to be on these missing persons instead."

Ithi leaned in, as did I. I hadn't seen the full list yet, and the amount of names that appeared was horrifying in its implications.

"Who are they?" She asked.

"Members of Imperial Intelligence who have been reported dead, marked as deserters, or went missing during a project." Jet replied. "Over the past five years."

Ithi's lips parted in shock. "...attrition's that bad in Intelligence?"

He snorted, fingers flying over the controls. The massive list slid to the right, and a new list not even a tenth the size appeared beside it. "This is the same list over the ten years *before* that."

"By the bloody... and this isn't known?" Ithi demanded.

I shook my head. "Not officially, no. There haven't been any alerts within the organization. Just general requests that we step up recruitment due to a shortage of assets. Jet? I want to see it sorted by sector."

"I can already give you the worst." A few taps dismissed the old records, then shifted the recent data into columns by sector. "Two thirds of the Far Reach department supposedly deserted or died within the last two years. Icar and Shaidan aren't that far gone, but they're in bad shape."

Resting an arm on the table, I leaned in, staring at the data.

It painted a far grimmer image on the horizon than I'd expected, and I hadn't expected the seas to be calm in the slightest.

I was only an Agent, true, but I would have expected to have heard *something* about losses at these levels. There should be hundreds of requests for help flying between the sectors. By the Aspects, I knew of at least a dozen Agents on Altair alone who were doing little more than busywork. Mostly assisting local security forces.

There was a bloody *war* raging in the Far Reaches, and the Ascendancy had splintered into a dozen factions similarly fighting it out to seize control of that nation.

Why weren't hundreds of Agents being transferred to those regions? To those projects?

"Imperial Intelligence is being attacked." I told them, "We can confirm that theory. We're under assault from both within and without."

Jet and Holde both nodded grimly, while the soldier among us took a long sip of her dark liquor.

She set the glass down, shaking her head. "That's why you dragged my unit all the way from the Contested Zone. You don't trust anyone else."

I tipped my head to her, flicking a tarah in agreement. "That, and I deserved the blows you gave me."

"Yes. You did." A finger tapped the side of her drink. "What are we going to do with this list?"

"Find them." I told her. "Find who took them. Find who in Intelligence is working for the Burned Hand rather than the Empire. Then we force them to tell us where they take those people they've made vanish."

Her crippled tarah tried to rise. "And then?"

"And then go there, find Ashe, find everyone else they've taken..." A growl entered my voice, "...and we kill everyone who tries to stop us."

71

VII

Regnon can really move, even when they're not really trying to.

He cut through the swamp in a quarter of the time that we'd taken, bypassing the space where we'd arrived on the barge. I kept a hold of a still tense Johanna, who was very much not relaxing like I was. I tried to talk to her a few times only to get silence back in response.

The sun had just set when our ride heaved himself out of the water, carefully picking his way through a thick cove of trees.

I nearly started crying when I heard a voice shout out in a thick Icar accent, "Stand down! Marzin is back!"

Flickering orange and red lights began to come into view between the dark trunks. The camp itself became clear as the Regnon, Marzin, slowed his pace to a crawl.

We were still in the swamp, but they'd picked a good spot for their camp. Bits of dry land held smoldering campfires, while broad platforms had been built among the branches of the trees. I could see curious faces looking down from a few, while others were emerging from hammocks stretched between the trunks.

All around us people were gathering. Not all, or even most, were Trahcon. I saw plenty of them, but there were also Thondians, Naule, even a brightly colored Mikira. Everyone was dressed differently. Some still had the same prison clothes I was wearing, others had added hide, or were standing entirely naked.

I wiped at my eyes. I didn't know anything about these people, but...

...just hearing so many voices speaking my language, seeing people other than Humans...

Marzin carefully dropped his meal next to one of the fires, "Eldest. I have returned, with recruits and knowledge."

The Eldest pushing her way forward wore a cloak made of animal

72

skins, though her own prison pants were visible beneath it when she walked. She was very tall, taller than me even, and fairly well built. Her hands pulled the hood back, revealing the worn features of an older guide, or maybe a young elder.

"You're supposed to take them to a cave first." She growled in a homeworld drawl, blue eyes slits while her tarah were angled up to display her irritation. "We've been over this a dozen times Marzin! You don't bring strangers straight to our camp!"

"I did not feel like it." He replied blandly. "Off, little friends. I wish to enjoy my meal before it rots, and you have an old woman to soothe."

Quiet laughter from the crowd told me that this was an argument that had happened before, and would probably happen again.

Johanna wasn't any more comfortable once we slid down than she'd been on Marzin's back. Nor did she relax when he lumbered off, vanishing back into the trees with his dinner. She kept looking around nervously, as if we were about to be attacked at any moment.

I took one step in front of her, drawing myself up into my best salute. "Rifle-Experienced Ashe'lori, seconded to Imperial Intelligence under Agent Rerth'Riah. Assigned to Altair."

The elder's tarah, which had just lowered, rose sharply once again, another murmur sailing through the crowd. Most of the Trahcon looked more interested in me, while many of the aliens merely shook their heads or simply wandered off.

"...Ashul'tasir, Director of Imperial Intelligence on Alum." The Eldest said after a long moment, waving off the salute.

"I... a *director*?" I blurted, my hopes of making a good impression melting into the ocean. "They captured a *Director*? How? I mean, I would have thought everyone would have heard about that."

Her lips thinned. "That is a long story, Rifle-Experienced. Who is your companion?"

I blinked a few more times, then recovered as gracefully as I could. "Johanna of the Ark Fleet. She was my cellmate."

73

There was a huff from her, and low noises of displeasure came from several of the people watching us. The few Thondians who'd stuck around to watch offered sharper glares, and Johanna slipped closer to my back.

"That explains why she's still trembling." The Eldest shook her head. "Probably thinks we're about to eat her."

Johanna found her voice, though it was shaky. "F-fuck off Imperial."

"Hmm. At least she speaks Caranat." Director Tasir crossed her arms, eyeing us both. "Well. You're both here, thanks to Marzin, so we can't kick you out. That'd be a death sentence, and I don't think we're quite that far out to sea just yet."

"Sir." I mumbled, still trying to recover from my shock at her rank. Or supposed rank, if I wanted to be paranoid about it.

She went on, "You both need a bath and food, Irkan will help with that. Then you and I are going to talk, Rifle-Experienced, about just what is going on in the galaxy."

"Sir." I said for the third time, earning a tired wave from her.

With that everyone still lingering seemed to lose interest, walking back to wherever they'd come from. The sole exception was the Mikira that approached, each step carefully chosen. Probably to make sure he didn't sink into the muck, I couldn't imagine it'd be easy to get him out again if he fell.

He was as short and squat as every other member of the species that I'd met. The shell covering his back and chest was a deep blue with bright green accents. That same green decorated the horn protruding from his snout, and the quills dangling below his narrow chin.

"Women of the savanna." He greeted us. "Follow this one to the baths, and he will provide you with food."

"Thank you." I said, Johanna echoing me a moment later.

He slowly led us through the camp, mostly walking on raised tree roots to avoid the water. We followed, balancing as best we could on our grime covered feet, until we reached a small alcove sheltered by more hide-blankets.

74

"The baths lay within." He instructed, speaking as slowly as he'd walked. "This sailor will bring the females water and food. They should clean themselves."

I thanked him again, then followed Johanna through the small gap into the covered space. A single lantern hung from the ceiling, revealing... well, the bastardized remains of a truck. A cargo hauler, from the looks of it. They'd cut off the roof, and trimmed the sides down to make a rectangular box, complete with rough benches inside.

A wooden tube ran down from somewhere, while another clearly served as a drain.

"Huh. Clever." Padding around it, I found a little plug and gave it a yank. Lukewarm water promptly began spilling down, slowly filling the make-shift tub.

"...are you sure about this?" Johanna asked just before I could pull my shirt off. She'd returned to her own language. A sign of her own paranoia I was sure. "How do we know these people will treat us any better than the others?"

I paused, exhaled, then yanked the wet clothing up and over my head. "We don't, but I'd rather take my chances here than with them. Do you disagree? Did you want to stay with a group already picking out which man would get to rape which woman?"

She turned away, as she always did when I stripped. Her voice was sullen when she spoke again, "You didn't give me a choice. Or explain yourself."

"There wasn't time." I countered. "Did you want to be a slave to Humans with guns?"

"...no."

"Did you want to try and live in the swamp, just the two of us?"

A very frustrated huff. "No."

I fought the urge to throw my hands in the air, mostly because what was the point of the drama if she couldn't see it. "Then why are you arguing with me? Please tell me it's not because *they* were all Human and everyone

75

here isn't."

Her silence went on a beat too long, leaving me to groan. "Ashahn's blood Johanna. Really?"

She spun around, fur whipping left to right, face flushed with either embarrassment or anger. "I'm from the Ark Fleet! Everyone out there, except the giant Dinosaurier, are our enemies! And he could eat me in one bite!"

I groaned, turning around to check the water. It wasn't even halfway up the sides of the 'tub' yet. "The Regnon have been fighting both beside the Empire and against the Empire since the Airalon wars. In more than two thousand years there's never been a recorded case of a Regnon *actually* eating a sapient being."

"That you know of." She muttered petulantly. "And there's still the Elfen out there. And the grays."

It was my turn to whip around, striding right up into her face. "Do *not* call them that."

Johanna flinched back at once, freezing when I grabbed her shirt.

"I..." I realized I was shaking a little. I was angry. I was *way* too angry. I was ready to...

"I'm sorry." I swallowed, trying to wet suddenly dry lips as I forced my fingers to let go. "I... I don't know what that was about."

"...tiny cell?" She said, voice very small. Eyes not looking anywhere near mine.

"...yeah. Let's blame the tiny cell." I took several more breaths, letting each one out slowly. I needed to meditate. I really, really needed to. "Talk in the bath?"

"...fine."

She still turned around again when I went to take my pants off, and refused to look my way until I'd climbed into the bath and closed off the pipe again. Then I had to close my eyes until she climbed in, which at least gave me a chance to let go of everything that wasn't my sense of hearing.

76

Wind rustled in the trees above. Distant voices spoke quietly. Water splashed as Johanna climbed in the far side, her breathing slowing as she got settled.

More quiet ripples and drops as she started trying to clean herself.

"I'm sorry." I said again, opening my eyes again. "I just... I've been called words like that so many times. I don't like hearing them. Normally I just get a little annoyed inside, but..."

Johanna sighed, staring down into the water. "Tiny cell."

"Tiny cell."

"I forgive you. Just... the Empire *is* my people's enemy, Ashe. You literally took our homeworld from us. The Elfen... the Thondians, they make us slaves. So do the Naule."

I sighed, nodding. "I'm not asking you to love them, to love us. Just, I don't know, try to keep an open mind? If Tasir's really a Director, I don't think she'd be tolerating anyone who's especially cruel or bigoted in her camp."

She grimaced. "I will... try, and hope they aren't going to kill us in our sleep."

"We've been hoping that every day for months now." I muttered. "At least if Tasir has us killed tonight, we'll probably die cleanly. Better than the barge."

That earned me a tiny snort, and even smaller smile. "True."

After that we focused on the actual mechanics of bathing. Washing our arms, and especially our feet. The clear water quickly began to turn a murky brown, which heralded the pair of us getting out far more quickly than I'd have liked.

The lack of towels didn't stop Johanna from quickly pulling her clothing back on, and making a frustrated sound when I didn't.

"What? I'm washing mine." I told her as I did just that, dunking them both and doing my best to scrape some of the grime off. Especially the lower parts of my pants. "You really need to stop being so hung up about clothing."

"Modesty." She growled without turning around. "People don't just strip down in front of strangers where I'm from."

"We're hardly strangers." I noted.

"People don't strip down in front of people they aren't having sex with." She amended.

"I bet your soldiers do, unless their barracks are very weirdly designed."

She grumbled and muttered some more, and was still at it when our food arrived.

Except Irkan wasn't the one holding a pair of bowls; that was Tasir.

"All we've got is stew tonight." She handed Johanna one bowl, then walked over to me. It proved to be filled with an orange colored liquid, along with a wooden spoon. "But it's got root vegetables and some grains. Should be safe for Humans."

"Thank you, sir." I took it gratefully. It was hot in my hands, and smelled... well, it smelled like not-gruel. That was enough to make it seem positively divine.

Leaning against the tub, I started sipping it as quickly as I could without burning myself. It tasted as good as it smelled, and I had to resist the urge to drink it even faster than I already was.

The Eldest helped with that, asking, "How were you captured?"

Swallowing a bit of stew, I answered, "My pack helped break up one of their operations in the Near Reaches. When we got back to Trinity, I went drinking with a different pack that I'm friends with. They drugged us at the bar, grabbed me, injected me with something else, and I then woke up on the barge."

"The typical story then." Tasir exhaled, "Pretty much every other Imperial here has told me a version of that."

"Are the others Intelligence as well?" I asked.

"No. Local authorities mostly, plus a few lower ranked officers who discovered the wrong things about their superiors."

I sipped more broth, licking my lips after. "Were you investigating them too?"

"Yes, but we'll discuss that later. We have priorities. Do you know where they implanted you?"

"Left shoulder." I nodded to where Johanna was quietly eating her stew. "Same for her. What is it?"

"Mixed tracking device and bomb, best we can tell." My cellmate and I both winced, which brought an unpleasant smile to Tasir's face. "Yes. Those will have to be removed as soon as possible. Tomorrow."

Johanna cleared her throat, "Um... medicine for pain?"

"We live in a swamp, girl." One tarah flicked. "Fortunately for you two, there is one Xenthan here. He'll dose you both with venom, which will make you luckier than the rest of us were."

My cellmate didn't look relieved, "You mean an actual Xenthan, or is he Kelthi?"

"Xenthan."

A wince. "Um, a... Taker?"

"No, thank the Aspects." Tasir said. "Point is, you agree to us taking those out and letting Marzin scan you for anything else, or you're leaving come morning."

I was already shaking my head. "Not much of a choice, sir."

We both glanced to Johanna, who let out a tiny huff. "No choice, but want answers. Where are we?"

Tasir scowled, both tarah flicking up and then down. "Your kind calls it Last Stop. A good a name as any. It's the dumping grounds for the Faithful, where they store the people they want to experiment on."

My contentment over having a bath and real food faded quickly. "...experiment on? Is that what the Culling is?"

"When they sweep up everyone and cut them open? If they're lucky? Yes. You don't want to know what happens to the unlucky ones." She said.

"You've seen a... Culling?" I asked.

"No, I haven't been here a year yet." Her chin jerked to one side. "Marzin has. He's one of the few who's been able to avoid them. Observe them. Everyone else gets taken in sooner or later, even the ones that try to buy them off. You want the horror stories? Go to him. He's got plenty."

I winced. "I've... had enough horror for a while, I think."

The Director snorted quietly. "It won't get any better, Huntress. For tonight, finish your food, then go to the second tent on the left as you come out. You two can sleep there. Tomorrow you'll get the chips out, and we see how bad a shape you're both in."

"After that?" I asked.

"After that? You join the rest of the Resistance. So long as you work, you'll get to eat."

"Work on what?" Johanna spoke up. "What are you doing here?"

Tasir turned away, speaking over her shoulder as she left. "What anyone sane is trying to do. Escape before we die."

VIII

Marzin's enormous head hung over me as I lay flat on a dry log, his moist breath impossible to get away from. And I was pretty sure I saw bits of Pferd-meat stuck between his teeth, which made me glad I'd already eaten. I'd have definitely been off my appetite for a while otherwise.

"Three devices." He said finally. "One in her shoulder, two in her left arm."

Khash himself must have blessed everyone here, to have Marzin around. The enormous Regnon turned out to have all kinds of cybernetic toys hidden away within him; everything from shield projectors to advanced medical scanners. It was that last that was probably the most important. The thing that let everyone get their tracking devices out of their bodies so that the... Faithful couldn't just blow everyone up at a distance.

"Um," I cleared my throat. "The left arm ones are my immunization booster and my hormone controller."

Tasir appeared on my other side, frowning down at me. "First is standard issue. Why do you need the second?"

I coughed a little, somewhat embarrassed. "My monthly cycle was extremely painful when it started, and it only got worse when I got older. I requested one during my second assignment, and I've kept it ever since."

She made a low sound of understanding. "Marzin, any sign of tampering in her arm?"

"I do not believe so... no. The only device is the usual one in her shoulder." He paused, tilting his head so that he could bring one glowing eye nearly down on top of me. "It's a new model. A disc instead of a tube. We'll have to be careful on removal."

"Always something new. Right, you're off." Tasir waved for me to move, beckoning my cellmate over. "Ark Fleet? Get over here, your turn."

I sat up once Marzin had pulled back, scooting off of the 'exam log' so that Johanna could take my place. Her hand caught mine before I could step

81

back, leaving me to settle in beside her as she laid down.

"Relax, little one." Marzin rumbled as he looked her over in turn. "I find your people to be cute, not appetizing."

Johanna inhaled sharply, "Um. That's nice. Your teeth are still larger than my head."

He chuckled, but took her hint and kept his lips over said teeth as much as he could. After a minute or so he pulled back, motioning for her to stand.

"Well?" Tasir demanded.

"She has the usual Ark Fleet assembly of implants. Two immunization boosters, definitely Kelthi manufactured, and an injection site in her left arm. I assume the device in her groin serves the same role as Lori's implant?"

We all glanced at Johanna, who turned a little pink. "Yes."

Marzin chuckled again. "Then the only device of concern is the fresh implant in her back. Should be a simple cut and pull, as usual. Just be wary of handling the new model."

"I've been an Intelligence asset longer than you've been alive." Tasir rolled her eyes, "I know how to handle a bomb. Ghost! Ginlos! Get over here, time to get to work."

I glanced over to where the two men had been lurking, and immediately wished I hadn't. Not because of Ginlos. He was a handsome old Guide, who somehow managed to make leather and prison garb look stately as he strolled over.

No, it was Ghost that was the issue.

I'd read that Xenthans, or their Ark Fleet Kelthi cousins, were uncomfortable to look at in person. At least if you weren't used to them. I was pretty sure whoever had written that textbook had been understating things for the sake of politeness. Focusing on him for more than a moment made my head start to throb.

There was no one thing that I could point to, so much as it was... well, everything.

82

His eyes were too big, his upper arms were too short, and his forearms were too long. When he grinned he showed off black gums that contrasted horribly with his chalk-white skin, and sharp canines that nearly cut into his own lips. His legs shared the same unfortunate sizing as his arms, which made his odd, swaying walk look... wrong.

Even his *fur* was wrong. The snow-white strands weren't smooth like a Human's or Naulian's. Instead they were... stiff, more like bristles. I was pretty sure I could actually hear the long mane on his head rustling when it swayed behind him.

Marzin was fifty times his size, yet wasn't nearly as strange to look at.

"Let us get this over with." His bright red eyes narrowed a little as he approached, one hand brushing the heavy fur of his mane away from his uncomfortable features. "Left shoulder on each of them?"

"Yes. Avoid the arteries." Tasir instructed. "How long for it to take effect on a Human?"

"Couple minutes. Dark or pale first?"

I cleared my throat. "I'll go first."

He gave me an annoyed little twirl of an overly long finger. "Spin around then, bare the shoulder, and don't scream in my ear."

I obeyed, suddenly feeling far less confident in all of this. It was my turn to grab Johanna's hand before she could pull away, holding tightly as the Xenthan stepped up behind me.

Strong hands pulled my fur back, then hot breath was on my shoulder. I'd just started to tense up when he struck; teeth sinking into my skin without any further warning.

I jerked in surprise, but honestly the pain wasn't nearly as bad as I'd thought it would be. I'd been bit harder by packmates for fun. This was more uncomfortable than anything else. Squeezing gently on my friend's hand, I kept my breathing even, counting to five before he pulled back.

"It'll be numb in a few minutes." He said brusquely, a black, forked tongue appearing to lick my blood off his lips. "Turn around."

83

Johanna looked a little green, probably from the way he'd clearly enjoyed the taste of it. "Ashe?"

"It wasn't that bad." I assured her, doing my best not to frown as my arm and shoulder began to tingle. "Five seconds. I'll be right here."

She swallowed, nodding tightly as Ghost walked behind her. Her fingers clenched down when he bit her, making me wince a little as she squeezed. Five long breaths later and he released his jaw, revealing four bleeding puncture wounds in her pale skin.

He wandered off without another word, leading Tasir to get us both sitting on the bench while we waited for the toxin to leave us numb.

She interrogated me while we waited. Asking just what kind of operations of the Faithful I'd broken up, how I'd gotten involved at all. I gave her the short version of what had happened on Oshflara, getting to the Burned Hand before I heard Ginlos move up behind me, Marzin taking a heavier set of steps to loom behind him.

"Burned Hand?" Tasir helped me get my shirt off, then got me laying on my belly on the log. "I've seen a few of the Faithful with burns on them, but I assumed they were battle scars. Your Agent thinks otherwise?"

I laid my cheek on the rough wood, doing my best to not pay attention to the men about to cut my skin open. "Yes. We thought it was ritual scarring. I saw it up close, and it was too even for a battle wound. Some of the ones we found dead later had similar markings in different locations."

Something tugged at my back. I started to turn only for Tasir to grab my chin, forcing me to keep talking with her.

"Their operation in the Reaches, the one you interfered with. Details." She ordered.

I gave them. I broke off once or twice, wincing as I felt things tugging at my body. Just because there wasn't any pain didn't make it comfortable. Especially when I realized that they'd gotten the device out pretty quickly; it was patching me back up after that was taking longer.

"A recruiting operation." Tasir mused when both I and they finished, leaving me with an awkward bandage wrapped around my neck and under my arm. "And a definite infiltration of Trinity's operations. Up, let's get you switched out."

My story time ended as we got me upright, then Johanna laying down. Tasir repeated her questioning, Johanna slowly giving a few vague details of where she'd been taken.

How their little mining colony had been overrun in a matter of hours, how they'd surrendered under the terms of the Compact. Described the Faithful promptly violating a half-dozen of its rules by executing every Kelthi still living, along with all of the wounded soldiers who'd tried to defend the Ark Fleet's outpost.

I tuned most of it out; I'd heard it all before. Instead I watched as a tiny projector emerged from one of Marzin's massive hands, red light tracing a small line on her back.

Ginlos, careful not to get in the way of the beam, leaned in with a medical knife that had seen better days. He cut slowly but steadily with one hand, the other holding a small tool I wasn't familiar with.

Whatever it was, he slid it inside as soon as there was room to do so, then quickly pulled it back.

A bloody silver disc came with it. He slowly walked away, setting it down next to the one he must have taken from me, then returned. He picked up a small canister of medical foam, bringing it near the wound. All that came out were a few drops that he carefully rubbed it into the bloody line he'd cut.

"...that was unpleasant." Johanna murmured when they finished getting her bandaged. "What will you do with them?"

"We bury them, leave them behind when we move camp." Ginlos replied, speaking for the first time. His accent was... a new one for me. It sounded like he was biting off each consonant. "Soon as the rest of the hunters get back, that's exactly what we're doing."

I grimaced, "Sorry. You'd have wanted to cut them out before we got here, wouldn't you?"

Tasir flicked her hard eyes up to Marzin. "Yes, and that's his fault, not yours."

85

"We were overdue to move anyway." The Regnon said in his own defense. "Speaking of, I will be departing soon to make sure our next site remains clear."

"Just be back in time to help us transfer everything."

He dipped his massive head before lumbering off. Ginlos vanished at the same time, stopping only long enough to pick up the two discs, carrying them with him when he left.

Tasir motioned for us both to sit down once they were gone, hands on her hips as she stared out into the swamp.

Several silent minutes passed, Johanna and I checking each other's bandages. Marzin's departure had clearly eased her mind, as had the removal of the bomb in her shoulder, leaving her finally looking relaxed.

Well, until Tasir started speaking again.

"We don't assign duties." The Elder said without turning. "Starting tomorrow, do whatever you want around the camp that you're comfortable with. Cooking, cleaning, repairing equipment, making clothes, whatever. Just do something useful and you'll get to eat."

I nodded. "Yes sir. When do we scout our captor's, um, the *Faithful's* positions?"

She glanced over at us, "You're both fresh off the barge. You're not in any shape for that, and we know most of what we need already."

"Waiting for the right moment?" I asked.

"There's no ships on the ground, not that we can tell." Her tarah lowered in irritation. "We'd have already tried our plan if there were."

Johanna frowned, "What about the barges? Or shuttles?"

"No routine schedule for either. They both come and go quickly, too quickly for us to try to storm them." Tasir huffed. "Which would end badly regardless. They have plenty of guns and powerful sorcerers. There's barely fifty of us."

"And collaborators." I added quietly.

86

"And those dead fish. Two major groups right now, one Human, one Thondian. They like to raid each other for slaves, or come after us when they can manage it."

I smiled a little. "Marzin scared them away pretty easily yesterday."

Tasir gave me a hard grin of her own. "He does that, but he's not always around. Doesn't help that there's a lot more of them than there is of us."

"There is?" Johanna asked. "More Humans?"

"Humans and Thondians are apparently their main focus. There's several hundred of both out there, living in little villages near the Faithful's base." She replied.

My cellmate visibly swallowed. "...can't be. Ark Fleet would know."

Gray lips twisted unpleasantly. "Don't be so sure of that, girl. If they can infiltrate Imperial Intelligence, they could have infiltrated your fleet as well."

"How? They're all Trahcon." She countered.

"Not all of them. They have... a Process." Tasir paused, grimaced, and shook her head. "At least that's what the half-mad fool we ran into called it. He wasn't sane anymore, but he just kept repeating that the Gods had Processed his soul, and deemed him unworthy. We didn't get anything else out of him."

That... didn't sound good.

"Is he still around?" I asked.

"Drowned himself." She said flatly.

We both winced, Johanna asking the next question. "Do... do you know what they did to him?"

"I have a theory." Tasir replied. "But I've been betrayed enough over the last few years. You'll be told once I'm either sure that neither of you is an infiltrator, or once it's time to leave."

Operational security. Ugh. "...yes sir. I understand."

"Good, because you don't have a choice." Tasir, it seemed, was rather blunt. "You can earn some trust right now."

"How, sir?"

She eyed me warily, which made me shift uncomfortably. Why would she be wary of me? I was thin, couldn't use my left arm, and didn't have any sorcery.

"You're history is impossible." I jerked in shock when she said that. "You've been in six packs? Seven now? No one in the Empire would have tolerated someone so clearly lost at sea. It's a good sympathy motive, but you should have thought of a better cover story."

"I... it isn't!" I protested. "It's not a story, sir. It's the truth!"

Blue eyes narrowed. "Is it, Huntress? Just like it's the truth that you just happened to stumble across an apparent agent of the Faithful on Oshflara? Then so quickly found another?"

"Th-there was nothing quick about it." I stuttered. "It took us months! And... and meeting the Burned Hand was the worst moment in my life! She tortured me!"

"Did she? Or did you volunteer to be marked to complete the story?" She demanded.

I felt my mouth drop open, hanging there in shock. Volunteered to be burned? To be tortured? For what!?

"I... I..."

I couldn't find my voice.

She'd... she didn't believe me. She thought I was some kind of agent, sent by the Faithful to do... something. That's why she'd waited to question me until I'd been drugged again. Why she was staying well out of arms reach. Why I could smell her sorcery in the air, ready to lash out.

She didn't believe me.

Ashahn's blood, I didn't know her at all, so why... why did that hurt so much?

"St-stop it." Johanna finally spoke, her voice trembling but loud. "She's not lying to you!"

Tasir turned on her. "Isn't she? What about you? You claim to be eighteen, that's a child to your kind. What was a *child* doing on an Ark Fleet mining colony? Why weren't you safely nestled on some ship?"

"I... not to you. I don't talk to you." Her Caranat started to fall apart as she got even more emotional. "Private. Ashe knows."

"Do you even have a family?" She continued as if Johanna hadn't. "Are you even from that collection of rusting hulks? You look more like a Thondian slave, withered and meek. A vulnerable little huntress, the perfect bait for an Imperial conscript cut off from her pack. Someone she'd instinctively want to protect, bond with, stay with."

"I... you rude! Cruel! We leave! Ashe, we leave!"

Tasir quickly brought a hand up, her posture draining of its tension. "Enough, enough. I had to know."

Johanna had already staggered to her feet, tugging at my limp arm with her working one. I rose shakily, finding my voice. "Know... know what, sir?"

"How you'd react." Her arms and tarah both slowly spread into a non-threatening position, her feet taking her one step back. "Whatever the Process is, one thing I know is that it does something to warp the victim's memories."

That didn't explain anything, and I said as much.

"I knew a man on Alum... a Human. Someone I now believe was Processed. He reacted... violently when I told him that his memories were impossible." Tasir frowned, as if in remembrance before shaking her head. "His personality changed in a moment. If you'd gone through what he had, you'd have reacted with rage, not tears, when I pushed you."

I swallowed, "...oh. Have you... caught anyone with that?"

89

Her voice was flat. "Yes."

"Oh." I said again, more quietly. That explained it, though it didn't explain just why I was so upset about it. "What happened?"

"A Thondian we rescued from a new arrival group, just like you. We got his implant out, and I questioned him just as I did you. He snapped and went for my throat within the first few seconds. Then two others did the same when it was their turn."

I winced, Johanna swallowing nervously. "That... oh."

"I don't know what the Process really is, or what these so-called Faithful are doing here." Tasir went on without emotion. "There used to be another group like ours. They were all killed two months ago. Marzin and I believe because a Processed infiltrated them, then called in the Faithful to wipe them out."

She paused, exhaled, and shook her head. "I will not apologize. Pressing you is the only test we have right now, and I had to know. You're both free for the remainder of the day. Rest, recover. Eat at any fires, I will make it known you're to be welcomed."

"...thank you sir." I mumbled.

Johanna didn't say anything, she just tugged me into motion. We slipped between the trees and alcoves, not speaking to anyone on our way back to our rough little tent.

Dark mutters and curses about Tasir in furious Deutsch filled the air as soon as we were inside.

"...we can't leave." I muttered before she could ask, sitting down heavily on the grass floor of our new 'home'. "We're in a swamp. We don't know how to hunt."

"Rude bitch. She... Ashe, why are you crying?"

"...I don't know." I admitted, staring at my bare feet. "I... don't know what's wrong with me."

Her legs slowly came into view, then the rest of her as she carefully knelt down in front of me. She nearly fell over, quickly throwing her working arm out for balance. "Ashe? Please... you're the strong one. Please."

I tried to take deep breaths. Tried to close my eyes, tried to meditate.

The sense of peace, of nothing but sound, didn't come.

"...hold me?" I asked.

She sat beside me, letting my head fall onto her shoulder, letting me feel the warmth of another person.

I closed my eyes, silently crying... unable to say just why.

Johanna held on until darkness claimed me.

IX

I paid more attention to my emotional state after that, trying to figure out just what was going on with me. The symptoms were pretty easy to identify, once I had a few days to really take stock of myself.

Everything was raw, overwhelming. Things that should have annoyed me made me want to attack someone. Something that should have upset me left tears on my cheeks. Startled jumps when I was surprised began turning into near-panic attacks.

Johanna wasn't any better. If anything she was even worse; I had to drag her off and hold her until she calmed down at least once a day. That or rub her back as she shook with fear, unable to be near Marzin or the Thondians in the camp.

I started meditating every single morning, sometimes for as long as an hour, just to prepare myself for the day. It seemed to help. A little, at least.

Eventually Johanna asked me to teach her the basics of it, and she did her best to copy me. I wasn't sure if she did because she hoped it would help, or if she was just bored and didn't want to interact with anyone who wasn't Human.

That last bit was still a problem. She may have kept her mouth shut, not actually *saying* anything that would upset me, but she remained obviously uncomfortable among so many aliens.

She'd taken to staying with me at all times, making us packmates in everything but name. I didn't really mind; it was nice to have someone I could confide in when few in the camp proved willing to talk to me.

"It is not the fault of the Imperial savanna." Irkan rumbled as we walked through the woods, everyone carrying as much as they could on the trip to the next camp. "All here are wary of newcomers. Few interact outside of their cliques."

"You do." I countered. "So does Marzin, and Tasir."

His chuckle was that odd, chirping noise that his people did. "This

92

one is the only one of his kind that remains upon Last Stop. The sailor prefers not to be alone. He takes companionship where it can be found."

Johanna glanced at him, doing her best to adjust the bundle of tent hides she was carrying on her back. "There weren't any other Mikira on your barge? I thought they brought people here by species."

"There were others of the sacred blood." He replied. "They were slain by the Thondian collaborators before we knew how to live on Last Stop. This sailor was the only survivor."

I winced. "I'm sorry."

His angular face cut in a shake of his head. "Do not apologize for those who died bravely. They joined our kin beyond the Veil with pride. The one who may be named Irkan would have joined them, but was ordered to retreat so that the Kings might know what has occurred here."

"...do you really have to talk about yourself in the third person like that?" Johanna complained.

"Yes."

"And not use our names?" She went on.

"Yes." He repeated, sounding amused. "The savanna people may throw about Names as though they are nothing, but those of the sacred blood treat them with tremendous respect. This one has not yet earned his name, and neither have you."

Johanna groaned. "Marzin apparently has."

"He survived many Cullings, and planned our eventual escape." Irkan explained. "Marzin saved this speaker's life when he fled the plains. He has earned his name."

"Has Tasir?" I asked, rolling my shoulders a little to try and stop the straps of my pack from digging into them. Just like Johanna I was carrying sections of the group's tents; the two of us were still too weak to haul anything heavier.

And the mixed hide, cloth, and ropes felt heavy enough as it was.

"The old shark has not." Another quiet laugh and a glance aside to Johanna. "This annoys her as much as it annoys the Fleet savanna."

She scowled, clearly not thrilled to have anything at all in common with the Director.

I brushed my fingers over her arm, smiling, which only made her huff.

"Aliens are weird." She muttered.

"That they are." Irkan agreed. "Did the Imperial savanna have other questions?"

I nodded, "I've... noticed that I've had a much harder time controlling my emotions since we arrived here. Did they do something to us on the barges, or is it just a side-effect of being confined? Or is it just a Human thing?"

"The Imperial savanna is wise for having noticed. Many do not." A clawed hand reached up, scratching at the quills on his chin. "No one is certain of what is done upon the barges, but emotional instability appears to be part of it. As does a certain damage to one's memories."

"Memory damage?" I swallowed, "Uh, what kind of memory damage?"

"The blur of the past. Of time. She claims to believe the trip lasted four or five months, yes?"

"Yes." I said slowly, "I'm pretty sure about that."

His follow-up chirping laugh somehow managed to sound bitter. "All are fairly certain of that, yet strangely all seem to agree that their voyage lasted that many months regardless of from where they were taken."

I flinched, making it Johanna's turn to gently grab my arm. "That's... how?"

"The old river-shark has a theory, which she will not tell." He said.

"You don't?"

94

He jerked his head in the negative. "It is of no consequence. The effect wears off in time, and our focus must be on the escape of this place. That is our priority. All else may be considered later."

That was probably the smart attitude to take, all things considered. It was the kind of attitude that Rerth would have told me to have, if she was here. Like how she had made sure I stayed focused on the project at hand, and put aside anything else for later.

I'd found that easier to do when there'd been plenty to work on. To distract myself with. When I'd had a real project in front of me, with months or years of work to look forward to.

It was a lot harder to focus on escape when we weren't trusted enough to be told anything. When we'd spent the last two days walking through a swamp, and now through the woods. When we had no idea where we were going, why we were on this planet, or where this planet even was.

"How long?" Johanna interrupted my thoughts. "Until we're back to normal?"

"A few months. Perhaps longer, perhaps shorter. Few shall take it personally if the savanna have problems. All have suffered from it." Irkan said.

That didn't make it any easier, but I thanked him for the information all the same. He waved me off, saying it was always pleasant to talk to new people. He'd picked up the pace a bit after that, moving farther ahead in the ragged line to speak with some of the Trahcon.

I'd have tried to join him, those three were all from Cathia, and I did want to know what life was like in the Far Reaches... but I was starting to run out of breath. My legs were burning from my hips to my ankles, and my back was protesting the weight on my shoulders.

"Tired?" I asked Johanna once he'd moved off.

She grimaced, nodding. "Tired and sore. You?"

"Same. Sunset soon, I hope."

"I hope so too."

95

That hope kept us going for the next hour or two, until Marzin and Tasir finally called a halt for the day. We didn't set up a full camp, we hadn't been doing that since we'd left. Instead we used bits of the tents to make awnings to sleep under, using the trees and crude spears driven into the ground to keep them up.

Food was, thankfully, a bit more plentiful. We'd been sticking close to a large river stocked with several kinds of fish that nearly everyone could eat.

Irkan and Marzin were apparently the exceptions. The former was making do with some kind of snakes he'd killed, while the latter claimed he was fine to not eat for a while thanks to some kind of implant. That he'd go back out to hunt again after we arrived.

For our part Johanna and I set up our own little awning fairly quickly, then divided into our usual dinner prep; She got the fire started while I fetched the fish from Ginlos, coming back with one each. Then she cooked them while I peeled the hard-skinned fruits someone had picked yesterday.

"Careful with that." I looked up to see Tasir approaching, her hood thrown back for the evening. "That's Stone Fruit from Alum, Aspects alone know why they planted it here. It'll break your teeth if you don't get all the skin off."

I nodded, "Thank you sir. Are you sitting with us tonight?"

"Not for long." She slowly got down to one knee beside me, tarah quivering a little as she tried to relax. "I'm getting too old for this."

Johanna pressed her lips together, saying nothing as she focused on our dinner.

She didn't like the Director much. Oh, she'd admitted that she understood why she'd done what she had. She just thought there had to have been a better way to go about it. One that hadn't set the both of us off when we were in bad shape physically and mentally.

I was pretty sure Tasir could have managed that too, but I knew better than to try and talk an Elder out of what they'd decided to do.

"We have three more days until we reached our next camp, provided that the weather holds." Tasir went on, "After which I will be leaving with some others to find the best path toward the Faithful's base."

96

"And do you have orders for me while you're gone, sir?"

She nodded. "I do. I want you to get into marching shape as quickly as possible. I've told Irkan and Ghost to work you hard on that. You will be accompanying me on a scouting trip after I return."

"Scouting who, sir? I thought you already had enough information on the Faithful." I asked, before realizing the answer was obvious. "Oh. The collaborators?"

"Yes. According to Marzin, they get an advanced warning of a Culling. The better to offer up everyone they don't want anymore. We need to keep a watch on them, so that we'll be ready to move when the time comes."

I swallowed nervously. "Just scouting? I... do not think an infiltration is a good idea."

Tasir snorted. "I may not trust you yet, huntress, but that doesn't mean I want you dead. That's all an infiltration would achieve. No. Consider this a chance to prove to me you've got actual training from an Intelligence Agent."

I perked up a little. That sounded a lot better. "I can do that, sir."

"Good. Your cellmate can accompany us if she can keep up. Otherwise she stays here."

Johanna scowled harder at the fish she was turning over. "I can hear you."

"I know, Ark Fleet." Gray hands pushed herself upright, another small groan coming out. "Eat well, rest well, and keep up tomorrow."

"Sir." I nodded, Tasir moving off after that.

"...she's still a bitch." Johanna grumbled, still in Caranat, well before Tasir had fully walked away. "Why do you have to call her sir all the time?"

"Because she's a Director." I replied tiredly. "That's a very high rank in Intelligence."

She glowered some more. "If she's so high ranking, how'd she end up here? Wouldn't your Empire have done more to protect her? Bodyguards and

97

big bases full of soldiers?"

I bit my lip, unable to think of a decent reply. I'd seen the kind of protections the Director on Trinity had. I couldn't begin to imagine a way that she could have been abducted the way that Tasir had apparently been.

Maybe things had been different on Alum? Its political situation was pretty odd, if I remembered right. Not an actual Imperial world at all, but not quite under Cathia's control either. Some kind of strange mess of two rivers slamming into each other or something.

"How is dinner coming?" I tried to change the subject.

Johanna wasn't having that tonight, though she at least switched to Deutsch. "I still think she's lying about who she is."

I let out a heavy sigh, replying in the same language. "She might be, and she probably thinks the same about us. About everyone else here, really. No one here can actually prove what they tell anyone, Johanna."

"...she's still hiding something." She mumbled.

"Everyone in Intelligence is hiding something." I smiled a little. "My pack plays a game where we lie to each other about things that happened in our pasts, or what we were up to when we go out alone. To see how convincing we can be. Practice for infiltrations."

She huffed, carefully pulling our dinner away from the coals. "You Imperials are weird. A bunch of alcoholics who lie to each other for fun. It's a wonder how you manage to get anything done."

"Well," I mused, taking my stick with its fish on it. "There is a whole lot of us. That helps. Fruit?"

"Did you finish getting the skin off?"

I held it up a bit, turning it over so that she could inspect it. Once she was satisfied she took it with a smile and a word of thanks, both of us settling in to eat. The fish proved to be tender and pleasantly flaky, but didn't have much actual flavor to it.

The fruit was sweet, with just enough tartness to be enjoyable.

My quiet snort at the thought made Johanna glance up as she finished picking at her fish. "What?"

"Two weeks ago I'd have been desperate for a meal like this." I told her. "Now I'm already thinking that it's just all right."

She blinked, then giggled. "Right? It's so bland. Did you eat fish a lot in the Empire?"

"All the time." I set my stick and its bones aside. "Fish are pretty easy to grow on almost any world that has water, so they're one of the main sources of protein in the Empire. What about in the Ark Fleet?"

"It varies. Depends on which farming colonies your flotilla is closest to when you have to resupply. Usually we don't get much meat like this though." The remains of her fish turned over in her hands as she looked down at it. "It's not bad, but I never really saw the appeal."

"...but do you get to drink?" I asked.

She laughed, "You're an alcoholic, Ashe."

I rolled my eyes, "You sound like my packmates. I didn't drink *that* much, and you didn't say no."

"We're not allowed to drink until we're twenty-one."

My mouth fell open. "What!?"

"Wait," She blinked. "How young can you drink in the Empire?"

"Soon as you're a Huntress." I said. "That's fifteen for Humans."

It was her turn to gape at me. "You started drinking at fifteen!?"

Finally being close enough to fluent to really talk about our pasts made it far more fun to talk with her late into the evening. We giggled over bits we'd misunderstood when we'd been talking on the ship, talking about our childhoods. How much I missed the simple times in my birth-pack, how much she missed her Onkel and the comfort of life aboard a ship.

We talked late into the evening, until it was time to rest before tomorrow's hike began.

X

Our destination proved to be a cave dug into an old hill near the river. It was pretty damp and generally unpleasant, but between the cave itself and the plentiful trees it seemed like as good a place to hide as any.

Concealing ourselves from the air was important, according to the older members of the group. The Faithful liked to send out drones to look for groups like us when they got bored. Anyone they spotted would be visited by hunting parties soon after; run down for no apparent reason beyond the fun of killing.

Hearing those stories fully convinced me that the Burned Hand's group and these 'Faithful' really were one in the same. It was all too easy to imagine them doing it, calling out to the 'beasts' they were chasing down to murder.

Tasir, Ginlos, and a handful of others vanished shortly after we'd gotten everything set up. According to Marzin, it was a two week trip farther down river to where the Faithful and Collaborators were setup, so it would be at least a month before we saw them again.

Johanna was completely fine with that. At least until Irkan and Ghost started showing up every morning to help us get into shape again.

They started by teaching us net fishing; making us wade deep into the river, sweeping a broad net between us. Then, once several fish were caught in it, we had to haul it back to shore.

Considering the current and sandy bottom, it was incredibly exhausting work, but it did help start to build our endurance back up. Well, mine at least. I wasn't sure Johanna had ever had much muscle to begin with.

She certainly had some after a few weeks of our new routine.

"Ark Fleet weakling." Ghost snorted when she went to bed early, as usual, leaving me sitting with the men around a low fire. "All she does is complain."

I gave him an annoyed look, poking the embers with a stick. "She complains, but she still does the work. And you complain just as much as she does."

The Xenthan bared his fangs at me, a hard toss of his head making his stiff fur rustle. "That is my prerogative. She's a child."

"Huntress." I corrected.

"I don't mean her age, Lori. I mean her attitude. She was sheltered in those disgusting hulks she called home, and all she wants to do is get back to them."

I upgraded my expression to a glare. "Her life wasn't pampered, and no one who traveled on one of those barges is a child anymore."

Irkan chortled, sending his chin-quills swaying. "The Imperial has a point, pale hunter. The Fleet savanna may complain often, but she still does all the tasks that are asked of her. It is commendable. More so than the sand-walkers among us."

Ghost let out a quiet grunt. "Hard to argue with that. At least old Narob has shut up with Tasir off."

"He still think he should be in charge?" I asked.

"Of course he does, but he's not stupid enough to confront Marzin about it." He brought a shoulder up and down in a Human-style shrug. "Marzin's made it clear he won't put up with their passive-aggressive power plays either."

I stared into the fire, trying not to scowl.

The Thondians among the group were... about as pleasant as the ones I'd met on Varur'fluro. They had some incredibly obscure way of determining rank and position among themselves, and constantly tried to apply that to everyone else. Mostly that had meant challenging Tasir's position as co-leader next to Marzin, trying to convince the Regnon to stop listening to her.

He mostly ignored them so long as they kept their complaints to words.

So far they had, though the tall aliens certainly liked to loom over everyone else whenever they could.

101

"How about we talk about more important things?" I asked. Not that I didn't want to know more about the group's internal politics, I kind of needed to if I wanted to keep myself and Johanna safe... but I also needed to know more about the men working with us.

Men who'd been frustratingly good at avoiding saying much about themselves.

"Like how we got here?" Ghost snorted. "You sure you're from an intelligence agency, Lori? You're as subtle as a supernova when you try to play the interrogator."

"I know better than to bother asking that question." I countered. "How about just what you two actually did for a living before you got here. Ashahn's blood, Ghost. I'll take your actual name."

A long finger wagged in my direction. "No. To both."

I gave him my best pout, which merely resulted in another of his unpleasant smiles.

"Irkan?" I asked.

The squat alien tilted his head, a low hum escaping his throat. "There seems little harm in telling a tale. The one who shall be named Irkan was a sailor in the navy of Scarlet Tears."

Ghost perked up, leaning in a bit. Apparently he hadn't known this. "An actual sailor? I thought you were just messing with us."

"The sailor quite enjoys machines in a way few of his people do." Irkan confessed, sounding almost... ashamed of that. "His blood stirred slowly in battle, to the dismay of his close kin. To operate the great ships of the stars is not a respected profession among the Kingdom."

I blinked. "Why not? It's kind of, you know, important for a nation to have sailors. Lots of them. Hard to run an interstellar kingdom without them."

"It is our way." He said simply. "We rely greatly upon Automations and those Clans of the Naule who joined with our Kingdom long ago."

"Huh." I shook my head, not really getting it. "That make sense to

102

you?"

"It's common knowledge in the Far Reaches." Ghost replied with another toss of his strange fur, "Mikira like being able to see who they're fighting. Always have. Fighting from ships is... not dishonorable exactly, but unpleasant. Or something. They're weird."

Irkan huffed out a laugh. "We are proud of our ways, as are all. But we speak away from the subject of this one's past. Before he was taken by the Faithful, he was the Officer of the Darkness upon a great cruiser. Its name would mean *Laughs with Chaos* in your tongue."

"...you commanded the night shifts?" I guessed at the meaning of his rank.

"Yes." He jerked his head in a nod. "In cruising. In battle, this sailor took command of the damage control teams. This was the duty that led to the Faithful's capture of an entire section of the ship's crew and this one's superior officer."

"Oh." I said quietly, "You don't have to tell us."

A stubby arm waved dismissively, "It is a good tale. One of warning. The Officer of Darkness and Officer of Daylight had noticed strange behavior among some of the crew assigned to the hours of darkness during a damage control simulation. Both began investigating them, and found several acting strangely when around River-Shark slaves who cleaned the ship."

I grimaced at the s-word, while Ghost openly scowled.

Irkan went on, not noticing or not caring about our opinion of his people's owning of other beings. "Both officers believed they were dealing with agents of the Crescent, or of the Riush of Terminus. They gathered warriors and set an ambush during the next shore leave. To their shame the ambush never occurred."

"They drugged you before?" Ghost asked.

"Yes." He confirmed. "Thirty of the Sacred Blood, laid low by toxins in the air while in a shuttle to the surface. When all woke, they were upon the barge."

I knew the rest of the story. They'd arrived on Last Stop, dropped off

103

almost on top of the Thondian collaborators. Mikira were tough little aliens from what I knew, but their enemies were nearly as strong, far taller, and more importantly; armed.

"Thank you for telling me." I said when he finished. "When we escape, are you going back to your Kingdom?"

"Yes." He said without hesitation. "The princes and kings must be warned. The Imperial must feel the same of her Empire."

"She does." I admitted. "Ghost?"

"Not even a question. The Elders need to be told, the Takers sent to hunt these Faithful." He paused, then grinned. "A pleasant image. The panic of the Faithful when we escape. When they realize just how many nations will be hunting them."

We all chuckled, imagining it.

"You think the Compact would be called?" I asked.

Ghost hummed, his forked tongue briefly playing over his lips. "The Faithful aren't a nation, but they *have* violated quite a few of its rules. And abducted members of a lot of signatories. I wouldn't be surprised if your Empire tried to call it."

"It would be the first Call of the Compact since..." My voice trailed off as I remembered the last time that the Compact had been called. "...sorry, Irkan."

"The Imperial has no need to apologize. All know that the Fool King was just that. We rightly cast the blame at him for his dishonor, and upon the Cathian fools that began that war. Not upon the Compact who ended it."

There was a quiet grunt from Ghost. "Cathia remembers your people being the ones to start that war."

Irkan shrugged. "They are wrong."

He rolled his eyes, glancing at me. "A word of warning, Lori? Don't get between the Tears and Cathia. That blood feud has been going since the Airalon Wars, and isn't ending anytime soon."

104

So I was learning. "Yeah. That war was just starting when I was taken."

A deep rumble of anger came from Irkan. "And this sailor is trapped here, rather than aiding his Kingdom in battle. It is... frustrating. What news of the opening engagements reached the Empire?"

"Uhh..." Fingers rose to rub my temples, as if that would help me remember. "...I think your side tried to attack Terminus right at the start, but were thrown back. Only other reports I remember Rerth getting were that you were hurting the Crescent pretty badly, but that the strange Trahcon Empress on Xentha was holding her ground."

He managed to look disappointed. "That is all?"

"My packmate had very firm ideas about staying focused on our assignment." I replied. "I got in trouble for even reading that much."

Irkan sighed, despondent, which made Ghost chuckle at him over the fire. "Don't worry about it. The Riush might collapse quickly, but you know that the Kolkris aren't going to die fast. Even if we're stuck here another year or two, you'll be back in time to see some action."

"...the Kolkris are worthy." Irkan admitted, looking a little cheered. "As is your Empress."

"She's more than worthy, but that's a discussion for another night." He pushed himself to his feet. "I'm off to my bedroll. I intend to leave early for a hunt tomorrow, it'll be more interesting than supervising a pair of flailing Humans in a river."

"We don't flail." I muttered. "We're competent now. You said so yesterday."

A hand waved dismissively as he walked off toward the cave's entrance. "Competent is still painful to watch."

The pang of hurt in my chest rose, but didn't quite breach the surface. I gave him a silent wave, Irkan still squatting by the the few flames still eating at the dry wood we'd fed it.

"Not tired?"

105

"Soon enough." He replied. "This one has been enjoying speaking with the Imperial. She is... more engaging than many others."

I blinked, feeling a bit of heat in my cheeks. "Oh. Um, I like talking with you too."

"Even with this sailor's strange ways?" He asked.

"Even with your very strange way of talking." I assured him.

"If it helps the Imperial, she sounds just as strange to this one."

I smiled, leaning back against the tree behind me. "It does help a little. May I ask you a serious question?"

"The Imperial may."

Taking a deep breath, I asked, "...the Faithful's outpost. What is it, really?"

Irkan stared down into the smoldering campfire. "...the Imperial asks a difficult question. One that is intended to lead to others."

"Yes." I admitted. "Are you going to answer?"

He took his time, clearly thinking about it. I'd begun to prod and poke at the embers again when he finally replied. "The outpost of the Faithful is many things. It is a military base. It is a place to experiment on those deemed lesser. It is a grand temple to their unknown gods."

The last made me frown. "They don't worship Aysh and the Aspects?"

"No, and they execute those that imply it." He said seriously. "A Clan of the Naule sought to collaborate, sought to appease. They built a statue to the shard of Dreams and Storms. The Faithful slaughtered them to the last, and hung what little remained in warning to those who worshipped false idols."

I swallowed against a suddenly dry throat. "Oh. Um... who *do* they worship then?"

"No one knows, save perhaps Marzin or the old shark. And they tell none their thoughts."

106

"Oh." I said again, more quietly. "How many of them are here?"

"Few between Cullings. Then there are many." His gravelly voice lowered further. "Do not speak this to the Ark Fleet savanna, but the chances of escape are poor for us all."

I'd... guessed that already. "...that bad?"

"This sailor believes that some will indeed escape, but only at the cost of many. The savannas' lack of sorcery will make it difficult for them to be among the living." He paused, then softly admitted. "This one does not believe he shall survive to flee either."

"...don't say that. We'll make it. You'll make it back to your Kingdom." Reaching out, I gently poked at the armored shell covering much of his body. "You've got armor after all."

Irkan blinked slowly, then his angular mouth parted in an amused look. "This one does indeed have armor. He supposes that the Imperial may even use it to hide behind, if she becomes fearful during battle."

"I may hold you to that. I'm not very good in a fight." I admitted. "My packmates were trying to help me with that, but I've always been pretty useless that way."

"Then we must fix that." He replied, as if it was that simple. "This sailor shall find you a proper tutor, and we shall begin tomorrow."

"...please tell me I'm not sparring with Ghost. Or you." I paused, "Or Marzin."

He let out a creaky, chirping laugh, slowly heaving himself to his feet. "Of course not. The Imperial shall spar with those most suited to teach her valuable lessons."

"...I'm not sparring with a Thondian."

His laugh continued... making sure that I wasn't going to have much of a choice in the matter.

Ashahn's blood.

107

XI

None of the Thondians were interested in training us in hand to hand, or with spears, or clubs.

Thank the Aspects for small mercies. I hadn't been looking forward to being pummeled by someone two or three times my weight. Neither had Johanna when I'd told her.

All Irkan was able to convince them to do was help teach us a bit of field craft... which mostly meant helping gather edible plants while they hunted. He wasn't interested in coming with, but Ghost had agreed to come along as an escort. Make sure that no one did anything to us.

I was pretty sure he came along out of boredom, but he was a reassuring presence among the towering Thondians all the same.

Well, for me, at least.

"I don't get why you're so nervous around Ghost." I said, yanking a Stone-Fruit out of the bush it had been nestled in. "He's obsessively private, and painful to look at, but he's less of an ass than most of the others are."

Johanna gave me a dark look, fingers taking the fruit from my hand and shoving it into her bag. "His people make drinking cups out of skulls as a way of boasting about how awesome they are."

I went silent for a moment, then had to admit. "...all right, that's more than a little disturbing, but Ghost seems nice enough."

"Ashe, he won't even tell us his real name!"

"And I work for Imperial Intelligence." I countered, carefully reaching past several thorns to get to the next fruit. "I probably shouldn't have even told you my real name."

"That's because you're nice and he's a bastard." She countered.

The words had hardly finished leaving her lips when said bastard came strolling into view, a bow that looked like it had been made out of shuttle parts held in his hands.

His sharp teeth were on full display before he spoke, "I freely admit to being a bastard, but I don't want to hear it from you, Ark Fleet."

Johanna let out a little whimper, her courage folding at once. "...sorry."

I grabbed the last fruit, pulling it out with a grunt. "Come on, Ghost. You know we're still having problems with that, you don't need to scare her."

"Of course I do. I'm Xenthan, she's Ark Fleet. It's a societal compulsion to remind her of her place." He swung his bow around, getting it up over a shoulder. "Come on. Nisco just found something ahead, need every hand to help check it over."

"Found what?"

Ghost shrugged, waving back the way he'd come. "Collaborator village, I think. The remains of one at least."

I perked up at once, curiosity riding an excited wave inside me. "Let's go then."

He gave me a far more friendly smile than he'd given Johanna, then turned and strode back into the woods. Shoving my last fruit into my bag, I quickly hurried after him, my friend following far more reluctantly behind me.

We moved down a very narrow path through the tall trees and thick bushes beneath, along what the others had called a game-trail. It was just flat enough, beaten down by the animals that regularly used it, that we made pretty decent time.

A quarter of an hour later and we emerged in a small clearing, several men and women already hard at work stripping whatever we'd be able to reuse for ourselves.

"You found the Humans. Good, they at least can be relied upon to do actual work." Nisco wasn't quite as towering as most of his species or gender, though he was certainly broad enough.

Unlike the rest of us, who mostly wore whatever we could that was

109

clean and protective, the Thondians had all adopted a rough 'uniform'; their prison pants cut off at the knees, wood and grass-rope shoes, and nothing else.

It certainly helped them show off their ridiculous muscles and cartilage armor, reminding everyone who wasn't Marzin that arguing with one of them carried the risk of the argument turning physical.

He sipped from a water skin, attaching it to a thin belt before stomping over to talk to us properly. "Ghost? Halluk and Khosh ran off just after you went off to find these two. Said they're hunters, not laborers. You want to try and find them?"

Ghost snorted, "After the third time they've split off? No. They can find their own way back, and explain to Marzin why they couldn't bother to follow his orders to stick together. We can all enjoy it when they squirm."

Nisco grinned, showing off his ivory teeth. "Figured you'd say that. Come on, we think we've found some good stuff in the main hall while you were gone."

The 'Main Hall' was just a really big hut built around a tree, its lower branches used to help hold up some kind of canvas roof. Narob was already hard at work yanking down what parts of it still looked good, while Tane was carefully sorting items she was pulling out from under dusty blankets.

"Ammunition." She reported, her Caranat thickly accented. "No guns yet."

I grimaced. "The Faithful would have taken them, wouldn't they?"

Tane gave me the usual look; a mix of disbelief that I could speak at all, and irritation that I'd dared to try. "Obviously."

It was my turn to let my emotions run stronger than they should have; anger at her sarcastic tone making me start to tense up before I realized I was being overly sensitive.

"...any evidence of the residents?" I forced myself to sound calm when I spoke again.

"No." She said shortly.

"Plenty of bullet holes and scorch marks." Nisco said a moment later,

110

his posture as rigid as his people's always seemed to be. Even his breathing hardly seemed to make him sway. "Mostly on the east side. The locals probably made a stand there, then ran into the trees when they broke."

I blinked in surprise. Nisco was usually the most polite of his people, but that didn't mean he spoke to us all that often. "You mean the Faithful attacked from the east?"

He gave me a tiny shake of his head, thick arms crossing his chest. "Bullet holes are all on this side of the buildings. The Faithful probably came in along the stream in the northwest, swept across the village, then pursued any survivors into the woods."

I nodded slowly, frowning. "Locals probably went out to greet them on that side, tried to offer up slaves, and got attacked regardless. Survivors ran east, held their ground, then fell apart."

"Likely." He agreed. "Not that it really matters. Poor bastards are dead at least a few years now. Not sure we'll find anything out there, but I suppose we can check."

Ghost snorted. "Even if they had proper arms they'd be rusted scrap after that long. No, we focus on what we can grab from the buildings, then we start making our way back to our own camp."

Nisco glowered a little at being given orders, but he tolerated it better than most. Of course he followed that up by immediately giving *us* orders, which probably said a lot about him. "You two, go check the west side of the village for wrist-comps, blades, or anything else usable."

"Sure." I shrugged, "Back in a bit."

Ghost was already poking around inside the main hall, so I left him to his business and tugged Johanna right back outside with me. She didn't resist, happy to go back to it just being the two of us once again.

Looking around, I counted five little huts on the west side, all of them built around trees just like the one we'd just left. Since there was pretty much no difference between them, I picked the farthest one out and walked over to it.

"Um... can I ask a question?" The fact that she asked it in Deutsch was enough to make me think she'd noticed a few of the things I already had.

"You know you can." I replied in her language, frowning as we walked inside. There wasn't much to see; a rope hammock hanging from the ceiling, a dust covered crate, and not much else. "Since when have things been like that between us?"

"Since this might sound racist." She replied, "But it isn't. I don't think it is, at least."

"Just ask." I told her. "I won't get angry. I promise."

She walked up next to me, giving me a level look. "Not that we can keep that under control, but all right. Um... was it just me, or was Nisco acting weird back there?"

I huffed, walking over and carefully nudging the supply crate with a toe. When nothing crawled out from behind or under it, I squatted down and carefully felt for its handle.

"You're not wrong." My thumb found a button, pressing down. "My working theory is that he's from this village, or knew someone who was."

She blinked, "Uh... oh. How?"

I nodded to the door, waiting as the crate slowly creaked open. "That door is Thondian sized, so was the one in the Main Hall. That was my first observation. My second was that Ghost made it sound like he came looking for us right after they got here, and Nisco implied they'd only had time to search the Main Hall."

Johanna nodded slowly, getting it at once. "So how did he know about the bullet holes on the east side."

"How indeed." Reaching down, I pulled out a bundle of cloth. Under that proved to be several bottles of actual soap, with two survival towels tucked under them. "I suppose he could have picked that up by walking through that side, but it was an odd thing to volunteer. Especially to us."

"Yeah... strange. What did you find?"

"Looks like an actual bath is in our future." I offered up the bounty that I'd found, soap on top for her to see.

112

"Real soap." Her groan was nearly lustful, worries about Nisco pushed aside in an instant as she took the bottles. "Plenty of it too."

I smiled, handing her the blanket and towels before standing up and poking around some more. Trying to see if there was anything else to find.

"For now, don't say anything about Nisco." I told her as I carefully paced around the small space. "It's just a theory, and we don't have much evidence for it. Even if we do, he had the good sense to run when the Faithful came for this place."

She frowned at me, "But he might have sold people to them, just so he could live a little better."

"Maybe." I admitted, "But we don't *know*. First and most important rule that my packmate taught me about information gathering is that you don't accuse without proof beyond doubt. Until then all you have is a theory, and you shouldn't even have a theory until you've got plenty of evidence in front of you."

Her lips turned down. "He knew what happened in a Thondian village, and he is a Thondian."

I glowered at her, that too-quick-to-rise anger welling up again. "*That* was too far."

She winced, clutching the blankets a little tighter to her chest, but her own tones turned hot. "...well he *did* know, and he *is* a Thondian! They're all slavers, Ashe!"

"Not helping!" I snapped.

"He..." She closed her mouth with an audible snap, clearly fighting down her own emotions.

We stood there, glaring at each other for most of a minute before she finally turned away, both of us trying to breathe. To stop from getting locked in a loop where we both lost control and took our rage out on one another.

I calmed down first, finding my voice again. "...we've got minimal evidence for the theory. We'll keep our eyes open around the village for more, but we're not accusing anyone. If he acts strangely on the way back, I will bring it up to Tasir."

"...Marzin." She mumbled.

I let out a frustrated huff, restrained myself from snapping at her again, and amended my statement. "If he acts strangely on the way back, I will bring it up to Marzin."

"...fine. I..." Her jaw clenched, then she managed to add, "And I'm sorry."

I took a deep breath, then let it out. "...sorry too. Tiny cells."

"Tiny cells." She agreed tiredly, quickly looking as drained as I felt. "Um. We should finish looking around."

"Yeah. Let's get this over with."

Sadly there wasn't anything else to find. Nothing was hidden in the floors or walls, only a few wooden plates even more crudely made than the ones we used back at the camp, and a few spare sets of clothes that had been mostly eaten by some kind of animal.

We moved on, sweeping through the next four homes about as quickly as the first.

Between us we slowly built up a nice little haul; one half-empty medical kit covered in Thondian runes, a utility knife, three empty travel bottles, a couple more towels, and a oddly preserved sonic toothbrush whose battery had probably died years ago.

Then I led Johanna to the east side, walking around the back side of the Main Hall so that no one would see us walk past the front door.

"...well, he wasn't wrong." I murmured, slowing my pace, taking a good look around. "They were definitely attacked from this direction, made some kind of last stand over here."

More than a dozen buildings had been built on this side, in four rows of three. Or as close to that as they could get while using the local trees as the center points of their homes.

That was interesting, but not as interesting as the fact that all of the buildings closest to the main hall had been utterly demolished. Here and there

114

a few walls were standing, blackened from old flame, but most of them had collapsed.

"What do you think happened?" Johanna asked quietly.

I licked my lips, then swallowed against painful memories of fire.

Shoving them back into my mental deeps, I let my eyes play over the wreckage, applying Rerth and Holde's training to make logical sense of what I was seeing.

"The... the rounds were all high. Very high. They weren't trying to hit anyone, just herd them. Make them take cover inside. Then..."

"...*mein Gott.*" She looked unwell. "They... burned them, didn't they?"

"Yeah." The faintest memory of my own skin burning made me close my eyes for a long moment before I got myself, and my stomach, under control. "Herded them into these buildings, then called up sorcerous fire. Burned most of them alive inside their homes, and shot down anyone who tried to get away."

"...when the Culling comes, this is what they'll do to us, isn't it?"

"I... think so." I said.

Johanna stepped up beside me, pale throat working as she swallowed. "...I need to learn how to fight. I... will not die like that. Not like that."

I reached out, squeezing her wrist. "We'll train together when we get back. I'm not the best, but I'll teach you what I can."

Her chin moved in a tiny nod. "Um... do we check these buildings?"

"Not these four, but we should check the rest. Do you want to stay outside, just in case?"

"In case you find bodies?" She shook her head. "No. I... I can handle it."

Thankfully her bravado went unchallenged, and I silently thanked Ashahn for that blessing. No bodies, no bones even. Just more dust, the vines

115

of encroaching plants, and little else. We added a single clip of Imperial-Standard ammunition to our haul, and another medical kit that had been mostly buried in a corner.

Ghost was waiting for us when we returned, not looking at all surprised to see us coming from the East side. "Anything good?"

"We'll give you a real knife to train us in hand to hand." I offered.

He snorted. "I've got one already."

I tried to imitate a sleazy salesman Jet and I had run into in the Near Reaches. "But you could have *two* knives, Ghost. Two whole knives just for you."

"Such an offer." His bright eyes rolled, "Get it all packed into your bags, then come in and help peel some of that fruit. We're going to eat and then start on the trip back."

"Sounds good."

XII

According to Ghost and Irkan, it took months to recover both emotionally and physically from the trip here.

There really wasn't anything we could do about the former, and the latter was tricky thanks to the fact that we'd been reduced to hunting and gathering. Sure, that meant a lot of walking and general physical labor, but it also meant we couldn't waste energy simply working out either. We just didn't have the calories for it.

The Faithful may have seeded this planet with plenty of edible plants and animals, but it was startling to realize just how much food fifty plus people needed to eat every day.

Especially when a third of us were Thondians who needed far more food than nearly anyone else, and when Marzin seemed like he could eat as much as the rest of us put together.

All right, that was probably an exaggeration. His implants let him go long periods between meals, but the Regnon still ate *a lot,* and was constantly going off on his own to hunt the larger prey animals outside of the forest.

Long story short, our sparring sessions ended up being pretty short because they made us hungry and exhausted, and no one was about to feed us extra to make up for it.

Short story shorter, with Marzin frequently gone, Nisco began inviting himself over to 'witness' my attempts to give Johanna a bit of training in hand to hand combat.

And after a few days quietly laughing from the sidelines, he decided to personally get involved.

I ducked a lazy punch, driving my own fist into his belly. It felt more like punching a wall than a person, and earned me nothing more than stung knuckles and a rumble of amusement as his other arm lashed out.

"Ow!" I yelped when his open hand slapped across my face, stinging badly. "A slap? Really!?"

117

"I could snap your neck with such a slap." Nisco countered, "Be glad I pulled the blow."

Irkan chuckled from the sidelines. "The Sand-walker exaggerates, Imperial, but a punch from that fist would have broken her jaw."

It probably could have, if he'd really put all of his strength into it.

Blowing out a breath, I got my hands back up to a ready position. "Your chest is either too armored or too muscled. Where in Ashahn's bloody name am I supposed to punch you?"

Ivory teeth appeared when his lips pulled back, "A teacher does not provide all the answers. Learn or suffer, that is our way."

Suffering it was then. It was clearly his preferred option for me.

Cautiously moving forward again, I eyed him as he kept his own hands lazily at his sides. Daring me to try and actually hurt him this time. So far I hadn't even made him shift his weight very much, or drawn more than a quiet grunt.

His throat had a bit of cartilage armor on it, but it was still his throat. That was probably my best target. That or... well, I could always try to knee him in the groin.

I went for the former first, trying to fake as if I was going for his side, then throwing my best punch up at his neck. Nisco was surprisingly quick; he leaned back just in time to avoid the attack, a hand snapping up to slap me again.

That time I took the impact with a quiet growl of pain, stepped in, and threw my leg up between his.

I'm pretty sure he let out a sharp bellow of pain, but I couldn't be one-hundred percent sure because my entire world turned into a blur a second later.

"Ashe? Ashe?" Spinning colors slowly formed into Johanna holding me in her arms, a hand in front of my face. "Can you see my hand?"

"...yes?" I groaned against the sudden migraine. "Head hurts."

"That's because he nearly crushed your skull. How many fingers am I holding up?" She asked.

"...three."

Johanna let out a quiet sound of relief. "Good. Irkan? Can you toss me that water bottle?"

She caught it a moment later, helping me sit up to drink from it. I downed about half of it in one go, and felt better for it. Being partially upright also let me see Nisco pacing around the little clearing we'd been sparring in, shaking out his legs every few steps.

"Pain for pain." He clearly saw me watching him, his deep voice sharp. "Do not do that to any man again."

"...will if they're trying to kill me." I managed to say in reply.

Dark eyes turned on me, narrowed in a glare. He kept it up for several silent seconds before a chuckle passed his lips. "I amend my statement. Do that to any follower of the Faithful you wish, but do it to me again and I will choke the life from you and enjoy every second of it."

There really wasn't anything I could do besides nod, then try and drink more of the water.

Johanna let me gulp the last of it down. Once it was empty she helped me stand, staying close as I carefully walked over to where Irkan was lounging in the shade of a tree. I wasn't dizzy, and my vision wasn't blurred, so hopefully I'd avoided a concussion.

Still. It would probably be best to stay awake and focused for a while all the same.

"How did I do?" I asked.

Irkan scratched at his chin-quills, "The Imperial did exactly as well as this sailor anticipated."

"...badly then." I sighed.

"The Imperial is used to fighting river-sharks smaller than she." He said, "It is obvious in the way she holds herself. Only time and practice will correct this flaw."

"That's... probably a fair observation." I admitted. "I'm not sure I'll ever be up for taking Nisco in an unarmed fight though."

Nisco slowly approached, remaining standing nearby. "You will likely never be. I have never heard of one of your kind defeating mine in such a circumstance. You are too small, we are too large."

Johanna huffed, sitting slowly and pulling me down with her. "Ark Fleet marines can beat Thondians in close combat."

"Xenthans." Nisco scoffed. "*They* are deadly to anyone."

"Humans too. We can get nearly as tall as you."

He brought a hand to his bare chest, two fingers flexing before he flicked the thick bands of cartilage over his heart. "They lack armor beneath their technology, and even the largest of your kind seem weak to those of the Warrior Caste."

"We've still won fights." She insisted.

"With weapons, no doubt." He rolled a stiff shoulder, tilting his head to the right. "Tell me you have ever met one of your kind who could defeat me with nothing but his fists, and I will call you a liar."

She grumbled something in Deutsch under her breath, but otherwise didn't bother replying.

Nisco grinned again, knowing he'd won the argument, and only then did he sit down across from us.

"The others don't like you much, Lori." He said, filling the silence that followed. "No group among us truly appreciates you."

I let out a tired sigh. "I know, and I don't want to talk about it."

"You should." He countered. "Those most disliked among us will be the first pushed aside when it comes time to escape this cursed world. That or someone might just grab you to use your body as a shield."

120

My brain promptly gave me a mental image of him carrying me along in one hand, holding me out to absorb bullets for him.

I winced. "Marzin wouldn't let that happen."

"Marzin's role in the escape will be as our only true source of firepower. He will not be in any position to argue or give commands." He replied, going on before I could, "And the Trahcon you are so fond of will be doing battle with their sorcery. It is the rest of us who need to find the shuttles, to swarm their pilots with numbers."

"...that's not a good plan." I said quietly.

Nisco gave me another stiff shrug, head still leaning to the right. "No, it is not, but our options are limited. We have few arms, no armor, no shields beyond what the grays can summon up."

"Stealth?" I suggested, forcing myself not to react to the slur.

Irkan replied, sounding tired. "Stealth will be required to approach the Faithful. Should they detect this group, all within shall be gunned down or captured long before they arrive at the compound."

Johanna winced. "...but we've got a chance, right?"

"We do, or else we wouldn't be bothering." Nisco replied. "But if you two don't start behaving politely then you're likely to be left behind. Or maybe pushed a bit closer to the guns than the rest of us when the time comes."

That made her go from grimacing to growling in a heartbeat. "I'm not going to pretend to be a slave or a low-caste or whatever, just to soothe your people's fragile egos."

The big man leaned a bit more to the right. "Then you'd best be ready to make your own way when the time comes, savanna."

"Du bist so ein Arschloch!" She spat, and it was my turn to wince, very glad he couldn't understand that language. "Ihre gesamte Spezies ist ekelhaft!"

Not that it stopped him from understanding her tone. His own voice lowered to a snarl, "Speak a civilized tongue, Fleet-Whore, or-"

121

"Enough!" Irkan bellowed, making all three of us jerk back from him. "This sailor is not in the mood. Sand-walker, be gone for the evening!"

Nisco growled, muscles visibly tightening as if he was struggling to hold himself back from attacking Irkan. The man who really was our only friend among the group let out a chirping challenge, jerking his head up and down to draw attention to the sharp horn rising from his snout.

It took him a moment, but the Thondian backed down. As big and tall as he was, his cartilage armor wasn't in the same class as the nearly bullet-proof shell worn by Irkan. And the squat alien was probably just as strong despite the enormous height difference.

Picking a fight wouldn't have been smart. Even if it took him a little while, he realized that. Powerful arms pushed himself back and up, his eyes glowering at us all before he strode off without another word.

Irkan let out a series of hissing chirps, then turned to glare at Johanna. "The Ark Fleet savanna must learn to control her mouth around those larger than her."

"...just because they're bigger doesn't mean I should have to obey them." My cellmate muttered.

"A sentiment this sailor would agree with, if the Ark Fleet savanna was holding a gun." He shot back. "She is not, and she would lose any battle she waged here. This sailor cannot always protect you, and neither can the Imperial."

Johanna clenched her jaw, calming down only when I put a hand on hers.

"Hey. Easy." I said, trying to keep my voice gentle. "Tiny cells, remember?"

She snapped her glare to me... then seemed to process my words. She still ground her teeth a bit, but she closed her eyes and started taking deep breaths to try and calm down.

"The annoying Sand-Walker is not wrong." Irkan rumbled, clearly talking to me and me alone now. "The isolation of the savannas in the group will do them no favors when it comes time to flee."

122

"I know, but... I'm not any happier at the idea of doing whatever Nisco tells me to do either." I admitted, "I keep trying to talk to the Trahcon, get to know them, but they're always out helping hunt or patrolling."

Well, that and the fact that Johanna didn't want to be around them. It was hard to both protect her and make contacts, not helped by the fact that we were both still overreacting to even the stupidest things.

"Then hunt with them." He suggested firmly, "And force the Ark Fleet savanna to get over her prejudice. Survival accepts no excuses."

The frustrated sound from Johanna made me sigh, patting her hand.

"He's not wrong. I'll ask them if we can go with and help tomorrow." I told her firmly. "We need more friends."

"...should just go with Ghost again." She muttered, drawing another rush of anger from within my soul. She didn't even *like* Ghost, but she'd still rather go be harassed by him rather than even introduce herself to the Trahcon among us. It was... ugh.

Tiny cells.

"Ghost mostly hunts with the Thondians." I countered, doing my best not to snap at her. "Would you rather go with them, or let me try and get us close to people whose culture I actually understand?"

"I... fine. Fine." Her head shook, pushing my hand off so that she could stand. "I'm going back to our tent to start dinner."

Her back was to me before I could say that I'd be there in a bit, her feet stomping heavily as she walked away.

Irkan shook his head in his odd, diagonal way. "This sailor would have thought that eight weeks here would have been enough to curb that one's opinions."

Eight weeks... Ashahn's blood. We'd been here for two months already? That was.... that meant...

It hadn't taken us more than a few days to catch up to the people we'd chased from Trinity. Even including the pause outside of Nueva Genova, it couldn't have been more than a week.

123

Two months. I'd been here for two months. That meant...

Rerth hadn't gotten a beacon on the ship. She couldn't have. She'd have been here by now.

Help wasn't coming.

"...not entirely her fault." I slowly got myself up to my feet as well. "Everyone else either insults or ignores her on a good day, apart from you."

"This is true." He allowed, "But it does not excuse how quickly she gave up, or how long the Imperial has allowed the other's opinion to hold her back."

"...I'll get started on it tomorrow. Night, Irkan."

"Sleep well, Imperial." He replied.

I barely heard him over the painful thoughts that continued to bombard my mental shores. That realization that I should have had weeks ago, that I must have been forcing myself to ignore. To not think about.

Rerth wasn't coming.

She wasn't coming.

I... was on my own here. With only a few people who tolerated talking to me, a cellmate as physically and emotionally fragile as I was, and without the vast resources of the Empire to support me.

No one was coming to rescue me.

"So stop whining about it." I hissed, tilting my head back to glare at the darkening sky. "Rerth didn't train you so you could give up. Stop whining about the fact that no one is going to rescue you but yourself. Do the one thing you're good at, and figure out what in the Aspect's holy names is going on here."

Figure it out, use it to escape, to get home.

And then stand at Rerth's side, watching as the might of the Empire obliterated the Faithful.

"...you've got a goal. Now make a plan."

I walked slowly back to the cave, to the tent I shared with Johanna, doing my best to plot out just how we'd survive long enough to escape.

With or without the group if need be.

Interlude
Rerth'riah

I ran through the pounding rain, feeling each impact on the hood over my head. The occasional sharp blow to my tarah making me wince and flinch until I finally reached the door of the inn.

The violent wind would have yanked it off its hinges if not for the massive bars that held it in place, pulling it closed once I'd staggered inside.

"Ashahn's blood." I gasped, feeling an ocean's worth of water dripping from my cloak. "Every time I visit this planet the weather gets worse."

A low chuckle came from the host; an older Guide holding out a hand. "It's just a little hurricane. You should have been here two weeks ago if you wanted a real storm. We actually had to close for a day."

"No thanks." I gave a theatrical shudder at the very notion. Well, half-theatrical, half-very real. A quick motion got the sopping coat off, letting him take it to be dried. "Reservation should be under Jukut. She here yet?"

"Yes, in the back corner." He provided, "The one with the screen above the fireplace."

I murmured a quick thanks, walking past him into the building proper.

It was doing a very brisk business despite or because of the ongoing storm outside. Men and women were packed in around tables, drinking and feasting in the cozy old space. Strike-Wave games from the Capital played on broad screens, and at least one group of conscripts was singing a drinking song at the bar.

Dodging a pair of staff carrying trays full of food, I found my target at a back corner table just as the host had promised.

Fyvn was seated in the very rear, a dark bottle in front of her and a worn pipe between her lips. Trails of white smoke were emerging from both it and her lips.

126

"Jukut." I greeted her by her alias, sliding along the booth. "What is that?"

"Chehala." She tugged the pipe from her mouth, leaning over to give me a quick kiss as I settled in beside her.

The too-sweet taste of the leaves made me wrinkle my nose, tarah flicking in displeasure. "Filthy habit."

"I know. Hard to find the real thing this far from the Ascendancy too." My old packmate sighed, extinguishing it with a tap. "How was your flight in?"

I gave the dark window to our left a pointed glance. "It's the Homeworld. How do you think?"

"Only a Level Two Hurricane this week." She noted.

"Still a bloody hurricane." I shook my head, lowering my voice. "How many are we expecting?"

"Just two more, as many as I'm willing to risk opening our cabal to." Teeth worked at the wood of her pipe, "How many on Altair do you have?"

"That I trusted to start digging into this? Seven others."

"About the same for me. " Her eyes flicked past mine in a warning.

I'd already spotted the oncoming waiter; a lean man who I'd have been very interested in a century ago. As it was he was still pleasant to look at, even if he didn't set my hearts to beating more quickly.

"Whatever your best dark is." I told him. "And some bread a little later in the evening."

"Of course. Another for you?" He asked Fyvn.

She shook her head, "No, I'm good."

Neither one of us spoke after he'd departed. I let myself sink back into the cushions behind us, Fyvn idly chewing on her unlit pipe. This close to the wall the steady beat of the rain drowned out most of the noise in the inn, the occasional sharp gust of wind rattling the reinforced glass.

127

My drink arrived at the same time as our next member; a woman who was the Intelligence ideal. Everything about her was bland, boring, and forgettable. I couldn't begin to guess her age... she could have been anywhere from ninety to four hundred.

"Jukut." She murmured, sliding in on Fyvn's other side. "This must be Altair."

"I am." I tipped my bottle toward her, guessing at her faint accent. "Icar?"

She nodded, "Yes. Sector names then?"

"Easiest." Fyvn murmured around a sip of her own ale. "Here's the last."

An unusually tall man took the spot beside me with a tired groan, his wet shirt betraying the fact that his coat must have failed him outside. Playing the part of an old packmate, I leaned over and gave him a quick kiss just as I had Fyvn.

"Evening." I gave his nearer tarah a gentle nuzzle with my cheek, "Finally in from Abantia?"

"Could say the same to you. You've been on Altair for too long. It's good to see you all again." He said, covering us as the waiter approached once more. "Something light."

Icar gave her own order, leaning back with an exhausted tilt to her tarah. We stayed that way until the server returned with the remaining drinks, only a few muttered complaints about the weather filling the air between us.

Only once he was gone again did we all lean forward, truly beginning.

"This is it?" Icar murmured. "A small circle considering the crisis."

I flicked my left tarah outwards. "Everyone who notices the crisis seems to end up dead. We're risking a great deal on uncertain seas. Four cells, four leaders, in four sectors."

Abantia grunted beside me. "Agreed. We focus on finding evidence now, we determine how to safely bring others into our harbor later."

128

When Fyvn and Icar both nodded in agreement, I spoke to the latter.

"Icar? You said one of your assets found a target?"

"Just the one." She murmured, resting both arms on the table. "He hit all of the marks you indicated. A perfect burn scar from wrist to elbow on his left arm, my people caught him torturing a Human male with sorcery, and he immolated himself with the Wrath before my Agent could take him alive."

I fought down a frustrated curse, "And the prisoner?"

"A Half-Sword Leader from Colony One. Picked off when he went to the wrong bar." Icar sighed. "He didn't know much. I'm keeping him on my ship for safe keeping all the same."

"Smart." Abantia's bottle rose and fell as he took a pull, "I've found two. One managed the Wrath as well, but we harpooned the other with drugs before she could. Interrogating her didn't reveal much."

I glanced at him, "Nothing?"

"Nothing on where they take those they capture. Sorry, Altair."

My fingers clenched around my own ale, a mouthful of the liquid not doing enough to calm me down. "What has she given up?"

His tarah lowered. "She was trained at that facility you tore apart. Graduated a few months before you called the Void Lord in to deal with it. I've got more than I wanted to know about their 'training', if you can call massacring aliens for fun training."

Tarah quivered, our power humming through the air. Our anger and disgust drew a few eyes from other tables until we managed to calm ourselves, quiet our sorcery to the point where the eyes turned back to their own affairs.

"I did confirm that it's a three stage process to join what she calls Those of the True Faith." He snorted at the name, "The ones you've been calling the Burned Hand are tier one assets. Anyone without a burn is just a disposable tool. She claimed to not know anything about those above her, save that they would invite her once she'd proven herself. The rest was just supremacist drivel."

129

Fyvn pursed her lips, "So the majority of those eliminated during the Near Reach operations were expendable to them."

"In theory. Just one interrogation means I can't confirm any of it."

I took a deep breath, letting it out with my words. "That is true. It's flimsy evidence at best, but right now it's the only evidence that we have."

He slid an arm around my shoulders, playing the comforting packmate well. "You haven't found anything?"

"I chased another smuggling ring from Altair to here." I said, leaning into his side. "A Delne'lir specializing in luxury yachts of all things. Supposedly they were being sold on Cathia, but we're already seeing number mismatches."

Icar frowned from her seat across from me. "Related?"

"When I say luxury, I mean fully wood paneled interiors from the forests outside of Zultic."

Her tarah rose sharply in surprise. "Ah. And any group calling themselves something so pretentious is likely to desire such luxury."

"Possibly." Even in the depths of my need to find Ashe I refused to create a theory in advance of the proper evidence. "I'm sailing after that lead right now. My packmate on Altair hasn't found any of the Burned Hands yet, or these... True Faith, Faithful, whichever. He does have more data for us."

Fyvn took a very long drink of her ale. "So do I, and it's not good... bread's coming."

Abantia casually leaned in even closer, nuzzling my cheek and tarah in equal measure. "You really need to come out and visit some time. It's been too long."

"We're not seventy anymore." I nudged him with an elbow, an easy grin coming to my lips. "There's a bathhouse next door if you're feeling young. There will be plenty of well toned young women in there."

He scoffed, giving the waiter a quick grin when the man set our snack out. "Huntresses are cute, sure, but sometimes you just need experience."

130

A chorus of snorts and chuckles came along with fingers tearing the loaf apart, each of us enjoying it while it was hot.

"Altair?" Fyvn said in between bites, turning back to our proper course once the waiter was gone. "You finish yours first."

I nodded, finishing my last piece before going on. "My reports on the incident that led to me bringing in my missing packmate were modified. Recently. Someone manipulated the information to make her seem far more at fault for the entire affair than she was, and removed any reference to the Burned Hand."

"...fuck." Abantia groaned. "DataNet Security is compromised?"

"Assuredly. The files on our Near Reach campaign were adjusted as well." I fought the urge to let my sorcery flare in anger. "We were already keeping copies on my ship, but consider that a requirement for everyone moving forward."

Fyvn nodded. "Agreed. Did your assets catch any of them in the act?"

"Yes." Jet and Huvu'ithi certainly had. There was just one problem. "One vanished, two more were found dead just as the Analyst on Trinity was. Suicide with missing packmates."

Icar let out a ragged exhalation, bringing her ale up and not putting it down until it was nearly empty.

"By the holy Aspects, these people." She muttered. "This is no game of the Federation or Concordat, that's for sure. We've sailed far beyond the Compact's horizons."

"Agreed." I turned my attention to my old packmate. "Jukut? What have you found?"

She took a deep breath, and began. "The Far Reach Director, Ashul'tasir, supposedly deserted just after the war out there began. I know that old fish. She's as crusty and jagged as an old reef, and utterly loyal to the Empire. The records of her last few months of communication don't make any sense at all, with one exception."

"Secondary channel?" I guessed.

Fyvn nodded, "Her Agent on Terminus sent it hard-coded, by courier right before she was killed and her supporting assets either died alongside her or else vanished. It was a plea for a mass influx of manpower, and a demand to know why the Oasis Commanders had ignored an Avalanche Declaration."

My hands and tarah both twitched sharply, Abantia's fingers digging into my shoulder in shock. "Ashahn's bloody ass. She went that far?"

Icar winced. "Blasphemy, Altair."

I waved her off impatiently, "You can't say it's unwarranted. How desperate would a Director have to be to invoke that?"

"...extremely." She admitted. "That's a destroyed Index and a guaranteed drowning on the Capital if her reasoning isn't perfect. Maybe even if it is."

Fyvn interjected there, "Exactly. Tasir wouldn't have gone that far unless she had no other options left. But between what we've found, and the physical message from Terminus, we have a chance for official sanction."

There was a skeptical hum from Abantia. "Two of you don't even have a Director right now, and I don't think I'd trust mine on this. Icar?"

She shook her head. "I hacked their message system. They're either unaware or uncaring that we're running at forty percent staff right now."

"Intelligence is compromised." I said, voice as hard and cold as ice. "We can't rely on it, or anyone outside of our greater packs. We have to go to a Void Lord. They're the only ones who will be able to give us official sanction and protection. The only ones able to act against a core Imperial institution on what limited evidence we have."

Fyvn took a slow, final sip of her ale, setting the empty bottle down. "Agreed."

"...agreed." Icar murmured.

"Yes." Abantia added finally. "Which one? Ahvith'srong?"

He was the oldest, and most respected, but... "I don't think he'd hear us out. Not when he's on the edge of retirement."

132

Icar shifted her weight, then said a name of her own. "Amiar'delarah."

I gave her a skeptical look. "The heiress? She's out in the Wastes, in exile for her adventurism taking over the Human homeworld without the Torlah's authorization."

"Yes." Icar agreed. "Exactly. She's been out there for five decades with the Watch. Well before any of this began, which means we've got some hope that her Void Fleet isn't riddled with the enemy's assets."

"And," Fyvn mused, "If any organization would be immune to this kind of infiltration, it would be the Imperial Watch. They're paranoid lunatics even when the seas are perfectly flat."

I considered that for a few long breaths, then nodded. "We've got one living prisoner, your hard coded message from Terminus, backups of hacked reports, and a small ocean of circumstantial evidence. That's something, but nearly all of it was gathered extremely illegally. Often against our own superiors' direct orders. Do you think she'll support us, or arrest us?"

My old packmate could only shrug. "I'll go to her directly and find out. If you don't hear from me in six months... dive as deep as you can, and I'll see you all when we join with Aysh in the beyond."

I nodded, offering a few silent prayers of my own that the youngest Void Lord would listen to us. Would sanction us.

Would give me what I needed to find my packmate, living or dead.

Would let me bring her home if I could.

Would let me avenge her if I could not.

133

XIII

I slammed my shoulder into Caliu's belly, bare feet digging into the muddy soil as I drove her back. The other woman growled, thrashing around as best she could to try and get her arms free.

"Push!" Jahgrah rushed in, pushing Caliu back into me before I could topple her. "Drive her furry ass back!"

"Team!" Olin called, appearing on my right, an arm wrapping around my shoulders. "Push!"

Our teammates were quicker off the mark than the rest of Caliu's. Hands and arms linked as they swarmed in, eight sets of feet driving the pile back toward the other side of our make-shift pitch. Caliu did her best to keep the 'ball', really a bundle of clothes tied as tightly as we could manage, only for her feet to go out from under her.

I landed on her with a huff, managing to shout, "She's down! Our shot attempt!"

Groans and cheers came from the two teams as everyone stopped shoving in favor of getting back to their feet. Olin offered me a hand, both of us smiling as I took it, "Thanks."

"Thank me by scoring." He retorted, catching the ball when Caliu tossed it to him.

I chuckled, holding my hands out. "That's asking a lot. I play goalie for a reason."

He laughed, passing it over. Around us the teams formed into ragged lines, everyone watching as I spun the bundle of clothing and tent fabric in my hands. Getting my grip settled on a bit of shirt, I brought my right arm all the way back before heaving it overhead.

More cheers and groans rose when it sailed between the two tree branches we'd settled on as the shot target.

"And that's ten!" Olin pumped an arm in the air, "Victory for the

Empire and the Homeworld!"

"Fuck off!" Jahgrah called back in his sharp accent, "Cathia and the Reaches forever!"

A few others offered their own comments, casual insults flying back and forth between those who'd been abducted in the Reaches and those born in the Empire. Despite the sharp words there were grins on their lips, their tarah relaxed.

No one was taking it personally. Species solidarity was still taking precedence over cultural identity among the Trahcon. That had been the main reason it had been a bit of a struggle to get them to accept me, at least at first.

It had taken some time, but I'd worn them down eventually.

I shook a few hands, hugged a few of my fellow Imperials, got my fur mussed by another. A couple of Cathians even came over, equally praising my skills as a Strike-Wave player and insulting my Imperial origins. I thanked them for the former, and rolled my eyes at the latter.

I'd have liked to try and reply in kind, but I was still a bit too nervous to try. Not when I was still finding my place in the group. It was safer to just exaggerate little things to make them laugh. I could work my way up to trying sarcasm later.

Olin walked with me back toward the camp as everyone broke up with the game over. "This was a pretty good idea, have to give you that, Ashe."

"Thanks." I replied, feeling as relaxed as he looked. "Really wish we had a real ball. Or an actual pitch."

"When we get home." He nudged me with an elbow. "I want to see if you're as good in goal as you claim. Not the same when we had to half-ass it with a bundle of pants tied together."

I couldn't help but agree. "Yeah. This is fun. I don't get to be a field player usually, but... I really like just being the goalie. If we had a real ball..."

He patted me on the shoulder, blue eyes alight with his grin. "Maybe we'll get lucky, and the next collaborator camp we find will have one. Or maybe Tasir will have found one in her wanderings. She's due back any day now."

That drew a snort, "I'll pray for that, but I'm not going to expect a miracle."

"Me either. Still, fun to dream. Want to bathe in the river?"

Considering that I was covered in mud, a bath was definitely in order. Sadly today was the Naulian group's turn to use the crude tub, meaning the cold river was the only option we had.

"Sure." I said. "Maybe you can tell me just why you think the Abantia League is better than Altair's."

The Sword Captain from Abantia threw his hands up as we walked, "Altair's hasn't won the Imperial League in seventy years! Everyone knows that."

"But we won sixteen championships in the twenty years before that." I countered. "And don't say it was-"

"-just because you had Amias'urral! That woman was the greatest Sail-Runner to have ever lived. Altair had no business winning half of those games."

I laughed, ducking under a leafy branch as we drew near the river. "Orry'reshin might have had something to do with that too you know."

It was his turn to roll his eyes, "Trust you to focus on who was playing in net. I bet your wrist-comp was full of pictures of her."

"...guilty." I admitted, a bit of heat rising in my cheeks. "I was hoping to hear her speak once, but I got transferred off world a week before she was through on one of her tours."

Olin shook his head, sympathy written on his plain features. "Ugh. Woman does know the game, that's for sure. I'd be upset too if I'd missed a chance to hear her lecture in person."

We kept talking about famous players until we reached the river, finding that a few of the other players had taken the more direct route. Everyone was diving in, rinsing off, then getting out of the cold as quickly as possible.

Taking a few deep breaths, I forced myself to plunge in alongside them. The temperature was biting to say the least, and I frantically scrubbed at my arms and shirt to get as much of the mud off as possible.

My teeth were chattering by the time I made it back to the shore, Olin splashing up right after me. There wasn't anymore talking after that; we were far too focused on making our run back to the warmth of the various cooking fires.

Johanna glanced up from ours when I approached, shaking her head at me. "You couldn't have dried off first?"

"C-Cold." I told her, dropping down and scooting as close to the smoldering wood as I could get. "V-very c-cold."

"Ag-agreed." Olin hunched in right next to me, his tarah shaking in time with his teeth.

"You're both children." Joahanna snorted, carefully turning the small animal we'd caught this morning on its spit. Its name was something unpronounceable in Naulian, and it looked like an enormous rodent, but it tasted good enough.

Plus, it wasn't fish.

It was very important that it wasn't fish.

Everyone was sick of fish after most of three months camped in this area.

"V-victorious children." Olin replied. "The Empire reigns triumphant still."

A month or two ago that would have made her scowl. Maybe even erupt with anger. Now it merely made her point a stick at him, "For that, you don't get a share until we're finished."

He groaned, putting a hand on his chest. "Just a bit? Look at me, I'm so small. You know how much harder it is to keep up with tall Humans when my legs are so little?"

"Then run your little legs back to your own tent." Johanna retorted.

137

"You can do your gross inter-species flirting thing later."

Olin flicked his tarah in amusement, pushing himself back to his feet, apparently warmed up. "Don't be such a prudish alien, Johanna. Tomorrow morning for another trapping run?"

"Sounds good." I said for us, breathing more easily as I dried out and warmed up. "See you at sunrise."

He gave me a final wave before walking off. I watched him go, enjoying the way his still wet clothes clung to him, before turning to find Johanna glowering at me.

"He's fun to look at, all right?" I said, somewhat defensive.

"That is still gross." She told me.

I groaned, "I thought you were over this."

"I'm used to dealing with them, and I'll... admit I should have been more open minded when we first got here." Johanna replied. "But that doesn't mean I want to sleep with them."

Reaching out, I turned the over-sized rodent over a bit more. "Well I do. Maybe not when we're stuck here like this, but I prefer Trahcon to Humans. They're just... more handsome."

Johanna gave me a flat look. "Ashe, he's not even five feet tall."

"He fits nicely under my arms." I confirmed. "He's nice and lean, and his tarah are wonderfully long. Not the most handsome face between them, I'll admit that, but they'd be fun to run my fingers along."

She made a fake-retching noise, "My god that's gross. Stop trying to rile me up. This is revenge for me trying to tell you what a handsome man should look like, isn't it?"

"Guilty." I admitted with a smile. "I've seen a grand total of one cute Human man in my life, and he didn't look anything like what you described."

"That's because you think men look like women." She shot back.

"They do!"

138

Bickering about our romantic tastes was becoming as routine as bickering about everything else. Eventually we'd get tired of it and move on to a new thing to banter about, just as we'd already moved past how we felt about the fur on our bodies and our favorite sports.

The conversation shifted when our meal was done cooking, both of us using sharpened stones to help cut off the little beasts' arms to nibble on.

"Did you talk to Ghost while we were playing?" I asked between bites. "About our next hunting trip?"

She nodded, swallowing quickly. "Yeah. He's going out with the Thondians again."

I grimaced, "Guess that means we're not going."

"No." She agreed, teeth gleaming as she took a sharp mouthful off the bone. Chewing quickly, she swallowed before going on, "He won't tell me why he puts up with them either."

"I still think he's keeping an eye on them for Tasir." I said.

"Maybe. Anything new on Nisco?" She asked.

It was my turn to take a big bite, working on it before replying. "Nothing new. He's an Aspect's cursed bastard, but he's one to everyone except for Marzin."

She huffed, "And you used to think he was nice."

"He used to be." I frowned, nibbling some more. "Not sure why he dropped the act. Maybe he was trying to lure us into something."

Her tone lowered to something dark. "Being his slaves probably."

That drew another grimace to my features. "Maybe. Marzin wouldn't have put up with that though."

"If you say so." She paused, staring at the leg in her hands. "I wonder what it's like to be Marzin. Have everyone be polite to you all the time."

I rolled a shoulder, wondering a little about that myself. It was hard to

139

be rude to a Regnon. Even if you didn't like them, you were *always* polite to the enormous alien that could kill you by accidentally stepping on you.

Although, speaking of our largest resident...

"Maybe we can go out on a trip with Marzin." I mused. "We should talk with him more too, and maybe we can find better varieties of food since he goes out so much farther than anyone else."

Johanna licked her lips between bites. "Uh... Ashe, I know he's surprisingly nice, but he's... still really intimidating."

"Of course he is. Think about it though. Maybe we find something new to eat, get a better view of the land. Even if he doesn't want to let us ride on his back when he goes hunting, he might be able to tell us better stories than Irkan has been able to."

"...true." She admitted, glancing down at the dimming remnants of our fire. "God. How is this my life?"

I winced. "Johanna, don't start that. Please... please not tonight."

Her chest shifted as she took a deep breath, letting it out before attacking her dinner again. When she spoke it was in a mumble around nibbles, trying to get the last meat off of the limb. "...sorry."

"It's all right." I said, my own eyes dropping to the little arm I was holding. Something I'd never, ever, *ever* have considered eating on my own, but what now seemed like such a feast.

A sharp shake of my head pushed the thoughts away. "We'll go and talk to him when we get back from setting the traps tomorrow. See if he'll let us come with when he goes out on his next hunt."

Johanna nodded, "...you want a leg?"

"Please."

She was just reaching out to start yanking them off when footsteps made us both glance up. Ghost emerged from the trees, his scarlet eyes glowing in the light of sunset.

"Up, both of you." He said without greeting us or even slowing

140

down. "Tasir and her group are back with news on the Faithful. Full group meeting at the river. Bring the meat, they need food!"

Tasir was back? With news?

I exchanged a quick, hopeful look with Johanna, then we were both scrambling to our feet, grabbing our rodent on a stick, and running to join everyone else at the river.

XIV

Tasir's small group refused to say anything until they'd eaten. Thankfully it didn't take them very long to devour the offerings we brought them. Meat, fruits, and root vegetables vanished into starving mouths, the scraps set aside for use as bait.

Everyone else sat or stood impatiently while they ate.

Nineteen Trahcon, twenty-seven Thondians, eight Naule, two Humans, one Mikira, and one Xenthan all doing their best to hide our collective eagerness for news. The sole exception was, naturally, our only Regnon member. Marzin had splashed into the river without a care in the world, rumbling something about the cold water feeling good on his scales.

"All right." Tasir said when she finished the rodent that I'd given her, the Director sitting on a small boulder so that everyone could see her. "First I'm going to disappoint you all. There's no sign of additional ships coming down yet. The collaborators weren't preparing their slaves for transfer either."

A chorus of exhausted groans came from many lips, while angry whistles came from others.

Tasir waited until the frustration wore itself out before going on. "There is good news. We've found a cave system close to the Faithful's base. It's not big enough to fit the entire group, but it'll work as a watch point. We're going to rotate teams through there to observe, and be ready to alert us when the time does come."

One of the Naule spoke up at once. "Can you see the collaborator's camps from there as well?"

"Yes." Tasir answered. "Good views on one, the other can be seen with a bit of work as well."

Narob, the oldest and apparent leader of the Thondians, raised his voice before she could go on. "How far is it from the base?"

"Close enough that I'm only going to send people I know can actually stay hidden." She replied. "The slope is severe enough that none of us will be

142

able to easily approach the base from that direction, but that'll work to keep anyone from stumbling across us either."

Ginlos spoke up in agreement, "Anyone up there will notice anyone coming easily enough. And before any of you get any ideas, it'd be suicide for any of us to try gambling on stealing a shuttle on their own."

His loud grunt said that he had been considering the latter. "And who will be in this group on watch?"

The Director gave him an irritated look. "A rotation, as I just said. Don't worry, you won't be among them."

The older man started to step forward, rigid posture all the more stiff with anger. He stopped rather abruptly when Marzin let out an annoyed huff, lifting his massive head to peer down at everyone from over Tasir.

"Tasir makes this call." He rumbled. "Not you, Narob. You shall listen when she speaks."

Narob kept his expression completely neutral as he slowly backed down. "As you say, Marzin. Who will be on the first watch?"

Tasir stared him down for a very long time, just to prove that she could. Only after more than a minute of strained silence did she finally give a list. "I will guide a team back. Irkan will be in command after I depart, with Ghost, Nisco, Caliu, and both of our Humans. They will stay there for four weeks, then send for a replacement group."

I was pretty sure that including Nisco was just to make the old man continue to back off. It seemed to work; he nodded in agreement. "Very well."

Irkan spoke into the silence that followed. "This sailor shall keep watch as ordered. Those with him shall not allow a chance to escape to pass us. All here may be assured of that."

Heads bobbed in acceptance, my own and Johanna's among them. Irkan was probably the only person here apart from Marzin who was universally accepted by everyone else. Mostly. At a minimum, he was respected, and that was more than good enough.

When no one else said anything in reply, I raised my own voice, "How far away is the collaborator's village?"

143

"The closer is at the bottom of the mountain, not more than five miles from the base." Tasir answered. "Their activity will be our main warning for when a Cull is about to occur."

Marzin let out another deep noise from his throat. "Yes. They always receive a warning in advance, to best prepare those they intend to sacrifice. When they are lucky, the Faithful only take their slaves. When they are not, all are taken."

"Yes." Narob agreed, his voice hard. "I have seen it as well. Who dwells in that camp?"

Tasir glanced at me, telegraphing her answer. "Humans. They've got some kind of pen set up, looks like they've got a handful of starving Thondians and Chezzek inside."

"Chezzek?" A Naulian man with dark fur, I didn't know his name, demanded. "We haven't seen any of their kind here before."

The old Thondian shook his head. "Again, I have. They are rare, but not unheard of."

"Agreed." Marzin added. "There have never been many, and they are always preyed upon by others. What is the layout of the camp?"

Tasir hopped down from the boulder she'd been sitting on, a flick of her tarah calling up her sorcery. A small stick obediently leaped from the ground to her hand, and she wasted no time in using it to draw in the mud and dirt.

"They've built it along their social divide. Here, in the center, is where their leaders seem to reside. In the direct middle there's a longhouse with multiple fires going every night, surrounded by a rough curtain wall." Her stick stabbed down just outside of it. "On the west and south, there's much smaller buildings. Roughly built compared to the main one, but they're livable."

We all watched as she pulled the wood left to right, sketching out a square. "Their pen for their alien prisoners is here. Far side of the village from us, so no real way we could get to the poor fools."

Narob grunted, stepping up again. "No cover to approach? I do not

144

like the idea of leaving my kin at the mercy of those furry beasts."

I glared at him, feeling Johanna doing the same, even if we both managed to keep our mouths shut.

Tasir gave him a flat look of her own, shaking her head. "None. They've cut down everything surrounding the village for their crops, and more pens for the herd beasts the Faithful have given them. You'd be in the open for more than a mile."

"River access?" He demanded, clearly not giving up.

"They're on a side-creek for water. It's a foot or two deep at most."

The old man grumbled, then whirled on Nisco. "Verify that. If there is even a chance to free them, we must take it."

Johanna's hiss in Deutsch covered up anything Nisco said in reply, "Hypocritical bastard."

"Hush." I murmured back, despite agreeing with her. I waited an extra second, then asked my next question to Tasir, "How far is our watch point from the river?"

"Close enough that we should be able to use a raft to get back here quickly, if a Culling is close." She replied. "Everyone in the first rotation? Expect to assist in building one of those once you arrive."

That would certainly be something. I didn't know the first thing about building boats, or even rafts. At least it would be something new to do. "Yes sir. When do we leave?"

"Tomorrow. Everyone on the team," Her hard gaze snapped from person to person, picking us all out, "Be ready by dawn. We'll hunt and scavenge along the way, and we'll be traveling light. Be prepared."

A forced march through the forest. Well, at least I wouldn't be in full armor while I did it... that was a bright side. Kind of. The lack of standard-issue boots was going to make it painful even if I'd been in the best shape of my life.

Which I wasn't.

145

I was doing better than I had been when we first got here, but I knew I was still lean and bony compared to what I'd been before I'd been taken. Johanna wasn't much better.

"Yes sir." I said, unable to say anything else. "We'll be ready."

"Will we?" Johanna whispered.

I murmured my own reply back to her, "Nein."

She grimaced, but stayed quiet as Tasir when through the motions of asking how things had been while she'd been gone. Everyone seemed to understand that she really meant if we'd spotted any collaborators or new barges showing up.

Tasir didn't seem particularly surprised when we told her that nothing interesting at happened. Or that a few more generic complaints about the food and the camp's location snuck in during the aftermath.

"Deal with it." She said after being told that everyone was getting tired of fish. "We're lucky that we've got meat here at all that nearly all of us can eat. We're not moving again unless we're spotted, or a Culling happens."

No one could really argue with that, but it didn't change the fact that the monotonous diet was getting to us. Especially to the Thondians; they couldn't eat the rodents we'd started trapping. Something about them made the big aliens throw them right back up, and the one woman who'd managed to choke some of it down had been inspected by Marzin when she fell ill the next day.

She'd live, but apparently the little beasts were completely incompatible with Thondian bodies.

Tasir put up with a few more complaints about the camp before ending her little session. "If that's it, I'm exhausted. Rifle-Experienced Lori! With me."

I followed her as the meeting broke up, Johanna in step with me. The Elder didn't seem surprised that I wasn't alone, walking with us a little ways down river.

As soon as we were a respectable distance from everyone else, she turned and spoke with her customary bluntness. "Will you be able to make the

146

march?"

"Yes sir." I said at once. "It won't be fun, but we'll make it."

Her old blue eyes regarded me without blinking, then flicked to Johanna. "And you, Ark Fleet?"

"I will keep up." She replied, far more frostily than I had.

"And what skills do you have?" Tasir demanded.

Johanna's eyes narrowed further. "Watching Ashe's back so that someone we can't know is actually a Director doesn't stab her there."

Tasir flicked her left tarah, something almost like approval in her voice. "Well. Perhaps you aren't a useless bit of driftwood after all. Lori. I want your analysis of our group now that you've spent time among us. Speak as if I was your commanding Agent."

A test? I settled my stance into an at-ease position, "Fully honest, sir?"

"Yes."

I swallowed, nodded, and told her. "It's a capable group, sir, but a heavily divided one. We're broken down by both species and region of origin in a way that will make escape difficult. The Reach and Imperial Trahcon are getting along better lately, but the Naulians and Thondians rarely interact outside of their cliques. I don't know how well they'd all actually work together without Marzin growling at them."

"I see." Her arms crossed, expression firmly under control once more. "How many agents do you believe the Faithful have among us?"

"I... we suspect one, but we have no proof." I admitted. "Is Nisco from a collaborator's village?"

Tasir grunted. "He likely is, not that he has ever admitted it. No one else?"

"No one is eager to interact with a Human." My shoulder rolled. "It makes talking with them difficult. I don't believe any of the Trahcon among us are agents, but they've only just begun to accept me among them. I only know a few of them, and not very well just yet."

She nodded, saying nothing, giving me the chance to ask a question of my own. "Do you suspect anyone, sir?"

"Suspect anyone?" Her voice shifted. Tones becoming raw, bitter, all while her eyes slid to stare into the distance. "I was betrayed by my own people, Ashe'lori. My own damned Agents turned on me when I tried to lead them to capture these criminals. Tried to learn just who they were. The people I trusted most attacked me, tied me up, delivered me to these bastards, and they mocked me as they did it. Do I suspect anyone? I suspect *everyone*. I doubt I'll ever stop."

I swallowed nervously. "...I understand sir."

"No you don't, Huntress." Tasir growled without facing me. "I don't need your sympathy, or your understanding. Just your obedience until we are out of here, and then a direct line to your Agent when we return to civilization."

"...yes sir."

She slid her arms down to her hips, eyes locking back onto mine. "We will speak more once we arrive at the watch point. Once we get there, I will also have a task for you. Something to help prove to me that you're actually from Intelligence as you claim."

"Yes sir." I repeated. "Analysis?"

"Something like that." Tasir nodded past us. "Go back to camp. Pack what you need, then sleep. I won't be pleased if we have to slow down for either of you."

I nodded one last time, giving her a sharp salute. The Director let out a ragged breath but returned it, only then waving us away.

A soft ripple in the water made me glance aside as we departed, letting me see Marzin calmly pulling himself out of the river. He stayed low to the ground, resting his head on the soil beside the elder. Tasir stayed motionless until we reached the trees...

And only then did I see her buckle, slumping into his side, clinging to his scales.

148

Johanna hadn't looked back, her voice a furious growl when she spoke. "I can't stand that-"

"Stop." I whispered before she could get started. "Just... stop. Please. Not tonight."

She blinked in surprise, then anger. "You're defending her still?"

"Yes... no." I blew out a breath. "I don't know. I need to think about it. Give me a bit of time, all right?"

"I... fine. All right. But you're packing our things for us when we get back."

I smiled a little. "That's fine."

That would give me the chance to think some more about what Tasir had said, what she hadn't said. How she'd collapsed in the aftermath. Physical exhaustion from the march maybe? I hoped so, because I was increasingly sure that the Elder was who she claimed to be.

What I wasn't certain of... was if she was sane anymore.

XV

I'd predicted we weren't ready for the kind of forced march that Tasir was going to put us through.

I wasn't happy to be proven right.

At least Irkan kept the pace slow. Not out of any personal choice, but because his stocky body made it his most comfortable speed. That helped, a little, but it didn't change the fact that neither Johanna or I were in nearly as good of shape as the others.

We were exhausted and hungry long before anyone else was ready to slow down for the day. It was all we could do to try and catch a fish or two when everyone else broke apart to hunt or forage when we ran out of food on the fifth night.

Ghost and Nisco wasted little time in mocking us. The latter more overtly than the former.

Irkan and Caliu defended us a little, and shared what food they could spare with us.

Tasir seemed content to ignore everyone else whenever she didn't need something. Instead she acted pretty much how I'd have expected a veteran member of Intelligence to act like: she sat quietly, observing everything from a distance.

She spoke little, but I would have put down good money that she could have recited back half the conversations we had on the trip.

Even the ones where she seemingly hadn't been around to hear.

All in all, it was a pretty miserable two week trek through the forest. Which made it all the more unpleasant to discover that we'd merely arrived at the base of the mountain; we still needed to ascend half way up its slope to get to the camp that Tasir's first party had created.

By the time we reached the small plateau, sheltered by a veritable wall of trees, my arms and legs were both shaking so badly that I could barely walk.

Johanna was even worse; Caliu had to half-carry her the last mile when Tasir's response to our request for a short break to catch our breath had been a terse 'no'.

"Here you go." Caliu gently got her seated next to me, both of us laying down on a gentle rise of soil as if it was a luxurious bed. "I'll be back for my payment when you're not panting like a landed fish."

The other woman mumbled something in between gasps for air, then simply let herself go limp.

I was ready to do the same when Tasir appeared above me. "Up, Rifle-Experienced. You have observations to make."

I'd never felt more like a Huntress than when I let out a tired whine. "Sir, please. A few minutes."

"That's an order. Up."

I don't know where I found the strength to obey. To shamble along in her wake, to ignore the blatant laugh from Ghost. At least Nisco was nearly as becalmed as Johanna and I. The big alien had ducked into the nearby cave, slumping down in the entrance to catch his own breath in something closer to privacy.

My feet carried me along, into the trees. A commanding motion from Tasir for me to get down, and her own crouch, had me drop to my knees. Then she moved forward quickly and quietly, like a professional soldier. In contrast I just crawled after her like a child.

Then we were at the edge of a very long drop, laying on our bellies, and staring out at a broad plain.

I felt myself wake up a bit when my brain recognized the signs of civilization that my eyes were looking at. To our left, near to the edge of the enormous forest, was what must have been the Human village. It was a lot bigger than I'd have thought from her descriptions... or maybe it was just more spread out than I'd imagined.

Of course that collection of wood and straw was far less important to me than the facility to our right, nestled between a pair of the mountain's

151

sloping arms.

"...that's an Imperial layout." I heard myself whisper. "Perfectly by doctrine even."

"Yes." Tasir murmured back. "More proof of how deeply those blood-eels are dug into our nation. Not that we needed it."

I dipped my head in a tiny nod, trying to pick out the details at this distance. "Three barracks?"

"Four. Layout 2-Del."

Meaning that extra barracks was hidden behind that shuttle hangar, at least from where we were sitting. "...there could be a full Squall Formation down there, sir."

"Could be." She agreed, her voice grim. "What else do you see?"

Biting my lip, I shut up and simply stared at the facility. This was definitely a test of some kind, and one that I needed to pass. I didn't know what would happen if I didn't, but at the very least she'd stop giving me chances to prove I wasn't an agent of the Faithful.

So I did my best to focus despite the exhaustion, to pick out anything odd or out of place that I could considering the distance.

"...there's not much traffic." I said finally. "There should be shuttles and trucks in the open, ready to transport goods or carry soldiers on patrol. There's half as many guards at the gate and on the walls as there should be. If I didn't know any better, from up here I'd say that the base was manned by a bare crew."

"It's not."

"Yes sir." I replied, not doubting her. "I'll have to watch it for a few days to know more for certain. Where are the Thondian collaborators?"

"Out of view over that hill, you can see their village if you go up higher." Her nearer tarah flicked once. "Give me your theory on the base."

"No theories without evidence, sir." I said at once. "It's my Agent's first rule, and I don't have much evidence right now."

152

For the first time in quite a while she gave me a low sound of approval. "A good rule. Give me your theories anyway."

Well, far be it from me to deny a direct order.

"...my first guess is that there isn't more than a single Arsenal in there." I chewed on my lip for another moment, then went on. "My second guess is that they work like a garrison at a penal colony. Minimal ships on the surface, bringing down large amounts of supplies just a few times a year instead of in a steady rotation."

Tasir nodded slightly. "We can't confirm the first theory. Your second matches what I've seen over the past year. No major ship or shuttle traffic coming down outside of Cullings. Supply runs seem to run on irregular patterns that we can't predict."

Which left us stuck just as she'd said when we'd first talked about escape. Our only good chance to get a ship and get off world was during a Culling, when there'd be plenty to choose from.

"Do more troops come down with Cullings?" I asked.

"Enough to replace the existing garrison." She rolled a shoulder, "At least according to Marzin. Likely more than that. They probably change whatever staff is conducting the Process, or experiments, or whatever they're doing in there."

I frowned at the base. "Where do they put everyone that they collect? In the barracks?"

"Underground is my guess." She nodded back the way we'd come. "I'm reasonably sure the tunnel over there connects to an old mining complex that runs through the mountain. Mikira built, from the other tunnels and caves I found farther down the slope when I checked it."

My breath hitched. "Mikira? We're in the Far Reaches?"

"We think so." A pause, then a scoff. "Not like that narrows it down much. Marzin and I hope that we're somewhere in the Kingdom of the Lost. Supposedly the old Mikiran Kingdoms had isolated colonies in this region before their wars with Cathia. If we're right, then we're close enough to civilization that we've got a chance to get home."

"...and if we're farther out?" I asked.

Her voice turned grim. "We hope their ships have enough fuel to get us somewhere we can resupply them."

"We don't have any money." I realized the problem at once. "And I don't think the Empire has friends out here."

"We don't." Tasir agreed with both points. "That's why we'll have to get down on our knees in the sand and beg for help."

I swallowed. "...barter maybe?"

The Elder scoffed ."With what, huntress? The ship that's going to be our only way to get back to the Empire? I doubt there will be anything valuable on it. Or were you offering to pay for fuel on your back with your legs spread?"

My stomach churned at the notion. "No sir."

"You'd better hope that Marzin and I survive then." She turned back to staring out at the two camps in the distance. "Narob would sell you as a slave in exchange for fuel the moment you made safe harbor. He might do it just for fun anyway."

"I... could guess that, sir. I'm going to stay close to Irkan when the time comes."

She grunted. "He's smart enough, and likes you enough to protect you. Too smart though. I don't buy his story about being a humble sailor."

"Do you believe anyone's stories, sir?"

"No." Tasir admitted without hesitation.

"Is there anything I can do to prove myself, sir?" I asked more quietly. "If you really are a Director, then I want to help you."

"If I really am?" Her eyes finally returned to me, another almost-approving look on her weathered features. "The Huntress learns quickly, I see. Doubting my own story then?"

"...yes sir." I admitted, though I did hesitate. "You act like someone from Intelligence, but a Director? Even if you're from a foreign station, I would have thought someone of your rank vanishing would have been a storm that even I'd have heard about."

Tasir stared at me in silence for several seconds before slowly turning away once more. When she spoke again that unstable anger was back in her voice, turning it lower and gruffer than usual. "So did I."

"Sir?"

"They isolated me." Her jaw worked, tarah rising in anger. "I figured it out too late. That they were modifying the messages I was sending back home. My communications specialist was one of the ones that held me down for the Faithful when they came for me. I don't know what he sent instead of my actual reports. How he changed my demands for more help. Only that he did."

I bit my lip, quietly asking, "You called for help?"

"More times than I should have." Fingers dug into the soil, clenching into fists. "It took me too long to realize just why the messages coming back were so damned odd. That storm cursed... I don't doubt he covered up my disappearance. Ashahn's fucking ass, he probably sent the Empire a letter of resignation with my key signed to it. That or a notice of desertion."

I winced, "Oh."

"Deadwood bastard probably hacked my personal system as well." She exhaled, hands shaking for a moment before she forced them to relax. "That was never my specialization. He'd have had full access to hold and rewrite anything I sent back home. The locations of every hidden Agent and Asset I had in the Far Reaches."

"You couldn't do a live transmission?" I asked.

A dark snort. "Huntress, I operated out of *Alum*. The Crescent would have drowned me the moment they thought I was making live transmissions back to the Empire."

"But... aren't there treaties there? An embassy?"

"Yes. I helped write the treaties when I was young. Doesn't change the

155

fact that they were more bluster than anything else. If the Ambassador or I did anything that Kolkris truly didn't like, we'd have been found dead in the bay before dawn. Assuming anyone ever found my body at all."

"Oh." I swallowed. "Do you think any of your Agents..."

"Lived?" Her head jerked forward. "I'm sure there's one or two here, somewhere. Either as Faithful, Processed, or prisoners."

"Some must have escaped or hidden." I tried to be positive. "Do you think any of them are looking for you, sir?"

She went still, a distant look of pain in her eyes for a bare moment. "The only one I'm sure was never with them died on Terminus, just before I was taken."

"Oh." I said again. "I'm sorry, sir."

The apology made her growl. "I don't need your sympathy, huntress."

"Yes sir."

"Do you feel better for having cleverly manipulated me into telling you more of what happened to me?" She demanded.

I flinched. "No, sir."

Her huff wasn't any more pleased than her prior growl. "Lying bitch. At least take pride in acting like an Agent. Pride's the only thing any of us has left at this point."

I had no idea what to say to that... so I did the smart thing and kept my mouth shut.

When it was clear I wasn't about to say or ask anything else, she spoke again, tones suddenly even again. "I'm leaving for the main camp tomorrow. Your group will be staying here for six weeks before you rotate back."

"...I thought it was going to be four weeks, sir."

"I changed my mind." She said flatly. "Get this camp properly set up for the group that will replace you, and get a raft built. We have no idea when

156

the next Culling will be, we might need to spend months or years waiting for our chance."

Years. It could still be years. "...let's hope it doesn't come to years, sir."

"You'll have to hope for the both of us. I've got none left." There was a pause, then she went on to say, "That's enough for now. You'll have plenty of chances to observe them later."

I crawled backward as obediently as I'd crawled forward, following her back to the camp. Well, to the place where everyone else had settled in to recover from our march at least.

"Rest." Tasir ordered. "Food will be cooked in the cave only. Irkan? You're with me on hunting duty. Caliu will stand watch."

More than grateful for the chance to lay down again, even on the dirt, I promptly collapsed next to Johanna for a second time. She let out a quiet chuckle at my dramatic flopping, though she sounded a little better when she spoke.

"What's out there?"

"Exactly what she said before we left." I replied, sailing on to give her the quick details.

"Huh." She looked a little taken aback by that for some reason.

"You thought she was lying to us?" I asked.

"No... well... no." She shook her head a tiny bit. "I just figured she'd left something out, I guess."

I let out an exhausted huff, getting my head situated in a little dip in the soil that would have to work as a pillow. It was about as comfortable as it sounded, but after the march and the conversation with Tasir, I just wasn't feeling like getting up again.

I didn't tell Johanna more about Tasir's past. She'd just try and poke more holes in the story, try to make me doubt the old Director more. I had doubts and worries enough of my own for now. I'd tell her later, when we were alone.

When I'd had some time to process it.

"Hey, Johanna." My half-closed eyelids opened at Caliu's call, finding her dropping to a seat right next to where our heads were laying in the dirt. "Time to collect my payment for carrying you uphill."

Johanna's pale cheeks turned red. "You were supposed to wait until Ashe was asleep."

"And I got tired of waiting." The other woman grinned, hands already coming down to bury themselves in Johanna's fur. "Mmm...."

I felt my lips curl at the aghast expression on my friend's face. At the embarrassed horror in her voice. "You're making it weird! You said you just wanted to touch it!"

"I did, and I am." She slid them up and down, thoroughly tangling the dark strands around her fingers. "Mmm. This is even more fun to play with than I thought. Why were you so against this?"

Johanna hissed, still more pink than pale. "It's demeaning!"

"Is it?" Caliu glanced to me. "Ashe?"

In response I got a tired arm up, waving it around until I got a hold of one of Caliu's wrists. Her small smile turned utterly delighted when I pulled it to my own scalp, a groan of pleasure escaping me when she began to stroke and tug at my own fur.

"Now you're both making this weird!" Johanna whined.

"Hush." I murmured, closing my eyes. "Never turn down a free massage."

Her petulant groans went on, drawing laughter and teasing from us both... and for a little while, things weren't so bad.

For a little while.

158

XVI

I held my torch high, the old branch burning away as I walked deeper into the old tunnel. "I'm not an expert, but I think the stone in here has been worked by something."

"This sailor is not an expert either." Irkan held his own torch closer to the wall, inspecting it with a yellow eye. "But he agrees. A secondary entrance to the mines, perhaps. That plateau would have been a decent landing field."

"Yeah. It would explain why there's only trees out to the sides. Someone cut down the rest to leave that open space, and they just never regrew for some reason."

Johanna crept up to my side, her own torch unlit, being saved for our trip back out. "Why wouldn't they have grown back though?"

"I'm not a tree person either." I rolled a shoulder. "Maybe we can dig down a bit back at camp. Could be concrete or steel just under the surface layer of dirt."

"Or the Faithful keep it clear so they can use these tunnels." She countered.

"...or that." I admitted. "I was really trying not to say that one out loud."

"Were you, or are you embarrassed that the big-shot Imperial spy didn't think of that before I did?" She asked, a rare slyness in her voice.

Irkan chuckled in that odd way that Mikira laughed. "The children should focus on the path before them, and seek to arouse one another later."

"We're not flirting!" Johanna said. "Or dating!"

"In the Empire we'd definitely be dating." I countered, picking up the pace a little. "We literally do everything together."

She let out a petulant little growl. "That's not *dating*. Why is everything in your Empire so weird?"

159

I huffed. "From my point of view, it's your Ark Fleet that's weird. How is going out to dinner a date? That's, like, an hour or two at most. You can't figure out if you actually like them from just that."

"That's why you go on more than one date." She said.

"And you'd need six or seven dates to cover the same amount of time as a single day of dating my way." I grinned at her expression. "It's called efficiency."

Johanna glared at me some more, but it was her 'I hate that you're right but I'm not admitting it' glare. And, sure enough, she avoided answering when she replied. "The point is that *we* are not dating. You like Trahcon, and I don't like other women that way."

"Which is also weird." I noted.

Her groan was as long as it was exhausted. "I'm not having that debate with you, *again.* I'm definitely not having it in a creepy tunnel."

Irkan chortled some more, long head swaying as he checked the roof and walls while we walked. "This sailor finds both of your practices strange, even disturbing, if that helps the pale savanna's mood."

"Oh no. I'm not touching your opinions on this." Johanna shook her head. "The first time was traumatizing enough. Can we please focus on the creepy tunnel? Please? I'd really rather figure out if there's anything in here that's going to kill us in our sleep."

"Or if this is another way to the base." I add.

"Or that." She agreed.

"This sailor doubts our torches would last so long." Irkan replied. "But the pale savanna's point is taken. No footprints are visible ahead. Are those of us who are walking leaving them behind?"

I glanced down at our feet for a moment, then back behind us. "Yeah. We're definitely leaving tracks."

"Then those who walk may assume this tunnel has not been used for some time."

Johanna nodded, "I guess that's reassuring. Could a hover cart have come through or something? Tunnel's wide enough for a small one."

"True, but not without throwing the dust up all over the place." My torch slid closer to the wall, "Looks pretty clean right down to the floor... I think we've got a side passage ahead."

We all slowed, eyes peering into the dark, picking out the barest outline of an extra curve in the wall. Moving closer let me see that it wasn't really a side tunnel at all. It was... an alcove of some kind. A truly ancient looking computer system occupied an entire wall, while a low table and strange chairs filled the rest of the space.

"Irkan?" I pitched my voice lower. "Is this Mikira made?"

Our only Mikira moved ahead of me, short arms extended as if he dearly wanted to, but didn't dare, touch any of it. "...yes. See how the chairs are built low, but strong. The better to support the weight of us."

Huh. Tasir had been right about that then. Good to know.

Johanna and I followed him, my arm raising my torch up to get a better look around. Apart from the table and the computer, there wasn't anything else to see.

"Rest stop?" Johanna suggested, waving at the table. "So that they could have meal breaks?"

I hummed an agreement. "Probably. Computer probably let them know shift changes... and it would have a map, I'd think."

She snorted. "There's no way you're going to be able to turn that thing on."

I shrugged again, and was about to say that it couldn't hurt to try... and then I remembered that it very much could hurt to try. "It might still have power, and it's dry enough in here. Not much chance moisture would have ruined the internals, but... if the Faithful are sitting on the main entrance to the mines, they'd have access to the old servers if they're still there."

"Assuming they're still working too." Johanna countered doubtfully. "This has got to be what? A thousand years old?"

161

A good question.

"Irkan?" I asked.

"This sailor will carefully check." He replied.

We stood back, watching as he approached the boxy old devices. Huffs of his breath sent dust into the air, revealing keyboards designed for clawed hands. More blowing let him pick out the thick cables connecting everything, and then the small latches that held the plating together.

He eased some of them apart, bringing his torch closer to inspect it. There mustn't have been anything to see because he closed it and moved on to another. That little routine repeated itself a half-dozen times before he made a sound of triumph.

"A maintenance log." He reported. "It is badly worn, but the date remains. Twenty-Five-Eight, of the Age of Triumph."

I shrugged, asking, "When is that in Imperial-standard?"

Irkan considered that as he closed it back up, still moving with gentle care. "The old shark was correct. That was the era in which the greatest Kingdom warred with Cathia for the fourth time."

I ran that through my head. "That's, what. Six hundred years ago?"

"Roughly." He agreed.

Johanna clicked her tongue. "Not much chance of turning it back on then."

"Probably not." I ran a hand up and through my fur, hating that it was getting so long. "Less odds that the Faithful would have bothered saving the old systems though."

"You want to risk trying?" Johanna asked.

"I...don't know." I admitted. "Irkan? What do you think?"

He jerked his head, quills wobbling on his chin. "This sailor must consider the matter. The most ancient computer shall not travel on its own.

Those of us here shall have time to reflect."

True enough. "I...don't think we should tell anyone about this. Let's keep it to ourselves."

"The Imperial savanna does not trust the others." He made that a statement rather than a question.

A statement I confirmed, "She does not. I want to trust Caliu, and maybe Ghost, but I definitely don't trust Nisco."

Johanna shook her head. "Ghost is an ass."

"But he's universally an ass." I said back. "And he's universally helpful even if he likes to insult you the entire time he helps you. Nisco would toss us both off the side of the mountain if he thought he could get away with it, and he'd laugh as he did it."

Irkan made a low, growling noise.

I quickly amended my statement. "Sorry, he'd throw all three of us over the side if he could get away with it."

The man among us huffed out an approval at the correction. "This sailor must agree with the Imperial savanna. The others should be told the tunnel extends beyond the range we wished to delve, and no more."

We both looked to Johanna, who merely shrugged. "I agree, I just think we should be just as paranoid about Ghost as we are about Nisco."

"Fair enough." I replied. "Should we try going farther, or turn back here?"

"Back." Johanna said, at the same time as Irkan said, "Farther."

They both turned to stare at each other, leaving me to smile. "Heh. Sorry, Johanna, but I do think we should go a little farther."

"...do we have to?" Her weight shifted in discomfort. "This is reminding me of the ship. And not in a good way."

I swallowed, my own memories of that darkness coming back at once. "I promise if we see a pair of eyes in the dark that we'll run as fast as we can the other way. Just a little farther."

She heaved out a sigh, her own hands rising to pull her fur out of her eyes. "Fine, but it better be just a little farther."

Irkan huffed a little at the delay, but thankfully didn't say anything when we got moving again.

In the end we didn't actually go all that far. Maybe ten or fifteen minutes passed before we hit a true split in the tunnel. The main run continued on, sloping only slightly downhill, while a smaller passage opened up on our right.

That one sloped almost vertically down, and we quickly agreed against exploring it when Irkan nearly slipped at the entrance. We made our way back to our little camp without incident... but I kept glancing over my shoulder every few steps all the same.

Watching for those eyes in the dark.

XVII

Our six weeks on duty passed without much of anything interesting happening.

We built a crude raft, then found a good stretch in the river to fish from. Nearby were several decent areas to forage for fruits and root vegetables, giving us a little variety in our diet.

There were so many edible plants around that I was utterly convinced the Faithful had seeded the world with them. That they'd prepared this world so that their prisoners could survive even outside of the collaborator's little farmlands.

Some kind of sick experiment was going on here, and we were all just test subjects.

I supposed I'd already realized that, but I was increasingly frustrated by my inability to tell just what this was all *for.*

Watching the village and the base didn't provide me with any clues. The Human collaborators tilled their fields, tended to their herds of pferd, and then gathered together for some kind of event every evening. I wasn't sure what that was about either, but I equally was sure that I was happier not knowing the details.

In contrast the base was utterly quiet. Once in a while we could pick out figures moving between the buildings. Spot a patrol walking the walls. There still weren't any vehicles, or shuttles.

Tasir didn't look terribly surprised at our report when she returned with the next group.

The march back to the main camp was easier than the march there had been, if only because Tasir had stayed behind to supervise the next group for a few days. Irkan allowed us a slower pace, with more breaks.

Not that it stopped Johanna and I from collapsing when we got back, but we lasted long enough to put our tent back up in its old spot first.

165

After that it was back to our primitive routine; hunting, gathering, and trying to build up our strength as much as we could considering how much time we had to spend on the first two.

"Pferd." Marzin rumbled, "So that is what they are called. An odd name. Are they bred as food stock?"

Johanna shook her head, the two of us carefully wading out in to the river to collect the traps we'd put down yesterday. "No. It depends on the breeder, but historically they're mounts. For single riders or for pulling carts in peace. Oh, or as cavalry mounts in war, back before we invented engines."

The huge alien hummed, sprawling out a little further on the muddy bank, watching as we worked. "That makes sense. They have a rather unpleasant taste, I could not imagine your people keeping them simply for food."

"...eating them is kind of a taboo, I think." Johanna said. "They're pretty well respected. Or at least they were, in the old days on Earth."

Marzin let out a deep chuckle. "I will not apologize. They are one of the few meals I can find that will actually fill me for a time."

"Just don't ask me to watch you eat one." She replied. "Once was disturbing enough."

"I shall not." He promised. "There was nothing else worth observing?"

I shook my head, reaching down to try and feel for the wooden box. "Not really. It was exactly as quiet as Tasir said it would be. Pretty disappointing really."

"As most things are at Last Stop." Marzin said. "What of the cave? Tasir was hopeful it might have enough room for the full camp, that we might move the entire group there."

"Definitely carved by tools, not naturally. We followed it as far as a split in the tunnel." I told him, not technically lying. Just not telling him everything we'd found. "I don't think you'd fit inside though. Well, you might be able to, but I don't think you'd be able to turn around."

A massive set of claws waved dismissively, "I never fit in such

166

spaces. Tiny aliens simply do not understand what the proper size of a building ought to be... or a proper tunnel in this case."

I snorted, grinning at him. "It's not our fault you're larger than most starfighters."

"Do not get me started on the way your people build ships either." He huffed out an enormous gust of warm air. "They need so many crew! It is incredibly inefficient."

"Not everyone wants to replace half their brains with cybernetics." My hands pulled the trap up, a grin spreading when I saw the small crustaceans trapped within. "Ha! These things worked after all. Finally something besides fish and rodents!"

Johanna let a cheer of her own when her own trap came up full of the little six-legged things. "Angry little Flusskrabbe... are we sure they're safe for us to eat?"

"Nope." I admitted, "You want to be the test, or you want me to?"

"You tried those rodents first. Guess it's my turn to hope the food isn't toxic." She turned, splashing water as she started wading back toward the shore. "Are you going to save me if I go into shock?"

The question had been aimed at Marzin, and he dipped his broad head as best he could while laying down. "But of course. You are far too adorable to die in such a pathetic fashion."

Johanna huffed. "Do your people keep Humans as tiny pets or something? Dress us up and pat our heads?"

He chuckled, watching as we both began laboring to get back to where he was laying. "I do not believe the Federation has many Human residents at all."

"But," I asked, "If there were, what would they do?"

"They would likely be the most exotic little pets." He admitted shamelessly. "It is not as though your people would be good for much else. We have plenty of Trahcon and Vekki for those times we need smaller beings to repair things we cannot reach."

167

My old cellmate shook her head. "Aliens."

"At least you didn't get angry." I noted. "Tiny cells."

"Tiny cells are wearing off." She nodded. "Mostly."

"Mostly." I agreed. "Come on. Let's get these back to camp so that our enormous monster can bathe himself without a pair of cute little Humans being in the way.""

Marzin let out the most petulant sound someone bigger than an aircar could. "I do believe you promised to help clean the scales behind my neck."

Johanna had come a long way. Instead of getting intimidated when she got close to him, she merely huffed, muddy feet already carrying her back toward camp. "That was before you told me I'd make a lovely little hunde for you to play dress up with."

"I may apologize if that would soothe her tiny temper." He offered.

She scoffed, making me laugh as I followed her. "Try again tomorrow, Marzin."

I heard him grumble something in his own language before he heaved himself back up to his six limbs. The massive splash of him plunging into the river came just as we got back to the trees, following the increasingly worn path ahead of us.

For once everyone was happy to see us, at least once they noticed that the traps we were carrying were filled with frustrated crustaceans.

"We've got a decent number!" I said, speaking loudly, "Uh, Akirak, you're supposed to be the expert on these things, aren't you?"

The black-furred Naulian grinned, quickly ambling forward to take the trap from my hands. One of the others ambled forward to take Johanna's as well, sharp teeth on full display at the promise of fresh food.

"Get some water boiling!" Akirak instructed. "They don't take long too cook, but they turn septic if you kill them first. Just toss them in with seasoning, then break them apart."

Ginlos and Rezzuk quickly did as instructed, getting one of our very few metal pots in place over a fire with plenty of water inside.

"Every part of them is edible to us," Akirak waved an arm at the rest of his people, all of whom looked eager for the upcoming meal, and who were getting a pot of their own set up over a different fire. "But we should start everyone else on just a leg each I think. Pure meat, no organs. Humans first since they brought them back. Who will try it?"

Johanna raised an arm, "Here, but I want Marzin back first."

That sentiment was echoed by Tane, the normally scowling woman watching the little creatures with interest. Apparently she was the volunteer for the Thondian toxicity test. "Are they sweet?"

"Very." He assured her. "Trahcon?"

Ginlos shrugged, holding a hand up. "I'll try it."

Akirak glanced to the white furred alien sitting by himself. "Ghost?"

The Xenthan waved a hand. "I have no need to risk my life just for a new meal. If you want to be that foolish, that's your prerogative."

Everyone glowered at him, myself very much included. Not that it stopped him smirking and turning back to his own embers, turning over the fish he was cooking directly on the coals.

With the volunteers settled, we all sat around waiting for water to boil. A Marzin dripping enough water to count as rain arrived back at camp in time to watch as our small group of Naule began devouring their meal, laughing as they dismembered the little things and slurped down the meat within.

The real moment of truth came as each of the volunteers carefully pulled a leg off of one. Starting with Johanna, they carefully bit the bit of meat hanging out, pulling it free before eating it.

And then we waited to see if any of them would have a reaction, just as we had for each of the other new types of food that we'd found.

"It was rather sweet." Johanna admitted, "It was good. Don't feel anything."

169

"We wait one hour." Marzin instructed, his tone brooking no argument. "I am scanning you all right now for signs of irregularity."

When that hour passed with no one falling over, or throwing up, Akirak began serving out more of the little arms for the rest of us.

"Mmm." I hummed around my own, "This is pretty good."

Johanna chuckled, tossing an empty bit of shell away. "It's probably really bland. We're just desperate for new flavor."

"Probably." I agreed. "These might go well on Jarak Noodles with blue sauce though."

Caliu let out a long groan across the fire. "Blue sauce. I would do anything for a jar of real blue sauce right now. Icar style."

I made a face at her, "Too spicy. Altair style or nothing."

"How do you even taste your food?" Her tarah flicked outward in amusement. "That's just sugar and blue food coloring."

Ginlos snorted in agreement. "It is sickly sweet, Ashe."

A finger rose to point at him, "I don't want food opinions from you, Sir We-Burn-Everything-Abantia."

He grinned, "At least we know what a grill looks like. You'd just lazily bake every-"

"Quiet!" Marzin's boom shut us all up, and made more than a few of us drop our meals in shock. "Something comes down the river. Defensive positions! Now!"

For a long second no one reacted, and then *everyone* reacted. Dirt was frantically shoved over the fires, dousing them all within moments. People shouted to each other in four languages, sprinting past one another as we tried to enact plans we'd practiced too rarely.

I followed Johanna back to our tent, yanking down the crude spears that helped hold it up. Thusly 'armed', we ran to find Irkan amid the chaos.

Trahcon raced past us, the ozone scent of sorcery filling the air as they

170

prepared to be the first line of defense. They mostly ran for the river itself; they'd hold up an attackers long enough to tell the rest of us what we were up against. In theory at least.

Behind them was the majority of Thondians and Naule, armed just as crudely as Johanna and I; with spears, clubs, and the occasional knife.

Only three men carried guns; Narob, Irkan, and Ghost. Well, and Marzin I supposed, though the massive rifle he had built into his back shamed their scavenged pistols. The four of them swept south, Johanna and I quickly following close behind.

"The savannas will remember their role." Irkan rumbled. He'd fallen to the back of the line quickly, letting us keep up with him. "Watch this group's flanks and rear. Be prepared to take this sailor's gun should he fall. Do not tend his wounds, his blood would kill them."

"We remember." I said around pants for breath. "We'll watch your back."

His follow up instructions were swallowed up by Marzin's, "I shall hold here. Move ahead thirty paces. That copse of trees shall be your firebase. Hold it until I instruct otherwise."

Neither Ghost nor Narob argued for once. They just ran a bit farther, then got themselves settled into cover. The larger alien even helped yank down leaves and sticks, helping to camouflage Ghost's snowy pelt.

"Here." I whispered, tugging Johanna into a small dip in the ground just behind the collection of trees. "We can see both ways from here."

"Al-all r-right." She stuttered, spear shaking as she ducked down beside me. Her follow up was in Deutsch, "Oh god. I'm not ready f-for this."

I swallowed, quickly shifting my spear to one hand so my other could grab her elbow. "Hey. It's okay. I'm right here. We'll get through this."

Her nod was nervous, and she scooted a little closer, but she gamely got her spear held level.

We waited there in silence for what felt like hours but was probably minutes before another bellow from Marzin reached us.

171

"It is two members of the watch party atop the raft! Return to camp, and begin packing as quickly as possible!" He called. "The collaborators have begun their preparations, and shuttles have been spotted! A Culling approaches!"

My heart skipped a beat.

"It is time!" He roared, "I am sick of this world, as you all are! It is time we depart it as free beings under the just laws of the Compact, or else make the Faithful suffer for the injustice they have delivered to us! It is time! Break camp! We march by sunset!"

He was right.

It was time to go home... or it was time to die trying.

XVIII

The entire camp moved as quickly as it could up river, following it to the base of the mountain. Our watch party was waiting for us there, Tasir and Marzin holding a private planning session well apart from the group as we took a single day to gather up as much food as we could scavenge.

In the evening we were finally given our briefing.

Everyone sat on the ground, sitting as closely to our neighbors as we could to see the map Marzin was projecting against a boulder. Tasir stood before it, pointing out various features with a hand as she spoke.

"We will remain within the mountain's treeline as long as we can." She said, tracing that line, "That will bring us within reach of the eastern walls, perhaps five or six hundred yards out."

One of the Naule spoke up, his voice a grumble, "An impossible distance without armor or shields."

Tasir motioned to herself. "The Trahcon among us will be in the lead. Our sorcery will call up barriers to protect us all on the approach. Our endurance will be limited, so that advance must be done *at speed*. A full sprint, from the treelines all the way up to the walls."

"That will exhaust you." Narob noted.

"Yes, but that's our only chance of making it to the base's exterior wall." She replied. "Marzin will breach them, and will be in the lead moving through. Any Trahcon still capable of wielding sorcery will be in the vanguard. Everyone else will move for the nearest landed spacecraft with the intent to board them."

More than a few people nodded, myself among them, but Narob wasn't done. "They'll still have arms."

I spoke up as loudly as I could to be heard, "Maybe, but on Nueva Genova the Faithful relied far more on sorcery than firearms. They might have far fewer guns than you'd think."

173

Ghost let out a long mewl, then surprised me by raising his own voice in agreement. "She's right, for once. And remember the bastards are sadists. They'll want to drag it out, which will give us all a chance to tear their throats out first."

The following rumble of approval was louder than the first. Tasir let it dance on the waves for a moment, then resumed speaking. "Our best case scenario will be to have two ships. Regardless of who makes it, your objective will be to get to the nearest capital world of a Compact signatory."

A deep huff from Marzin followed her words, "We believe we are near the Far Reaches, perhaps within or near the Lost's Kingdom. Any ship that escapes should make for Terminus, Xentha, Cathia, or Lushrivers. They are bound by the Compact to protect us all, and to punish those who have done this to us."

"And if we're not near the Reaches?" One of the few Trahcon I didn't know called out. "What if we're on the far side of the Storm of Curses, or in the Airalon Wastes?"

Tasir shook her head, "Then use your bloody *brain* and find the nearest safe port. And don't stop moving until you get back to civilization."

The speaker ducked his head, chagrined, while his neighbors chuckled and patted him on the back.

Our eldest waited until she was sure no one else was going to interrupt before she resumed the briefing. "Marzin and I will be the last to board any ships. If you're not on before we are, you're being left behind. Keep that in mind, and keep track of where we are at all times."

"That," Marzin rumbled, "Will be easier for me than her, perhaps. But make the attempt regardless."

Johanna and I were among the many who chuckled at that, the big alien clearly pleased that his joke had helped soothe us. He went on, "Keep close to your companions. I will not tell you what you already know about our odds, about how many of us will live to see freedom. I will say instead to rest well tonight, and in the nights to come. Take comfort where you may."

Silence and solemn nods were his response that time.

"Get some sleep." Tasir barked out, "We move at sunrise. According

174

to those who've been here long enough to see one, the Culling usually takes several weeks. That means we'll have an opportunity to pick our moment, but only if we get there soon! Be ready for a forced march!"

That time I stayed quiet, not joining in the groans and complaints. Another forced march wouldn't be fun, but I'd expected we'd have to pick up the pace at some point.

"This will be our last decent night of sleep in a while." I murmured to Johanna. "Come on. Let's make sure our packs are settled."

She nodded, the two of us among the first to stand and slip away. More followed, though many seemed content to continue questioning Tasir's rough plan.

I couldn't blame them. She'd been extremely light on the details....

"...but then, we don't have much of anything to work with." I muttered, following my cellmate back to the area we'd claimed for ourselves. "Not much point in having a more detailed plan. Not until we're there and can see what we're going to be up against."

Johanna must have heard me, because she called back in her native tongue. "You think so? I'm.... not really confident in our chances after that."

I sighed and replied in the same language. "You saw the base. Can you think of anything better?"

"No, but I'm not a military officer. I kind of expected more than something an eighteen year old girl could have figured out."

"I'm sure we'll get more details once we're closer." I said with a confidence I didn't really feel. "Until we know where the ships are, how many Faithful are on duty, it's kind of hard to really plan more than what she already gave us."

And besides. Lead with the sorcerers, hope our few people with guns don't die, and pray everyone else gets into melee range was about the extent of our tactical options considering the fact that our group wasn't a real military formation.

Ashahn's blood, we were still pretty much divided up by species. Events like finding new kinds of food were among the few that could actually

175

get everyone working together for a little while.

There'd been no real drills, no general practices of battle tactics. Maybe if we'd been defending a location Tasir could have given us more to work with. But as it was... well, we *had* to attack their base across mostly open ground. That was a bad enough idea even with a real military unit.

Which our little band really, *really* wasn't.

"I guess..." Johanna mumbled.

Another sigh escaped me at her less than hopeful tone. I caught up to her when she got to our packs, the both of us dropping back down onto the hard dirt under an old tree. We'd been trailing behind during the march, as usual, and had ended up at the outskirts.

That suited Johanna just fine, even if I'd have preferred to be a bit closer to where most of the Trahcon had started to put up their tents.

"We'll make it." I told her quietly. "We'll get on one of those ships, and we'll both get to go home."

Johanna looked away from me, head slowly bowing. "I... do you promise?"

"I promise." A hand found hers, squeezing. "I'll get us on one of those ships."

Her fingers tightened as well, "All right. Are you staying over here tonight, or are you going to go off with them?"

"Them?"

At her nod, I turned my head around to see more people trickling back to camp. More than a few of the Trahcon were already reaching out, caressing each other's tarah. Caliu had a handsome young man on one arm, and an equally handsome woman on the other, while Ginlos was similarly enjoying the attentions of several admirers.

"Oh." I shook my head, understanding what she meant. "No. Not tonight."

"Not your thing?" She asked.

"Not really." I admitted. "I prefer to know them as packmates first. Going outside of that is... not for me."

"Oh." She echoed, watching for a moment before forcing herself to look away. "At least we're far away from where they'll all be. Um, do you want to set up our tent, or just use it as a blanket tonight?"

"Do you want to have to take the tent down in the morning?" I asked in return.

"Blanket it is."

We got the leather and hide cloth unwrapped, then arranged our packs into pillows as best we could. That didn't take very long, thankfully, and within a few minutes we were cuddled up under its protection. Johanna's back to my chest, one of my arms draped over her waist.

Quiet conversation filled the camp. It seemed the Thondians weren't any more fond of the Trahcon's ways as Johanna. Their volume rose to cover up the sounds of people enjoying themselves for what might be the last time, a careful look letting me see small campfires being set up to roast bits and pieces of food.

I watched until Irkan slowly approached, giving me a nod before he carefully laid himself down nearby; between us and the bulk of the camp.

"Protecting us?" I asked over Johanna's head.

"Until the savannas no longer require this sailor's aid, he shall do so." He replied, slowly dropping down to his belly with a tired groan. "This sailor shall keep pace with them tomorrow."

I smiled at him, "You mean we'll need to keep pace with your short legs."

"Is that not what the sailor said?"

Johanna chuckled in my arms, "Maybe we could bribe Marzin to ride on his back."

"There's an idea." I mused. "Not sure he could carry Irkan though. He looks heavy."

177

The Mikira tried to growl at us, but there was an amused chirp in his slow words. "This sailor is quite light for one of the Sacred Blood. The savanna would do well to not accuse him of obesity."

"Well you *are* pretty wide." I teased.

"The savanna's tone remains-"

The thunder-crack of a heavy rifle cut him off.

For a long moment there was dead silence, everyone freezing in place.

Then the rifle boomed again, and a man began screaming in agony.

I shot upright, frantically kicking my way free of our make-shift blanket. Irkan was similarly heaving himself up, Johanna gathering herself into a panicked crouch.

"What in Ashahn's name is-"

Rapid fire guns began to go off on the far side of the camp, chattering in quick bursts. More screams came, mixed with the harsher cracks of combat sorcery being brought into play. Blue-white flames became appearing and vanishing as power was called into reality.

My own heart began to race. Limbs unprotected by armor, not even by a shield brace, began to tremble.

"Faithful!" Someone shouted, voice booming out. "The Faithful are attacking!"

I found the speaker, Narob, standing sheltered behind a distant tree, waving the gun that was his symbol of authority. "Form up! Form up, now! We hold-"

A round slammed into his wrist, blowing his hand and its weapon off of his body. He fell to his knees with a scream, swallowed up by the rush of people racing around the camp.

"What do we do!?" Johanna screamed.

I....

178

Three more Thondians were cut down by an unseen gun, felled by a single burst.

I... made the only decision I could. "Run! Get the packs and run! Irkan!"

"Yes!" He had seized his own bag, already breaking into his best run. "Run!"

Johanna and I yanked our bags into our arms, paused just long enough to grab our crude spears, and then sprinted after him. I felt my feet digging into the soft dirt, sticks breaking under my calloused heels as we ran for our lives.

Marzin roared somewhere in the distance, his orders affirming my panicked decision. "Scatter to the woods! Regroup at our first camp! Scatter and regroup!"

I saw him far to the right, his huge body splashing into the river. The gun on his back was glowing red hot, tracers spitting out into the darkness. Incoming fire slammed into barriers over the Regnon, sent water splashing up when they missed.

Then he was deep enough to begin swimming with the current, long body vanishing around a copse of trees.

We ran away as our little band of survivors continued to die. I saw blue-white light gather around distant forms; a collection of Trahcon trying to retreat together, their sorcery overlapping. Strobe-lights went off right before them, deafening cracks sounding in time with the flash-bang's detonation.

Our people staggered, protections failing them.

Their dead bodies fell, riddled with bullets seconds later.

We ran into the forest, scrambling up the earliest slope of the mountain.

We ran, and listened to everyone else dying behind us.

We ran, and we lived.

179

XIX

We followed the river north, scrambling over the low hills, trying to stay in the thick woods as long as we could.

Terror kept my legs moving. Kept me pulling Johanna along. Let us keep to Irkan's relentless pace until the first lights of sunrise began to color the sky.

It was only then that Johanna simply collapsed, unable to go on. I tried to get her back up, and found my own knees striking the dirt a moment later.

"Can't..." I gasped, shaking arms barely keeping me from falling face-first into the ground. "...we can't..."

Irkan was breathing heavily as well, his wide body heaving with the effort of it. "Find a ditch. Shelter. This sailor will retrieve water."

I nodded, pushing myself back so I was at least upright, if still kneeling. It let me get a better look around us.

We'd stumbled into a tiny clearing amid the underbrush, near the base of a great old tree. The river was somewhere nearby, the sound of the rapids coming down from the mountain audible in the distance.

The roots had disturbed the ground enough to create broad furrows just a few yards away. Good enough to hide us, if we collapsed within them instead of in the open. I hoped.

I just had to move her there.

My first attempt nearly had me collapse on top of her, leaving me wheezing and shaking beside her. "Ashahn's... blood...."

Johanna's quiet whimpers seemed to agree with the sentiment, even if she didn't have the strength to reply. I reached down, my trembling hand touching hers.

"Come... on. Just... over there."

Tears were running down her cheeks. "...can't."

"You can." I convinced my fingers to wrap around her wrist, a light tug all I could muster. "Come on. Just... just over there. Safe. We'll be safe there. Come... come on."

She slowly, painfully slowly, rolled onto her stomach. We didn't manage to get back up so much as we managed to crawl on our hands and knees. We didn't lay down inside the ditch either; we just fell over when we arrived, bodies slamming into the dirt.

Irkan returned before I could do more than roll onto my back, and he didn't come back alone; a drenched gray form was in his arms.

"...who?" I rasped.

"The eldest." He rumbled, carefully setting her down on her side beside me.

Tasir was covered in mud, scratches, and was shivering badly. A make-shift bandage was wrapped around one hand, but had mostly come loose in the water, letting me see missing fingers and burn scars over the stumps. She still had her thumb, but the others were gone.

"There is another." Irkan was already moving away. "Rouse her."

It hurt to get my arm up, to give the elder a gentle shove. Then another.

She didn't stir.

Groaning, I corrected my aim, getting two fingers around the tip of her right tarah.

A sharp pinch made her hiss, one eye fluttering open. "...fuck?"

"Wake...up... sir." I rasped at her. "Wake up."

"Lori?" Both eyes opened, her voice as rough as mine sounded. "Oh. We're alive."

I nodded, letting my head fall back until the dirt cushioned it. "For

181

now... sir. What... happened?"

She gave me the tiniest shake of her head, "Don't know. Drone maybe. Traitor maybe. Expected problems ahead. Came from behind instead."

I swallowed. "Anyone... did anyone else...?"

The sound of Irkan returning made me look up in time to see that he didn't have a second person in his arms. His long head jerked in a negative motion.

Tasir saw as well, sighing as she let her head fall back down as well. "Ginlos."

My eyes closed, a tear rolling its way down a cheek as the great waves of reality washed over me. As I was forced to face the stormy seas swirling all around.

Four of us.

Four of us had made it.

Four of us out of more than sixty. Many of whom I'd started to get to know. Had started to like. Ginlos, Jahgrah, Caliu, even Ghost... by the holy Aspects, even the Naulians had started to warm up to us on the march. We'd all be excited, eager. Ready to make our great attempt at escaping this prison.

And now we were all that was left. Two Humans not even fully recovered yet, a wounded Elder, and one Mikiran Sailor.

There was no way we'd be able to storm the compound with four of us. The idea was laughable. Every plan we'd had to get out of here had just been broken against the cruelest shores. What was left was... I didn't even know what was left.

Irkan kept us all awake long enough to make us drink water, to clean off Tasir's wounds. Then he vanished for a few minutes, returning with his shell covered in mud to conceal it, carefully laying down nearby.

I woke up sometime in the late afternoon, as best I could tell from the position of the sun overhead. Tasir was still sleeping, as was Irkan, but Johanna woke up when she heard me pulling fruit out of my bag.

Between us we shared a Stone Fruit, then crept off to relieve ourselves closer to the river.

By the time we returned our alien companions were awake as well, sitting on the tree's roots.

We sat as well, the four of us staring at one another before Tasir spoke.

"Well. That's that then." She shook her head. "We're not breaking into the base with four of us."

"No." I agreed, eyes falling to the ground. "What are our options, sir?"

The Elder sighed, sounding utterly defeated. "Find Marzin, if he's still alive. Any other survivors. Set up a new camp farther south, and try all of this again when the next Culling comes around."

Johanna cleared her throat, "That would be... more than a year, wouldn't it?"

"At least." Tasir said. "Probably two years, three at the outside."

Her pale throat worked in a swallow. "I... no. No. I can't do it. I can't do another year here. Not more than that. There's... there's got to be something else."

"There isn't." Tasir's voice was flat. Broken. Her usual timber of command was gone, and nothing had replaced it. "Numbers and surprise are the only chance we had, and we lost both. There's enough food here that we can survive, so long as the Faithful don't find us. We rest today, we cross the river tomorrow."

Johanna turned, giving me a desperate look.

I... another year?

Another *year?* Minimum? With the gamble of having this happen all over again three years from today?

"...no." I heard myself whisper. "I... won't make that gamble, sir."

Tasir went still, turning slowly to face me. Some tiny crest of anger made her sound more alive when she spoke again, "What was that, Rifle?"

It was my turn to swallow, to lick my lips. "Another two years here, sir, is just a gamble that this won't happen again. I... I'm with Johanna. I can't spend that long here, doing nothing but wondering if the next time will be any different."

An irritated huff escaped the Elder, "And what's your alternative plan, Rifle?"

My plan... I needed a plan. We couldn't approach as the group had intended. Even if we got close enough, the four of us would never survive the run across the kill-zone. That left us with only two real options that I could see.

First option, we could try to infiltrate the collaborators. Pose Tasir and Irkan as prisoners... no. It was a terrible idea. They'd know everyone in their little village. Know who their prisoners were. Maybe if we stayed the year, that could work as an infiltration plan for next time...

But I didn't want there to be a next time. I wanted to go home. To find Rerth. To get Johanna back to her home. I wanted to know just what was going on here, who the Faithful were, why they were doing what they were doing.

And then I wanted to watch as the Empire dispensed its justice for their crimes.

That left just one option.

"The tunnels." I said simply. "The mining tunnels. We use those to approach by stealth, sneak into whatever facility they have underground, whatever is inside the mountain, under the base. We infiltrate, and we find and steal the first FTL spacecraft we can."

Her expression was flat. "They'll have sealed off the mines from anything they've built down there."

"Then we spend a few days wandering around in the dark, sir." I countered, "And then we turn around and head off to find Marzin like you want."

Irkan nodded, very slowly. "The Imperial savanna has a point, eldest. The Faithful are no doubt hunting for survivors. A few days underground may conceal this group's survival, even if no way into the base is found."

Tasir lowered both of her tarah. "That's days of food that we'll need to eat, days stumbling around in the dark where we could trip any number of alarms. We only know one way into those tunnels. It would take them no effort at all to bury us if they know we went in."

"Unlikely." Irkan countered for us. "A tunnel so high in the mountain? It must be secondary. For air or escape. There will be more."

I nodded, "It's not a good chance. I'll admit that, sir, but is it any worse than our plan to charge the gates?"

"We'd at least have had the distraction of the collaborators bringing in their prisoners." She shot back. "We won't be able to time that right with your plan. We won't have any idea as to what's going on once we're underground. No."

Johanna started to speak, stopped herself, then turned to me. "Ashe. I'm not going back south."

"I know." I said quietly, steeling myself to do the one thing I swore I wouldn't do after the mess on Oshflara.

I prepared myself to disobey a direct order from a superior officer.

"Director... we're going into the tunnel. We have to at least try."

Her bright eyes stared into mine, tarah twitching once. "I see. Irkan?"

"The sailor is with the savannas." He replied. "Let this group at least try, eldest. If it should fail, then we shall simply flee to wait until the next culling as she says."

Tasir hadn't looked away from me. "I see. You know this is direct insubordination, don't you?"

"Yes, sir." I said quietly.

"And what that could mean if we ever get home?" She asked.

"I would be consigned to a penal colony, sir." I replied. "I'm one severe demerit away. I'm not even sure they would give me a full hearing for it."

"And you do this regardless?" She demanded.

"Yes, sir." I said.

"Why?"

I swallowed, but didn't otherwise hesitate. "Because Johanna isn't going to stay sane if we stay out here for three years, sir. She's the closest thing I have to a packmate right now. I won't let that happen to her."

Johanna blinked rapidly, skin coloring a light red.

"And," I went on, trying to keep my voice firm despite the roiling storm of fear inside of me. "I... have to know what is going on here. I have to know *why* they're doing this to us. If you're right, and they have facilities underground, then that's our best chance for both answers and escape."

My superior officer pursed her lips, "Ashahn's ass, you're as stubborn as Kean ever was. Bloody Humans... although..."

"Sir?"

"I do want to meet this Agent of yours now." She shook her head, "Even with all of our plans stormwrecked, our entire camp dead, and you're still determined to get answers. She trained you well."

I felt my face heat up slightly. "I... was like that before she trained me, sir. It's why I have so many demerits. Agent Rerth'riah just made me better at finding what I'm looking for."

Tasir snorted, "Then she has Khash's own luck, to find you. Fine. I'm not in any shape to force you three, and you've made it clear that you're not following my orders because of my rank."

"You're still our leader, sir."

A quiet grunt came from her throat. "Then our plan for today will be to move farther upriver and start gathering as much food as we can for the trip into the mines. We'll need more torches, and that sap to fuel them as well. I'm

186

drawing a line in the sand though. As soon as we're halfway through our food, we're turning around if we still can."

I nodded at once. "Yes sir."

And with our new plan in place, those few of us that remained started making our slow trek to the north.

Interlude
Rerth'riah

The hovercar slammed onto the ground far harder than it should have, but I didn't really give a damn.

Shoving the door open, I trusted Holde to shut the machine off as I jogged over to the house currently surrounded by a full Sword's worth of veteran soldiers.

In any other circumstance it would have been a fairly lovely home in Altair's rural countryside. It was big enough for either one large pack, or perhaps two smaller ones. A nice garden, a broad garage for tinkering, and an excessively large pool to one side.

Of course that loveliness was marred by the fact that the home had seen a tidal wave of violence. Half the windows had been blown out, and most of the remainder had impact points where bullets had torn through them. The front door was splinters, the yard torn up by the trio of assault shuttles that had made combat landings upon it.

"How many?" I demanded upon reaching the first of the soldiers.

Huvu'ithi pulled her helmet off, falling into step beside me. "Three of them are still alive, we've got a nullifier tied into the power grid. Six are dead. We tried to save a fourth, but our medic couldn't stem the bleeding."

My tarah quivered in anticipation, pace picking up. "Three is still more than we've ever caught before. Losses?"

"A few wounded, but none dead. They had no idea we were coming until we breached."

Excellent. That meant our informational security was still intact, at least for now.

Striding through the shattered door, I followed the trail of destruction to the main living space. There I found two women and a man bound and gagged, nullification bars already locked over their tarah. Honestly those made the heavy nullifier overkill, but I appreciated Ithi's thoroughness.

188

The corpse of a fourth was laying near the couch, the holes in her chest betraying her cause of death... but it was the perfect burned ring on her wrist that betrayed the reason for that death.

Surrounding the surviving prisoners were six more soldiers. Three with their guns ready to aim, another three looming behind, ready to either remove their gags or simply execute them.

I waited for Holde to catch up, my bond brushing a hand over mine before taking up a silent vigil to one side.

"All right." I finally spoke, looking at the three survivors as they stared up at me. They'd been stripped down to nothing, revealing that all three had at least one unnaturally shaped burn somewhere on their bodies.

Finally, I had real prisoners to work with.

"It is good to see you all alive." I told them, meaning it. "We'll get started with something that a friend of mine advised me to experiment with. Let us see how you react to this particular noise. Are you listening?"

Furious glares were their only response.

"Blessed is Ashahn, bringer of Inspiration." I said, noting the way all three quivered, snarling through their gags. "Wrathful is Ashahn, the stormbringer. Comforting is Ghath, teacher of healing. Frightful is Ghath, who brings madness. Soothing is Iriahn, who advises indulgence. Covetous is Iriahn, the greedy hoarder."

The woman on the right twisted, muscles bulging as she tried to rip apart the bands locking her arms in place. Three Aspects was apparently her limit.

"And the first has reached the shore." A wave saw one of Ithi's soldiers step up, pulling the gag out of that one.

The screeching started at once, "Cease your prattling about your false gods! We of the True Faith will never bow to such pathetic idols!"

I snorted, dropping into a crouch in front of her. "I know. I just wanted to confirm that you were one of those maniacs. Seems you really can't resist when someone prays to an Aspect, can you?"

189

She bared her teeth at me, blue eyes narrowed. "You... ah. I know you. You're Riah. The Agent who loves the furry little creatures more than anything else."

"And you," I replied, "Are the woman who's going to tell me everything she knows about her organization."

"Or what?" She sneered. "Torture? Pain? Drugs? I have already passed through the trials of my faith, my soul affirmed through agonies you can't even begin to imagine."

I met her gaze, considering her. "I believe you. How about we cut open your tarah then."

The sneer faltered.

"I'm sure you can handle the pain, even there. Wouldn't scream when we started separating the nerve endings, began pulling the organs out." I mused, watching her, watching the way the others began shifting in discomfort.

I sailed on, voice a quiet promise. "You revel in your sorcery. You rain it down upon all of those who lack it. Would rather wield power than simply pick up a gun. How would you live without that power, I wonder? How would live just as so many aliens do?"

"...you wouldn't." Her bravado had drained away in moments, replaced with a Huntress's fear. "You wouldn't do that to a fellow Trahcon. The Compact-"

"If I am right, you're a rebel." I reminded her with forced patience. "A criminal, a traitor to the Empire. You have no protections under the Compact. And, well, if I'm wrong? Then as you said, I'm hardly operating under Imperial law."

She swallowed, closed her eyes, and seemed to recover. "I... will tell you nothing, faithless. You won't do it."

I exhaled, pushing myself to my feet. "Your kind took my packmate from me. Whatever I am, I am *Trahcon*. I will do whatever I have to do to get her back, no matter how dark the sea becomes. Holde?"

My bond stepped up, hands pulling his bag off of his shoulder. "Time to see what lies within this bloody sea. Hold her down, and restrain the others as well."

The soldiers wrestled two of the prisoners back, shoving the third onto her belly. Her thrashing lasted until a pair of them simply stood on her limbs, drawing a pained cry.

Holde injected the first vial into her arm a moment later. "Give it a few minutes and she'll be unable to move, but should still be able to feel what we're doing. Let's start with simple questions. If you answer them truthfully, we won't have to go as far as my lovely bond suggested."

Turning away, I left him to his work. "Where's Jet?"

Ithi motioned for me to follow, "This way."

We left the living space, moving down a short hallway. On the far side proved to be a dining room overlooking a sunlit patio. In the center of the room was a broad table playing host to eight different wrist-comps, each one wired into the heavy tablet in Jet's hands.

"Did you crack any of them?" I demanded, angling to look over his shoulder.

He huffed, "Of course I did. Five are disposable pieces of driftwood, still at factory spec apart from some minimal accounts. I've got two of Ithi's soldier types tearing apart the rooms upstairs to see if there's real ones hidden somewhere."

Damn. "The others?"

"We're famous." He replied dryly. His hands brought the tablet up a bit more, letting me see the current display. "Their orders."

"...eliminate Agent Riah and associated packmates at once for continuing interference. Interrogation before execution preferred but not required." I read aloud for Ithi's sake. "Anything on our Dual-Commander?"

Jet shook his head, dark fur rippling. "Not yet, but I'm still running queries. It'll be a little while before I can be certain."

There was a strangled cry from the living room. I paused just long

191

enough to make sure she wasn't going to scream again before I asked my next question.

"Any locations? Channels to be used?"

"Looks like they're supposed to send off a confirmation when they kill us, then await pick up." He tapped rapidly through a few screens. "Here. Got the address. What do you think, boss? Been a few years since we had to fake our deaths."

I flicked a tarah. "We may have to, depending on what our prisoners give up. Keep diving deeper, I want anything actionable as soon as possible."

He nodded, already focusing on his work once more.

My attempt to head back to observe Holde was ruined by Ithi giving me a sharp nudge, the armored elbow bruising my chest. A sharp nod toward the patio told me what she wanted.

A few minutes later we were both outside, chased by a second howl of pain from the living room. Probably a drug induced one from the tone; he wouldn't start on her tarah for a while yet. Not unless she really kept her mouth shut.

"Can we trust anything that one says?" She asked, closing the patio door behind us to cut off the noise. "I was taught information extracted that way was rarely reliable."

"It isn't." I crossed my arms, steadying my breathing, my heartbeats. "But right now there's nothing else to use."

Ithi huffed, armor creaking as she walked over to join me. "And you won't tell me if any of your other people found anything. Or what you and Holde had to do running all the way to the Homeworld and back."

"Operational-"

"-security." She interrupted, ruined tarah trying to quiver, straining the muscles in her cheeks. "I *know*. Doesn't mean I like being kept in the shallows. Not when it's been a year since you lost Ashe."

My jaw clenched, head turning away from her. "I know."

192

"...that Naule in there is convinced she's been dead for months now."

"He's told me." I said, voice short. "I forgave him only because he's not a Trahcon."

Her grunt was approving. "Good. You ever let him convince you otherwise and I'll finish what I started when we met."

"If I ever doubt she's alive, I'll let you." I told her.

She nodded slightly. "What's our next plan then? Faking your deaths, ambushing the retrieval team for those burnt fish?"

"Assuming they do not give us better information under interrogation? Likely." I considered it for a moment. "Ideally not. It's harder to fake your death than you'd think, but it may be our only option... hm. Maybe..."

A quiet chime from my wrist-comp interrupted my train of thought. I brought it up, a tap bringing the message up.

Both of my hearts felt as if they stilled, then sank ever so slowly into crushing depths.

"...go inside." I said. "Tell Holde to stop. Your soldiers should assemble, disarm, and stand down."

Ithi's eyes narrowed at once. "What is it?"

"My wrist-comp was just disconnected from the Intelligence network."

I'd hardly finished speaking before Jet yanked the door open, "Rerth! I just lost connection!"

"Yes, yes." Exhaustion seemed to roll up, washing over me as I waved him off. "Send back-ups to the *Posa'volt* at once, then order them to go to Void Lord Delarah. They are to give her all of our information, and ignore all other orders that don't come directly from a Void Lord."

He nodded grimly, ducking back in.

"...Ashahn's blood." Ithi turned, already searching the sky. She must

193

have spotted something because I saw her go still, eyes slowly tracking movement. "Your superiors finally saw our sails, didn't they?"

"Yes." I said.

"And we're surrendering?" She demanded.

"We're not shooting our way off of Altair." I chided her. "An old friend is on her way to Delarah. She'll come for us. We just have to live until then."

Ithi let out a heavy breath, carefully pulling her rifle off her back. A toss sent it clattering to the ground. "And if your friend can't convince an exiled Void Lord to come sailing all the way here?"

I rolled a shoulder in a shrug. "Worst case? Penal colonies filled with people I put there, who tear us apart in anger. Assuming that the Faithful's assets in Intelligence don't torture us to death first."

"...damn. What's the best case?"

"Delarah saves us." I paused, leaning back as the first of several dozen assault craft began to close on the house. "Middle case? The Faitful make us vanish... and we find Ashe that way."

Ithi's response was lost in the roar of engines, and bellowed orders to surrender at once.

XX

I crouched down behind a boulder, eyes locked onto the flying wing as it circled above the forest.

"Another drone." I whispered to Tasir, the Director sitting with her back to the stone. "I can't tell how many miles away... hard to see it except when the sun catches the wings."

Her tarah flicked in frustration. "They know we're alive then."

"Likely, sir." I bit my lip for a moment, thinking on it. "Maybe they took some of the group alive. Interrogated them."

"Possible." Her eyes narrowed to angry slits. "Or there was a traitor among our number the entire time. Either way, we're going to have to cut our hunting and gathering short."

I nodded, returning my attention to the distant drone, finding it again when the sun hit it just right. "Yes sir. Do you think we should start our descent today?"

"No choice now." My elder growled. "They've got the way south watched by air. It's either underground and trying to escape, or it's trying to circle the mountain and strike east."

"What's east?"

"Twenty more miles of forest, then flat plains." She replied. "The problem is that the plant life gets hostile about two miles upriver from here. Meant for any Chezzek they grab, I think."

I swallowed, remembering a few lessons from my early training. "And Chezzek food is toxic to pretty much everyone else."

Her grunt confirmed it. "You're lucky if you only start throwing up the lining of your stomach. Back off slowly, Lori. It's time to go."

Obeying, I slid myself backwards as slowly as I could. Hoping that none of the drones caught the subtle movement, that none of them had a

195

camera pointed my way. That any trackers on the ground hadn't found our footsteps, food scraps, or waste.

Too many hopes to be realistic.

"...they're going to know where we went, aren't they, sir?" I asked.

"Of course they are." Tasir was already moving in a low crouch, forcing me to follow her through the dense undergrowth. "We moved fast, not stealthily. We're a few waves ahead of them, but they'll catch up soon if we don't keep up the speed."

I took the hint, picking up the pace and keeping my mouth shut.

We moved uphill as quickly as we could, stopping only to pick up the water-skins we'd been filling in the creek before I'd spotted the distant machines searching for us. Slinging them all over our shoulders, we snuck up as close to the entrance to the cave as we could, looking over our old campsite in the process.

"And *that*," Tasir growled, "Is going to be an enormous fucking arrow pointed right at us."

"Nothing we can do about it, sir." I replied. "We didn't have any reason to clean it up, no reason to think we were ever coming back here."

She gave me a flat look, both tarah lifted. "*You* obviously thought about it, huntress."

I swallowed, "Well, yes sir, but it was more... um, an escape plan. If the group turned on Johanna and I. I didn't intend for it to be a back-up in case of everyone else being killed by the Faithful."

Tasir flicked her left tarah down, then up again. "A paranoid escape plan in case of betrayal... an escape plan that gave you a long-shot of getting off world without our help even."

"And answers, sir. I want... I need answers."

Something close to a smile tugged at her lips. "If you'd been like this when you'd first arrived, I think I'd have liked you better, huntress."

"I don't think I was all that stable when I first arrived, elder." I said.

196

"I'm kind of surprised any of us are, after the tiny cells."

One of her shoulders rolled. "I don't think any of us are stable even now, girl. Can you see the drone?"

I crept to the edge of the bush we were hiding behind, doing my best to search the sky.

"...no sir." I said finally. "I can't hear one either."

"Slow and casual to the cavern entrance." She ordered. "Stay low."

I obeyed once more, forcing myself to slowly crouch-walk from our hiding place toward the tunnel's mouth. I saw the drone again just as I got there, still far off in the distance, still swooping in lazy circles in the far skies.

Swallowing, I kept moving, picking up the pace a little once I was moving across stone rather than dirt. Tasir was right behind me, the two of us straightening only once we were swallowed up in the darkness.

"Hand." She said.

I held one of mine out, feeling her calloused fingers wrapping around mine. My other arm rose until I could feel the smooth side of the tunnel, trailing along it as we walked through the pitch darkness.

We walked in silence for several minutes before Tasir spoke again, her voice low. "Never tell your Fleet girl this... but she's right. The darkness reminds me of that damned barge."

I smiled a little, even though it wasn't at all funny. "Yes sir. They played light games on yours as well?"

"From the very start. I think it amused them to see how close to the breaking point they could push us." Her fingers tightened for a moment. "My cellmate broke. Stopped eating. During one of the dark cycles they took him while I was asleep."

That smile died at once. "Did you know them well, sir?"

"Ullra'thros." The name was a murmur. "A dumb Hunter from Trinity who caught a Faithful agent cutting a deal with Thondians to buy slaves. He was too clumsy to get away clean, and they caught him. Little fish clung to

197

me the entire time, until those last few days. I tried to force food into him, tried... tried everything I could think of."

"...I'm sorry, sir." I murmured.

"Don't be sorry, be angry." She countered. "Be as furious as the seas of the Homeworld. Remember him, remember the Humans that died on your ship. Anger is determination, and only determination combined with sheer bloody stubbornness might let us pull off this insane plan of yours."

"Sir." I gave her an invisible nod... and remembered.

Michael and Wolfgang, in the cell beside ours. Their slow warming up to us. The stories we relayed up and down to try and help everyone cope. The way they'd fought and argued when Michael had caught Wolfgang staring at me when I'd been washing my clothing.

The way their blood had covered their cell from floor to ceiling.

Emma and Ida on our other side. The way they'd spoken with Johanna in the days before I'd learned their language. How cheerful the rippling stories through the cells had made them. The hard way their moods had crashed upon the shores when the light-games had started. The way they'd gone silent, just waiting for their turn to die.

They'd survived, but they'd have been taken by the collaborators along with the rest. Doomed to be kept as house prisoners, as slaves. Abused until it was their turn to be given over to the Faithful for more torture, for whatever the Process entailed.

And for what? Why? What was the Aspect's damned *point*?

I let myself get angry... let the fury set my mental seas to boiling. Felt my fingers squeeze tightly on the Elder's as we walked through the dark.

"We're getting out of here, sir." I said as we finally saw the distant torchlight of our friends. "We're going to find out what this is about. And then we're going to come back and watch the entire Compact flatten this disgusting place from orbit."

Tasir's growl was approving. "Stay in that frame of mind when we're starving in the dark, huntress. Keep that anger."

"I will, sir."

We said nothing more until we arrived in the small alcove, Irkan and Johanna sitting at the small table. Our packs covered the surface of it; everything we'd carried spread out as they tried to figure out what we needed, and what could be left behind.

Both of them tensed as we arrived, relaxing only when they recognized us.

Tasir gave them the bad news, "Change of plans. We leave as soon as possible, there's drones hunting us. Irkan, Lori. Check the computer for power. Ark Fleet? Start getting the packs filled with all of the food and water we've got."

Irkan heaved himself to his feet at once, "The sailor shall do so. Can the Imperial savanna bring the torch?"

I quickly picked it up from where it had been carefully propped up on the table, following him over to the ancient device. This time there wasn't any reverence; he yanked one of the panels off, dropping into a crouch to start rifling around inside.

Behind us Tasir and Johanna struck up a quick conversation, the Elder shaking her head dismissively several times as they grabbed what we'd need in the dark.

"If the Imperial savanna could angle the light?"

I held my torch up a bit closer to his shoulder, tilting it when he motioned for me to turn it a bit more. "How does it look?"

"The Imperial savanna's hopes were correct." He replied, arm deep into the old computer. "Something is still providing this machine with power. This sailor cannot guarantee it shall activate, but there is hope."

That was good. And probably bad at the same time.

"Do you think it will have a map of the mining tunnels if we turn it on?" I asked.

"It may." Irkan replied, "But there is every chance that the Faithful shall notice it was accessed."

199

I bit my lip, chewing on it for a moment before calling over, "Sir? There's power after all. Last chance to decide if we risk turning it on."

She didn't even look up, her intact hand still shoving a water-skin deeper into her pack, followed by the only proper bottle we had. "Can you maintain a sense of direction in an underground environment, huntress?"

"Point taken, sir."

Irkan grunted, twisting his arm once. The quiet hum of a fan began sputtering to life somewhere within the old machine, dying off almost at once. I watched nervously as several lights tried to light as well, only to dim before any of them could truly brighten.

But where *nearly* the entire old computer stayed dark, a single display at the far side stubbornly flickered to life. Text scrolled rapidly by for several seconds, and I felt myself release the breath I'd been holding when it flashed to show some kind of home screen.

"Quickly." I urged him, "Let's not keep it on for long."

Irkan grunted, extracting himself from the guts of the thing. He rapidly lumbered down to inspect what was being shown. "This sailor shall find a map. The savanna should regain her pack."

I nodded, carefully setting the torch down beside him in case the the already dim screen lost power. He jerked his head in a thankful motion without looking away from it, and I slipped away to get the last of our things ready.

Johanna quickly pushed my bag over when I got to the table, waving to the various bits that she'd removed. "You sure we won't need any of that?"

"No." I admitted, looking over the bits of cooking supplies that I'd accumulated over the past few months. Our badly carved bowls, cups, and plates. The very battered cooking pan we'd been given to use. "What's left inside?"

"Rope, your stone knife, your spare shirt, two water skins, and a mix of stone-fruit and those green root vegetables we found." She said.

"Torches?"

200

She grabbed two of them, handing them over, "I'm tying mine to my bag."

I quickly began to do the same, "How much of that sap do we have left?"

"Three jars." She hesitated, "Is that enough?"

"I don't know."

Tasir grunted from my right, "Probably not. Less talking, more packing."

Johanna glowered at her, while I merely ducked my head, murmuring, "Sir."

We got the rest of it organized within a few minutes. Each of us had an even share of the food, one knife, and three torches. Tasir and Irkan each had their battered old guns, though both were low on both power and ammunition. I still would have taken one of those over the wooden spears that Johanna and I would carry.

I helped Tasir get her bag onto her back, tightening it a little, and then helped make sure nothing rattled too loudly when she moved.

My diligence earned me a quiet word of approval, which gave me a little bit of hope that this wouldn't end with me on a penal colony after all. Maybe, just maybe...

Of course, to worry about that, we had to survive getting out of here first.

Johanna and I got our own packs settled just as Irkan pulled some kind of tablet out of a port on the machine. The main computer shut down a moment later, the thin device in his hands glowing in the flickering light of my torch.

"The eldest and the savannas should inspect this." He held it out for Tasir. "To determine our route."

Grabbing his pack, I brought it over as we all huddled up around his little screen.

201

"...that's a lot of tunnels." Johanna murmured, staring at the white lines winding their way down through the mountain. "Where are we?"

Irkan used his clawed hands to manipulate the image, rotating the display. "Here. The label in the old tongue calls it the emergency exit."

I hummed, glad to have that confirmed. I reached out with a hand, tracing a line down from where he'd pointed. "This is the tunnel... it takes us right to some kind of vertical shaft. We'll have to avoid that, right?"

"Obviously." Tasir shook her head. "Even if the lifts work, which I doubt, they'd be centrally controlled. The Faithful would just lock us in one to kill at their leisure."

"Or to capture again." Irkan rumbled.

Johanna cleared her throat. "Um, where's the exit?"

We all stared at the confusing mess of tunnels and lines for a few moments before Irkan tapped a point with a claw. "It is here, Fleet Savanna. This text calls it the primary entrance."

I fought down the urge to wince. It was much farther down, and much farther away, than I'd hoped. From Tasir's displeased grunt she had done the same math. Johanna's drawn features compelled me to at least try for some optimism.

"There's plenty of ways into that area, at least." I murmured, pointing to them. "Look. It's even more of a mess down there. If the Faithful have turned that into some kind of base, there should be plenty of ways for us to sneak in so long as we're careful."

Tasir gave me a somewhat sour look, but didn't shove me back into the tide for once. "We'll concern ourselves with that part once we're closer. For now we focus on getting down to the levels below us."

"Yes sir." I tapped three other points. "One of these routes then. Each one spirals downward and connects to other tunnels. That nearest one?"

Our Elder considered, eyes locked onto the image once more. "No. Any pursuit would assume we'd take that one since it's closest, and they'll know we're in a hurry. We take the farthest. It comes out near that large

202

cavern. Irkan? What's that mark?"

"Refining Station Three." He supplied the label's meaning.

"That will be our first destination." Tasir decided. "There's a dozen routes in and out of it, and hopefully mining equipment we can camp out behind to get some rest."

The rest of us nodded, but the Director stopped us from starting our march through the dark with her next words. "We need to move light, and move fast. If any of us is too badly wounded to walk, we can't spend the time pulling them along."

I swallowed, getting her meaning. "Yes sir."

Johanna's pale skinned paled further, but she jerked her head in another nod. "I... don't let me be captured by them. Not again. I can't do that again."

"We won't." Tasir's voice was grim. "We don't leave anyone behind alive to be taken. Irkan? No matter what, we each save four rounds in case we need them."

The only male among us tipped his head, "The sailor shall do so, eldest."

With our final pact made, I picked my torch back up so that I could lead us farther into the darkness.

XXI

We couldn't have been walking for more than a few minutes before Tasir said the words I'd desperately hoped she wouldn't.

"We're being followed." She murmured.

I grabbed Johanna around the shoulders before she could turn around, forcing her to keep walking beside me. "Don't look back."

She staggered a step, recovering, and had the good sense to keep her voice quiet as well. "Are you sure?"

"Yes." Tasir rolled her neck, shaking out her arms. "We hear better behind us than ahead, Ark Fleet. That drone must have spotted Lori and I after all."

"Yes sir." I whispered. Trying not to think about the fact that we were probably extremely easy to spot with our little torch, the red flame bobbing along in my hands.

Silhouetting us perfectly for anyone with a gun behind us.

"Orders?" I asked.

"How far to the first passage down?" She asked.

I tried to remember, only for Johanna to beat me to it. "Not far. It was a few hundred feet away at most."

Tasir grunted. "Good. Keep walking calmly and silently until then. We use it as cover to see what's behind us."

My tongue ran over my lips, "It's too steep. Irkan nearly fell down that path last time."

There was a low growl of frustration, "Then we watch our feet. It's our only option."

The comfortable silence of our prior walk was replaced with a tense one. All four of us straining our hearing to try and pick up what Tasir had. It was hard, over the sound of our own footsteps, but I started to hear it after a few minutes.

An echoing clicking repeating somewhere in the tunnel. Behind or in front, I couldn't say, but I trusted Tasir's better directional hearing.

That we were being followed at all wasn't good. What was worse was the fact that I couldn't place exactly what the noise was. It didn't sound like boots on stone. I'd heard that rhythm more times than I could count in my fairly short life. It... sounded more like claws on stone. Maybe.

I was strangling my need to speak my thoughts out loud when we arrived at the side-tunnel, just as quickly as Johanna had predicted.

"Irkan." Tasir motioned to the left, "There. Lori, behind him, spear at the ready. Ark Fleet, get one of my torches off my pack."

While Johanna quickly began tugging a torch free, I slid over to crouch behind Irkan's broad shell. Keeping my torch angled backwards, I stared over his shoulder as we both tried to get our eyes to adjust to the darkness.

Irkan slowly got his old pistol set in his broad hands, aiming it back the way we'd come. I got my spear settled in my other hand, resting it against his shell, murmuring a quiet prayer. "Ashahn, don't let them have guns... don't let them spot what we're doing."

"Light it on hers, and take it so she's got her hands free." Tasir's whispered order had me turn my torch a little, letting Johanna take it from my grasp. She did, quickly igniting the other one she was holding. "On my call, throw the old one sideways, far as you can."

Johanna was shaking, but she nodded gamely. "Ready."

"Throw."

She brought her arm back, then hurled it forward. The torch spun around, already heading for the tunnel floor, then a hiss from Tasir changed its trajectory. Her spell gently caught it, propelling it farther and faster than Johanna could have ever managed.

I watched it sail away... flying over the heads of the shaggy,

205

lumbering *things* crawling along the floor toward us.

The torch hadn't finished tumbling to the ground behind them before they let out high-pitched shrieks, bounding forward on six limbs as they charged.

"Fuck!" Tasir's curse was followed by orders, "Irkan! Fire one!"

He pulled the trigger once; and one of the loping animals yelped and tumbled. The others simply trampled over their wounded comrade, picking up speed.

"No barriers!" I called, guessing why she'd only told him to fire once.

"Kill them!" She barked a heartbeat later.

Our mere two guns began barking in a steady rhythm, Irkan and Tasir both refusing to waste rounds with hurried fire. Each shot sent a creature to the floor, wounded or dead.

I straightened up, felt the spear's end rattling on the ground in my shaking hands. "Tasir! The torch is being smothered! Too many of them still coming!"

"Run?!" Johanna asked.

"Stay!" Our eldest barked, her gun going silent. I twitched sharply when the scent of ozone flooded the air, her tarah quivering madly as she called up power.

Her mangled hand rose when the nearest animal was hardly a dozen paces away, and dark blue fire screamed out from where her fingers would have been.

She didn't aim it at the horde; the torrent of flame roared upwards, above them, hammering into the ceiling and cracking stone. The mountain itself seemed to groan under the force of the spell, the noise growing when she snarled, keeping it going in a steady stream of fire and force.

But below it, the horde didn't stop. Not even when stones began falling onto them, crushing limbs and heads.

Irkan shot down the first that got close, then the second, but I saw a

206

third rushing Tasir. I heard myself let out a high-pitched yell of my own, lunging forward with my spear.

It was a terrible thrust, I'd fully admit that, but the thing didn't even try to dodge. The furry animal hurled itself onto my spear, nearly twisting it from my hands, all six of its limbs thrashing as it tried to claw at me.

Heart hammering inside of my chest, I shoved it back, down, pinning it to the ground. I must have gotten something vital because its movements slowed quickly, then went still when I yanked the wooden shaft back.

And as I stared at the corpse, horror made me want to throw up when I realized what I'd just killed.

I was trying to settle my stomach and spear alike, to get ready for any other attackers, when the tunnel finally lost its battle with Tasir.

A tremendous snapping sound came, all too similar to the noises Marzin made eating a Pferd, and then a rain of stone and dust began flooding down from the roof.

"Back!" Irkan boomed, already trying to get back as the tunnel continued to groan and rumble.

"I've got her!" Johanna's shout drew my attention to see her catch Tasir before the elder could fall into the side tunnel.

The Director's eyes had rolled back in her head, and she was wobbling badly even with Johanna holding her up. Her gun dropped from her loose fingers, bouncing toward the long drop.

Strike-Wave reflexes had my leg lash out, kicking the pistol, sending it spinning the way Irkan was already running. The blessings of the Aspects ensured that the thing didn't go off anywhere in there, and I wasted no time in grabbing Tasir's other arm to help Johanna pull her along.

More cracks began to appear above us, dust making the torch flicker. Small stones pelted my shoulders and head as they fell from the ceiling, the cave-in chasing us deeper into the mountain.

I don't know how long we ran, our only stop to scoop up the gun.

We stumbled along, pulling Tasir between us until she managed to

207

start bearing her own weight, cursing in a raspy voice. I couldn't say how long the dust cloud chased us until it finally began to settle. How long it took the tunnel to grow still and silent once more.

We were all out of breath by the time we found a small alcove. A dozen paces deep by half that wide, a battered table betraying its purpose as a rest stop similar to the first one we'd found.

I whispered a quiet thanks to the Aspects for providing it to people who badly needed rest, collapsing onto one of the low seats. Tasir did the same across from me, still unsteady.

Johanna carefully set our torch down, leaning it against a chair to keep it upright, then settled in beside me.

"...what now?" She asked, voice very quiet. "We're buried alive. Aren't we?"

"...water." I groaned, "We need water, and we need food. Irkan? Get Tasir's out for her. She needs it."

He jerked his long head in a nod, carefully getting to work on the elder's bag. Johanna and I started getting our own open, and within a few minutes we were all drinking from our little water skins. Those of us that could eat them ate the green root vegetables we'd found, while Irkan contented himself with dried snake meat.

Tasir recovered enough to speak once she had some food in her, "Ark Fleet's right, for once. We're buried alive."

"This sailor does not believe so." Irkan rumbled a polite rebuttal. "There were many routes in and out upon the map. We simply must reach them."

I nodded, reaching out to put a hand on Johanna's shoulder. "He's right. All we lost was the easy way back out. We just... have to keep going down. Just like we planned anyway."

The elder huffed quietly, "Doubly forced to go with the ridiculous plan thought up by a pair of unstable Human Huntresses. I'd say there's no point in cursing fate written by the Aspects, but I'm getting sick of their disdain for me."

208

I licked my lips, then quietly admitted. "My packmates called me an Avatar of Khash. A bringer of bad luck."

"I'd wager mine is as bad as yours, Lori." Tasir sighed, "But there's no point in arguing it. Did any of you get a good look at what those things were?"

My stomach rolled despite its recent meal. "Yes sir."

When I didn't go on, all three of them seemed to know it wasn't going to be a pleasant answer.

"Out with it." The Director ordered tiredly.

"...Naule."

She went still. "What."

I swallowed, hand sliding off of Johanna's shoulder to find hers. She knew what I needed, quickly wrapping her fingers around mine in support as I forced myself to go on. "They were Naulians, sir."

"Naule don't have claws like that." She countered.

Irkan let out a quiet chirp of agreement, "Nor are their back limbs so long."

"I know, I know." I shook my head, "But the one I killed... it was a Naule. It had the face of a Naule, the shaggy hair of one, the arms of one. I think... I think it had cybernetics of some kind, but I didn't get more than a quick look at the one I stabbed."

Beside me, Johanna's weight shifted. "Marzin... Marzin said that the Faithful experiment on the slaves given to them. Do you think they... did that to them? Turned them into attack hunde?"

"They do call us beasts." I said. "I... think they might have."

"Why?" She whispered.

I looked down at the table. "Experiments? Sadistic fun? I... I don't know. We'll find out when we get to their base. We have to find out why."

Tasir let out a nearly silent sigh. "I don't think any of us are going to like those answers, huntress."

"No sir, but we need them." I replied.

"True enough." Movement made me look up to see her planting her good hand on the table, pushing herself up with a wince. "We need to keep moving. If those things were sent in to flush us out, we can't stay on this level."

Irkan heaved himself up as well, "The eldest river-shark is correct. This level holds no places in which our group may hide, may lose pursuit. Rest must come later."

Both unable and unwilling to argue with that logic, the pair of us stood up in turn. The four of us shuffling back into the dark tunnels, following that constant slope downward.

XXII

We moved cautiously after that, descending ever deeper. It was impossible to tell how long it had been since we'd entered the tunnels, but Irkan seemed confident it hadn't been more than three days, give or take a few hours.

Nothing much of note happened over that time. I should have been relieved by that. More relaxed. Instead I felt myself growing more anxious with every hour we plunged deeper into the mountain. More convinced that we were sailing on borrowed winds that would be taken from us sooner rather than later.

We slept in shifts, hidden in small alcoves, or behind long ruined tunneling machines. Hid our waste as best we could in those same places when we left, while rationing our limited food kept us hungry.

Especially Tasir. She'd spent a lot of her calories on the enormous spell that had both saved and buried us, and she didn't let herself eat nearly as much as her old body needed to recover.

It was on that third or fourth day, when we were about halfway down by Irkan's map, that we started to find proof that the Faithful used these tunnels. Started to find boot-prints in the dust, see claw marks on the walls, smell bodily waste that wasn't ours.

Worse was when we began to hear the echoes of movement; the sounds of claws on stone.

We'd split off from the main tunnels then. Plunging into the narrower, less direct paths down. Doing our best to move through spaces that would conceal our torchlight, make it harder to follow us. Tasir spent precious energy on tiny spells, hurling dust up behind us to cover our tracks. We spent long periods with no light at all, walking single-file with our hands on each other, on the walls.

And we started moving faster.

That worked for us for about a day, maybe. Until we finally reached Refining Station Three.

"And you're sure this is the only way down?" I whispered to Irkan.

"Unless the Imperial savanna wishes to cross the entire mountain." He murmured back. "Only to then use Refining Stations One or Two."

I grimaced. "And you're sure you saw something in there?"

"Yes." He sounded certain. "A single form, moving rapidly away from this sailor."

Ashahn's blood. I'd really hoped we'd be able to avoid running into anything else until we got closer to the Faithful's base, but Khash apparently wasn't in a very giving mood today. Not that he ever had been.

I licked my lips once, fingers tightening around my torch. My eyes stared out at the edges of the light, where the dimmest outline of the Refining Station's entrance could be seen.

"Let's get back to the others and figure out how we're going to cross it." I said finally. "Hopefully they'll have your tablet fully charged up again."

"This one has hope." He replied, turning to lumber back the way we'd come. I followed suit, though I walked backwards for the first few paces, and only turned once I couldn't see the tunnel's exit anymore.

Splitting up hadn't been our first idea, but Tasir was breaking down physically even if she was doing her best to hide it. Between her wounded hand, her stressing her sorcery, and her general age... she needed far more rest and food than we could afford to give her.

The Elder was doing her best to push on as stubbornly as ever, but she'd taken Johanna's place as the weakest among us. That she knew it wasn't improving her state of mind in the slightest.

I sighed, shaking my head. At least we'd found an exposed power conduit with some charge left in it. Finding a place to recharge our only device with a map had left us all in a better mood, and given us a chance to let Johanna and Tasir rest while Irkan and I scouted ahead a little.

That was good.

That he was sure he'd seen something wasn't.

212

"It's us." I called quietly when we reached the bundle of cloth pressed up against the side of the tunnel. "We've got news."

The repurposed tent shifted, Johanna pulling the mix of fabric and hide back from where she and Tasir had been hiding the glow of the tablet. Our Elder was examining the map once more, and nodded for us to get on with what we'd found.

"It's just ahead, but Irkan saw movement inside." I reported.

Tasir's face drew into a scowl. "More Naule?"

The Mikira shook his head, "Too tall. This sailor heard nothing else within. Only silence."

Johanna bit her lip before speaking, "Then it wouldn't be those Naulians again. We've heard them, and they're anything but quiet."

"True." Tasir grunted. "Dammit. Irkan, keep watch in case whatever it is followed us."

He nodded, moving a few paces away with his back to us. While he moved she went on, "This is our only way to the lower levels. We're already running out of food and torches. We can't try and go around."

"Yes sir." I agreed. "Plan?"

Her eyes dropped back to the tablet in her hands. Well, hand, considering that her mangled one was simply supporting the back of it. "Zoom in, Ark Fleet."

My friend complied, adjusting the image until it was zoomed in on the broad cavern we were just outside of.

"We're here, three levels up." The Elder murmured, "Our exit is here. Should be a pretty straight run along this side of the Station, then down and out. After that we can lose ourselves in that maze of tunnels again."

Reaching out, I pointed to one run in particular, tracing it slowly down. "That one should take us straight to the main entrance... more or less. From a side approach too."

213

Tasir nodded slowly, "Best we can do. It'll be slower than the straight route, we'll be hungry and thirsty, but it gives us better odds that we'll avoid their attention for longer."

"So..." Johanna glanced between us, "What do we do about the thing Irkan saw?"

"Run." Tasir said simply. "Fast as we can through that cavern."

That looked to be the answer she'd expected, if not the answer she'd wanted. "...all right. Um, should we reorganize our packs first?"

I was about to say yes when Tasir shook her head. "Not yet. If we're attacked out there, we want our supplies spread out. If we put all of our remaining food in one bag, and that poor fish gets speared, the rest of us starve."

Johanna winced. "Oh. Right."

I gave her a gentle pat on the back while Tasir got the tablet powered down. We didn't need any orders to get our spears in hand, and I passed the nearly spent torch to Irkan to get a two handed grip on mine.

He took the lead, pistol ready, torch held high with Johanna and I on either side with our spears. Tasir followed close behind, her own gun in her working hand, most of her attention behind us.

We paused at the tunnel's end, just long enough for everyone to take the final breaths before the plunge.

Then Irkan took off at his best sprint, the three of us right behind his bobbing shell. His flickering torch barely lit any of the enormous cavern, leaving us surrounded by the shadowed forms of ancient machines.

Scaffolding loomed all around us, walkways stretching out into nothingness from the ledge we ran across. I could see chains hanging from things far out of view, giving only the barest impression of how massive a cavern this truly was.

I was looking out into that darkness when I saw them.

Two dots of blue light, perfectly keeping pace with us.

214

"Tasir!" I hissed, "Right!"

"I see them." She growled back, "Keep moving!"

I ran, jerking my attention back and forth to avoid running into Irkan while also keeping track of whatever was out there.

Those blue dots moved in a perfect line, then rose as if their owner was clambering up something... and then we could all hear the feet pounding on metal as it ran along a machine.

"Ashe." Johanna gasped, her own head snapping around just like mine. "The eyes from the barge!"

On the barge, they'd been red, not blue, but I couldn't fault her. I was starting to shake from those same memories of eyes staring at us in judgment.

"Just run!"

Irkan led us down the long stone ledge, following it as it became a ramp to the cavern's floor. Rows upon rows of dust covered carts and other mining equipment awaited us, all neatly organized as if the owners had simply gone home at the end of their shifts instead of abandoning the entire world.

Blue eyes struck the ground on the far side of them, still keeping pace.

"Kelthi." I heard myself gasp, unable to keep my thoughts inside my own head. "Has to be a Kelthi, or an Xenthan. Experimented on, like those poor Naule."

"Shut up, Lori." Tasir growled. "Focus!"

"Yes-" My attention turned to the front just in time to see a white-furred blur emerge from behind a parked cart, slamming into Irkan before he could bring his gun around. "-Irkan!"

Our friend let out a roar, bracing himself as his attacker tried to wrench him off his feet.

Johanna let out a startled cry, lunging forward with her spear, but the alien twisted away before she could connect. I raced forward as well, lashing out with the wooden weapon, driving it back a few more paces.

215

The Xenthan snarled at me, baring metal fangs so long that they were tearing its own lips open when it tried to close its mouth. Its eyes were gone, replaced with the red glow of cybernetics, with more lines of metal tracing its head, neck, and down across its chest.

Matted white fur was so covered in dust it looked more gray than anything else, but enough of it had been shaved away to let me see that the poor alien was male, and was more metal than flesh below the hips.

He growled at us like an animal rather than a person, flinching when Irkan used the chance to shoot him. The round struck a barrier over its face, making the Xenthan flinch, then snarl as it came at him again.

Behind us Tasir fired twice, "Flanker!"

I jerked my head away from where Irkan had collided with his opponent once more, seeing a black-furred Kelthi version of the tortured Xenthan bounding at us over top of the parked carts.

Tasir's rounds sparked off their barriers, drawing a mocking cackle from torn lips. Ignoring the Elder entirely, its mechanical eyes locked onto mine as I raised my sharpened stick.

The Kelthi blurred forward on all fours, already awkward limbs now unnaturally long. A hand shoved aside my spear, her other going for my throat. I barely tucked my chin down in time to get my face grabbed instead, biting down on panicked reflex when her hand covered my mouth.

Her skin tasted like dust and blood, and her startled shriek hurt my ears. She let go at once, darting away a half-breath before Tasir could jam her pistol against her side to bypass whatever barriers she had.

"*Kusho!*" The word was the first either had spoken, somewhat mangled by her metallic teeth. "*Shay'ko!*"

Tasir didn't waste another bullet, she just moved up right behind me, staring her down while our companions fought hers. I didn't risk looking away to see how that fight was going; but I heard the Xenthan yowling in pain.

The Kelthi jerked its attention that way for a bare moment, snarled again, then turned and sprinted away on mechanical limbs.

Only then did I turn in time to see Johanna rapidly stabbing down

216

with her spear, Irkan staggering back from the white furred form as its thrashing began to slow down.

Running over, I brought my own spear around, thrusting down at its throat.

The Xenthan let out a final snarling rasp... and then its head fell limply against the stone.

"Irkan?" I surprised myself by not being out of breath. It was only then that I realized that the entire event couldn't have lasted for more than a minute. Two at most. "You all right?"

"Yes." He replied, shaking himself. "The Process took its mind. It tried to bite through this one's shell."

Looking around, I found the torch on the ground. It was sputtering when I grabbed it, and even a few frantic waves only drew a meager flame to it.

Good enough to check over Irkan's back, finding scratch marks all over his spiked protection, but nothing worse than that. Thank the Aspects for that... if he'd started bleeding, we wouldn't be able to help him. Not with how toxic Mikiran blood was.

"Johanna. Johanna!"

My friend jerked from where she'd been staring at the body, bloody stick held in both hands. "Ashe... I... he..."

I couldn't grab her hand, mine were full, but Tasir grabbed her by the shirt for me. Her voice a rough growl, "Not now. These things probably have cameras in their eyes. We need to move."

Johanna stumbled along for a few steps, then started properly jogging. I kept our torch up, leaving the corpse behind as we ran for the exit. The lingering flames began to die out just as we reached the narrower space, forcing us to slow up again so that we could use it to ignite one of the last two torches we had.

I looked back while Irkan got his last torch out... and found two blue eyes staring at me in the darkness.

217

"She's coming back." I hissed.

The others all turned around, Tasir and Johanna readying themselves for battle, Irkan lighting his torch so that I could drop my spent one to get my spear settled.

We stood there, waiting... and the Kelthi never appeared. Her eyes simply glowed in the distance, stopping in place.

"Attack it?" Irkan suggested, already taking a step forward. We all followed him, only to see the glow shift as the alien drew back, not letting us get close.

"Sir?" I asked quietly. "Can you...?"

"I'm starving." Tasir replied just as softly. "Back up. One person watching the back at all times. We draw it into the narrow tunnels."

I nodded, taking one slow step back. Then another. Irkan turned, the only one of us truly able to turn his back on her, and began leading the way. We moved, and the eyes seemed to follow, staying the same distance.

We retreated.

The eyes of our enemy followed.

XXIII

The Kelthi vanished when we made our first turn, plunging into a tunnel barely wider than Irkan. We moved along as quickly as we could, taking two more side routes, hoping to throw our pursuit off, and then found an alcove to try and rest.

Johanna's scream woke us all up in time to see the Kelthi snap her spear in half, backhand my companion across the face, and then dart off into the darkness once more.

We moved on, exhausted, and tried to sleep behind an old mining drill. Irkan was able to get a few of the lights on, saving our last torch and the batteries on our tablet. Even better, there was only a narrow path between the machine and the wall of the cave. The Kelthi couldn't approach us without plenty of time to spot her.

She didn't even try. She just crept up on the far side of the drill and began beating out a rhythm on the metal with her claws.

And when we drove her off, tried to sleep, she returned and started doing it again.

"This one is smarter than the other." Irkan huffed, returning after an attempt to play bait away from the group had only drawn the Kelthi toward us rather than him. "That one was a mad animal. Clawing and biting armor it could not hope to breach."

I nodded in exhaustion, eating the last piece of my stone-fruit in the dim glow of the tablet. "...yeah. This one can still talk, think."

Tasir grunted around her own final bit of fruit. "Or it's being remotely piloted."

The notion made me wince. "...can that be done, sir?"

"Anything can be done with enough cybernetics." She replied. "Can't think of any nation where it's legal, but the Regnon could probably pull it off if they wanted to."

Johanna shuddered, finally looking away from where the Kelthi's unblinking eyes were watching us eat our last meal. "Maybe Marzin was the traitor. Maybe they controlled him too."

"It's a thought I've had." Our Elder admitted, "But we can think about that later, if there is a later. That dead fish over there is definitely broadcasting all of this for the Faithful to get off on. We've got to kill her."

Irkan let out a frustrated huff. "This sailor agrees with the elder river shark, but cannot see how. Our weapons are too poor to breach its barriers."

"And you can't do more sorcery." I nodded to Tasir. "So what do we do, sir?"

Tasir reached down, tapping the map with a finger. It vanished, and she carefully poked another icon. None of us could read them, but Irkan had told us the bare minimum to open other useful tools on it. Just in case he went down.

The text editor open, Tasir began scrawling out words as quickly as she could with one hand. I leaned down, reading her plan, biting my lip when I realized what she intended.

"I'll do it instead." I told her, reaching down and writing a quick addition of my own. "I think that's all I'll need."

"Rifle-"

"You're wounded, sir. I'm... not good at it, but I've got two hands." I paused, then added more quietly, "And you might use sorcery on reflex, sir. If you do you won't have the strength to go on."

Her expression told me that I was right, but that she didn't like that fact.

She didn't argue though. "Packs off, everyone. Carry your last water skins over your shoulder. Ark Fleet, give Lori your knife and the last spare torch."

Johanna did so, passing over the brittle stone weapon once she'd gotten it out of her bag. I got the torch tied to a bit of rope around my shoulder, letting it dangle, and checked the knife to make sure it was still sharp.

220

It was, thank the Aspects.

"What's the plan?" Johanna whispered.

"We're leaving the tunnels early." Tasir said flatly. "There's an emergency exit on this level. We have a better chance of losing her in the wilderness, and finding enough food for us to recover."

She froze. "We're... giving up?"

"No." Tasir said firmly. "Cullings last for at least a month, we've got time."

"But... Marzin told you that." Johanna countered, not sounding at all reassured. "He could have been lying!"

Irkan's voice was gentle when he spoke, "Then this group is already doomed, young savanna. The plan is a good one."

"I can't read Caranat! I don't know what the plan you wrote was!"

"I know." Tasir growled, "Shut up and drop the pack, we're going to move as fast as we can to get back outside. We lose her in the forest, get more food, get more torches. Come on."

Johanna wasn't exactly willing, but when Irkan and I stood up she hesitantly followed suit. I offered a hand to Tasir, the Elder taking it, letting me haul her to her feet. Adjusting pants that were barely holding together, I fell in beside Johanna in the back when we began moving again.

It was easier without the crude bags on our backs, letting us get up to a quick jog without making too much noise.

"It'll be all right." I whispered. "Remember my promise. Okay?"

"...yes."

"Stay close to Irkan." I told her.

She blinked, glancing at me as we began jogging along. The bouncing light of the tablet barely letting us see each other's faces from a few feet away. I think she got it when she glanced down, realizing that I was still holding her

221

knife in one hand, my spear in the other.

Or maybe she just saw my nerves in my eyes. She jerked her head around, looking behind, whimpering quietly to tell me that the Kelthi was still following as tirelessly as ever.

"Ashe..."

"We'll be fine." I said quickly. "Just keep moving, and stay quiet."

I think I saw tears well up in her eyes. She stumbled for a few steps, then caught herself, forcing her feet to keep moving.

She'd definitely figured it out, then.

I felt the shaking start again when we drew near the side-tunnel that lead back towards another exit. When everyone else turned to the left, vanishing down it.

When I kept going straight, plunging into the total darkness ahead.

I counted each step, the numbers coming from my dry lips as I jogged with no idea of what lay in front of me. "Twenty one. Twenty two. Twenty three."

To my vague surprise the Kelthi didn't sprint after me at once, though a quick look back confirmed that she was chasing me rather than the others. Going after the idiot who'd run off alone as a sacrifice play.

When my count hit fifty I slid to a stop, turned, and dropped to one knee.

The Kelthi seemed to draw up short as well, eyes going motionless. Watching as I set my weapons down, as I pulled my torch and water-skin off my shoulders. The latter I carefully set aside, and the former I used my last bit of flint-stone to ignite.

Lucky me, this part of the tunnel seemed to be more natural than artificial. There were plenty of small rocks and cracks in the walls, and I had no issues wedging the torch into a small fissure at my shoulder height.

Then I walked back to my weapons, picking them both up just as the Kelthi casually strolled into the flickering light. Her too long fingers flexed one after the other, showing off the metallic claws that had been added to the tips.

"*Ackisho.*" A toss of it head sent the enormous mane to rustling behind her, the black fur glistening in the torchlight. Mechanical legs slowly brought her down into a ready crouch, hands pressing against the floor as she prepared to leap at me. "...worthy. Prey."

"...mind if I pray first?" I asked.

She hissed between metal teeth. "No. Masters... hate."

"Really wish I knew why." I swallowed, shaking my head, bringing my spear around to point at her. Holding it with my knife in my strong hand wasn't easy, but I wasn't about to drop the blade. "Ashahn, weaver of dreams, grant me-"

The Kelthi became a blur of motion, bounding forward. Having learned my lesson, I dodged right and didn't thrust with the spear, instead lashing out with the back-half of it like a thin club. I caught her on the hand, driving it away before she could maul me.

She snarled, planted a foot, and spun in place to kick out with the other. Her kick had enough power to snap the spear in half, the wood shattering into splinters that pelted me. I couldn't stop a yelp when both pieces were wrenched from my fingers, scrambling back before she could break a bone or five with another kick.

To my surprise she didn't follow-up, instead moving back a few steps as well.

"...ready.... yourself... prey." She rasped, lips tearing a bit with each word. "Fun."

I swallowed, shakily getting my stone knife settled up. "Ashahn, grant me the inspiration I need to see the path through the-"

Claws nearly took my eyes out, my frantic slashing with the knife only making her lean back to avoid the clumsy attack. My right arm suddenly burned when she raked a hand down it, skin tearing open.

I screamed, thrusting desperately with the blade, and managed to catch her own limb before she could dodge back once more. The Kelthi snarled as I cut her flesh open, blood matting her fur, her other hand whipping up in a slap that sent me staggering.

She followed that up with a sharp backhand that left my vision blurry, then a sharp slap on the wounds on my arm that drew another howl of pain. Desperate slashes from my blade hit only air, then her fingers were around my wrist, wrenching.

The stone blade tumbled to the ground, and a single stomp of her metal foot shattered it.

She shoved me back, to the edges of the torchlight, a raspy laugh emerging from her throat.

When she spoke again it wasn't with her own voice. It was too even. Too smooth. "Ah. I recognize those scars on your bestial face, you're that little creature that was sobbing on Oshflara! I had hoped we'd meet again."

I tried to get up, but the tunnel kept spinning around me. My knees hit the floor as I gasped for breath, felt my blood trickling down my arm. In a way I was grateful for the pain; I hurt too much for my mental seas to drain at the sound of the Burned Hand.

"...been looking for you." I gasped, "Been here?"

"We shall speak later." She said through her puppet. "And then I can finish what I began with your face."

I couldn't stop a fearful shudder. "...the path through the mist. Ashahn, bringer of storms, unleash your-"

A furious growl came out of the Kelthi in two distinct tones. "Choke the thing until it shuts up about its false gods. Do it before the others double-back and complete their oh-so-clever trick."

The Kelthi was on me within a breath, bearing me down to the floor. She crouched over me, chuckling with glee, hands wrapping around my throat.

Rerth had told me that a trained Agent could choke out most species in a matter of seconds... or that they could make it agonizing for more than a minute.

My opponent made it hurt.

There was no chance of staying calm when I felt my air began to run out. When I heard my blood pounding in my head, my body flailing on instinct to try and protect my vulnerable neck.

Metal teeth tore at her lips as she smiled down at me, mechanical eyes so close to my face.

Irkan's distant bellow made her head snap around, her mane of stiff fur covering my face. "We come!"

"Finish it!" The Burned Hand snarled. "Bring it to me-"

The gunshot cut her off, the Kelthi jerking in pained surprise, head slowly turning to stare at me.

I shifted the angle of the gun I'd pulled out of my pants. Felt my lungs finally fill with air when her fingers lost their strength.

"In the Aspects' names," I rasped.

"Kill-"

I pulled the trigger again. Then a third time.

The Kelthi collapsed, right limbs giving way, heavy frame slamming to the ground beside me. Three holes in her chest leaking dark red blood, her body twitching a few times before going still.

I didn't get up when my companions ran over. I was too busy enjoying being able to breathe again. Someone took the pistol out of my hand, Tasir murmuring. "I'll get the torch and her water-skin. You two get her up, we have to get her outside to bind those wounds."

Johanna and Irkan picked me up, helping me walk on unsteady legs back the way we'd come.

My mental seas had stopped churning about by the time we made it to the side tunnel they'd pretended to go down, Tasir ordering a quick halt to see to my wounds.

They weren't as bad as I'd thought when she shined the tablet's light

225

on them. Four marks were all bleeding pretty badly, but they looked shallow.

"It was playing with you." She grunted, "As arrogant as her masters. Shirt off, it's the only bandage we've got."

I hissed in pain, but got the old prison shirt off. "I noticed. She could have broken my ribs or my legs easily."

"Or the Imperial's neck." Irkan rumbled, taking the cloth. It tore easily in his hands, the strips handed off to Johanna who began tightly wrapping them around my arm. "Who spoke through it?"

"...the Burned Hand." I said.

He paused for a moment, then gave over the last bits of my shirt. "The one who scarred the Imperial savanna."

"Yeah." I swallowed as the old fear crept in. "I... ow!"

Johanna tightened the cloth even further, making me whimper. "Can we talk about that after I yell at you for all of this? When we're outside, maybe?"

I winced at the mix of hurt and anger in her tone. "All right. Sir?"

Tasir huffed out a breath, nodding once. "Let's go."

Taking the last scraps of my shirt from Johanna, I pushed them into my pockets. Then I snapped my left arm out, grabbing my cellmate before she could start down the side tunnel. She jerked to a halt, turning to frown out at me.

"What..." She saw my fingers in front of my mouth, and quieted at once.

Then she realized that Tasir and Irkan were moving the other way, heading back toward where we'd left our bags behind. We stopped there, just long enough to take out Tasir's spare cloak, draping it over my bare chest.

The rest we left behind when we ran to the tunnel that would take us farther down, hopefully leaving any pursuit behind long enough for us to finally rest.

226

XXIV

We made our last rest stop one level above where we prayed that the Faithful's underground base would be. A small alcove nearly identical to the first one we'd found served as our hiding place, the four of us squeezing into the back as best we could.

With no food left, we drank what little water remained before setting aside the water skins. Then we shut off the tablet, curled up without bothering to set a watch, and got what little sleep we could on the stone floor.

I woke up first, some indeterminate amount of time later. My arm itched, badly, and I felt Johanna's back against mine. Her breathing steady as she slumbered.

Getting up as quietly as I could, I crawled away from the others. A hand on the wall directed me along until I reached the main tunnel.

I sat with my back to the wall, taking stock of... everything.

My stomach was very empty. I was thirsty. I hadn't been in very good shape ever since I'd first woken up on the barge, and I doubted I was any better now. Johanna and I had one stone knife left between us, along with one half of a barbarically primitive spear.

Spear. I kept calling it that, but it was really just a sharpened stick of wood.

If I included what Tasir and Irkan were carrying... we had two barely working pistols, a wooden stick, and three stone knives. Not exactly the kind of armaments you wanted when breaking into an enemy fortification. Definitely not what you wanted to go up against enemy sorcerers.

We had no nullification grenades. No stunners. No technicals. Our only sorcerer was so hungry she probably couldn't manage even a moderate spell on her own.

I had no idea how we were going to fight the Burned Hand if she found us.

227

When she found us.

The woman who had haunted my nightmares for more than a year was somewhere on this cursed world. She could be directly below me, for all I knew.

My arms wrapped around me as a full body shudder ran from my head to my grime covered toes.

"You're going to break when you see her." I whispered, "You know you are."

And how could I not? I'd lost track of how many nights of sleep she'd ruined. How many times I'd woken up, convinced I could smell my skin melting under her touch.

Even without all of that... if she really was a trained battle-priest, she could kill all four of us with a casual wave of her hand. Ashahn's blood, even if we'd been in full armor, with every technological toy available in an Imperial Armory...

Johanna's combat experience was non-existent. As was her training.

I'd never been the best combat soldier.

Irkan was a sailor.

Tasir was our only true warrior, and she was falling apart physically.

I let my head fall back against the stone, felt my lips move as I murmured. "You've avoided thinking it for so long. So long. Now..."

Now I could admit that we were doomed.

How could we not be? We had no idea if the Faithful even had a facility below us. If we could use these tunnels to break into the base. If we could slip through whatever patrols and staff would be within. If we could find a shuttle. An FTL capable shuttle. If we could take off without being shot down. If the shuttle had enough fuel to make it to a friendly world.

If. If. If. If. If.

I'd forced myself to be optimistic for so long. I'd promised Johanna

228

that I'd get her off of this world.

I'd promised myself that I'd find the answers I needed.

I don't know when I started crying. When I had to wipe my face free of the tears silently running down my cheeks.

"Wasting water." I swallowed, shaking my head. "Can't fall apart now. Not when we're so close."

Close to being captured again. Close to dying of dehydration in these tunnels. Close to finding a cavern full of those poor Naulians, those poor Xenthans.

Quiet, heavy footsteps warned me that Irkan was awake long before he reached me. Before a hand cautiously found my shoulder. His massive bulk settling down onto the floor beside me.

"Do the savanna's wounds hurt her?" He spoke as quietly as his deep voice would allow. "This sailor can tend to them."

"No, I'm all right." I whispered back. "Just... needed a moment."

I heard him let out a soft hum. "The river-shark who maimed her is on her thoughts."

"Yeah."

"My people would welcome such an opportunity. To avenge a past wrong." He told me.

The laugh I let out was weak, raspy. "Irkan. I don't have a gun, or armor, or grenades, or... anything I'd need to fight someone like her."

"The savanna lacked those things when she fought the Kelthi." He replied. "Yet she prevailed, even when the plan called for her to merely stall. That this one was supposed to arrive sooner, to deliver the killing blow."

"I got lucky."

He huffed. "The savanna made her own luck. She is clever, and quick. For her protests of being a poor warrior, she is an able killer."

229

I swallowed. "I..."

"It is a good thing, in this dark universe." Irkan rumbled on. "It is filled with those who believe themselves strong, powerful, wise, when in truth they are little but thugs. Spinning in place amid the great dance, convinced that they are unique, when the universe has already made a million just like them."

"So..." I worked at my lip for a moment, "...I'm what? Not spinning in place?"

"She is not. She is weak, and small, and a poor fighter, yes." He said.

"...thanks." I muttered.

It was his turn to chuckle. "She is those things, but she is aware of them. She relies instead on her greatest assets. Her stubbornness, her cleverness. She knew her enemy would bait her. Refuse to kill her quickly or cleanly, and she took advantage of that. As she will once again."

"I don't think the Burned Hand will let me get that close with a gun in my pocket." I said.

"Likely not." He agreed, "But this one is told it is poor form to repeat such a trick regardless. The savanna will simply have to come up with a new trick."

A new trick? To beat the Burned Hand?

I bit my lip for a long moment. "...we don't have much to work with."

"No." He agreed.

"...do you really think we have a chance?"

Irkan went silent for a long moment. I heard his quills rustle, a claw scraping at his chin as he considered the question.

"These four souls never had much of a chance." He murmured finally. "In truth, this is farther than this sailor believed they would ever go. They have emerged victorious from more chances than this one thought possible. Now, they must survive the next."

"We're out of food. Water. Almost out of weapons."

He chuckled, "Yes. This one eagerly looks forward to how they might overcome this next challenge."

I blinked. "Eagerly?"

"Of course this one is eager. How could he not be? To survive as he has, to traverse a mountain in such conditions, to breach an enemy's holdfast? This one does not know how we will overcome our challenges, but he expects us to do so. And when we do, he shall name his companions."

Expects us to do so? "You're just... that confident, huh?"

"This one does not fear death. He only looks forward to our victory."

...Ashahn's blood. That was a kind of confidence that I wished I could have. Was it that easy for him? To simply not care that we'd already surpassed every reasonable expectation for survival?

Tasir's rasp came from the back of the room. "Fury and stubbornness, Lori."

I had no idea how long she'd been awake, how long she'd been listening. "I'm... trying to find it again, sir."

Irkan huffed. "The savanna merely must feel her bones. Her kind is always stubborn, down to the marrow. It is in her nature."

"Stereotype much?" I whispered.

"With justification." He replied, "How long did it take the Ark Fleet savanna to admit she judged aliens too harshly?"

That drew a groan from Johanna. "I wasn't that bad."

I felt myself smile. "Johanna. It took me more than three weeks to convince you that you'd survive a few hours without me while I talked to the Trahcon at the camp."

"...it wasn't a full three weeks."

A chuckle came from Irkan at that. "It was longer."

231

"It was not!"

"Heh." Tasir's own snort came with the tablet powering up, throwing her worn features into relief with its green light. "You can lie to yourself, Ark Fleet, but not to Imperial Intelligence."

Johanna's face appeared as she sat up beside the Director, a scowl on her pale features. "Is that your schlagwort or something? Uh, the phrase that describes Intelligence?"

"No." The Elder paused, hummed, then glanced at me. "It should be, though. When we make it to Altair, remind me to demand the slogan be changed to that."

"Yes sir." I groaned, pushing myself up to my feet. "It's better than Vigilant In Storm. Might be harder to fit on those logos at headquarters though."

"True." She watched as I walked over, Irkan following slowly behind. The pair of us sitting down once more, leaning in to best look over the map. "Right. To work. As best I can tell, we're here. We're going to use this shaft here to drop down to the main level, and approach the main chamber."

We all watched as she traced a finger along the map, finally tapping the enormous space.

"Based on this map, that exit should come out right next to the northeastern wall of the Faithful's base. More likely it's directly connected." Tasir pursed her lips, tarah drooped in exhaustion. "If it isn't, there should be some kind of traffic between the two. If it's vehicular, that'll be ideal. We cut the throat of a driver, take their truck, and I'll drive us through any checkpoints."

I nodded, "Their base layout should have their main hangar right next to that side of the wall, if I'm remembering right sir."

"Yeah. We pull the truck right on in. If Khash is with us, we'll emerge in the late evening."

Another nod from me, but puzzled looks from Irkan and Johanna. I explained, "The Faithful seem to be mostly sticking to Imperial procedures. Anyone assigned to maintenance tasks for the day will be finished and

232

returning to barracks by the early evening."

"Oh." Johanna said. "What if there's lots of shuttles coming and going?"

I hummed, thinking about it for a moment. "I think we'd still have an opening. The hangar of their base is pretty small, meant for small sized but regular traffic."

"So there wouldn't be room." She got it. "And if anyone was still working, they'd probably be outside."

"That will be our hope." I agreed, trying to find that wellspring of hope and optimism once more. "I think that's our best plan, sir."

Irkan bobbed his head. "This sailor agrees. It is past time we earned our names, and departed this world. The sooner our group is in orbit, the sooner we might finally eat a proper meal."

My stomach promptly rumbled, drawing heat to my face. "A meal sounds really nice right now. When we do leave... where do we go first?"

"Cathia, or Lushrivers." Tasir said. "Whichever is closest. Irkan's Kings aren't Trahcon, and there's no chance someone at that level was processed. And Kolkris might be a maniac, but she's her own maniac. She was hunting for answers on these Faithful just as I was."

I nodded once, then again.

I still didn't know if we were actually going to get out of here. If I was going to start screaming in terror if we saw the Burned Hand again. If I truly believed I was going to keep my promises.

But... dammit. Irkan was right. I might have been a failure of a soldier, of an Imperial spy, but I was more than stubborn enough for this. I was *not* going to give those driftwood bastards the satisfaction of falling apart. Of letting them cage me again.

We were going to get out of here. We were going to get answers.

And we were going to bring the fury of every nation of the Compact down on these Faithful for what they'd done.

233

Interlude
Rerth'riah

It had been a while since I'd been on this side of imprisonment.

Some if it had been easy to remember. The tight quarters, the lack of clothing, the absence of my packmates. Irregular and terrible food, games with the lighting. Variance intended to leave me constantly unsettled, destroy my body's natural rhythms. To leave me vulnerable and desperate for stability.

But in truth? It was the boredom that I'd forgotten.

"That's really the most effective part of this." I told my interrogator, stretching out as best I could considering that they'd chained me to a chair. "The rest isn't all that much worse than when those pirates captured me a few decades ago."

The woman, I vaguely recognized her as an Operative, huffed as she took the more comfortable seat across from me. "I saw that event in your index. Two months imprisonment, and they were going to use you as a blood sacrifice to the old Naulian sun gods."

I rolled a shoulder, making chains jangle. "Not the most orthodox way to track down a pirate group, I'll admit, but we made it work."

"And what? You're portraying your own Empire as the pirates this time?" She asked.

"Not the Empire, no." My tarah tried to rise, only for the nullification bar to keep them weighted down. "Just Imperial Intelligence."

She nodded agreeably. "Because we have been infiltrated by this mysterious cult."

"Your tone was a little too mocking." I chided her. "The expression was good, but you need to make me truly think that you believe me."

The Operative's tarah flicked, the only sign of her discomfort at my banter. "You will find that I am more than qualified to run this interrogation, Riah."

234

"I am sure you are. That is why you're in here." I said agreeably, pausing for a long breath before saying, "See? That's how you say it."

"Mocking now?" She made a tutting sound, rising slowly to her feet. I watched as she casually strolled around the table, vanishing behind me. "You know that I have full clearance to determine just what you are truly doing. Full chemical interrogation."

Of course she did. "That will be unpleasant."

"Oh yes." Her head appeared over my shoulder, whispering into my tarah. "Your bond was put through it yesterday. He was extremely resilient. He stuck to your story through the entire voyage."

My eyes closed, my focus on my breathing, keeping it even. Level. "Much better, Operative. Now I have to fear for my bond, my packmate. Not knowing if you truly tortured him or not."

A hand patted my shoulder as she pulled back, resuming her circle of the small room. "How glad that you approve. This is your last chance before we begin. Who are you truly working for? Why did you co-opt a full Sword worth of veteran soldiers, illegally hack Intelligence files outside of your projects, and murder Imperial citizens?"

"Because Intelligence has been compromised. Those citizens were involved in the group that abducted my packmate." I said, just as I had every time they had asked. "Because DataNet Security is compromised, and my reports and files hacked, changed."

"And your proof?" She asked, just as the first man to question me had.

"You took all of my evidence." I replied.

"And there was none. Just mad ramblings about a cult."

I shrugged once again. "Then you didn't read what we'd accumulated, or whoever you tasked with that duty changed the data."

"So quick to blame others." A hand knocked hard on the door, "Let's get started."

235

I took deep breaths when the door opened, two more women entering with a full interrogation kit between them.

My chair whirred, rising, tilting back. Within moments I was laying rather than sitting, giving them free access to my arms and legs. They were quick and efficient, I'd give them that.

Injectors were strapped to each bicep, another pair to the ends of my tarah. Monitoring patches slapped down on my chest and thighs. One left after that, while the other sat at the table, bringing a console view up.

"Baselines set, sir." She tapped out a few commands. "Ready to begin."

"Let's start slowly."

I got one more deep breath in before fire flooded into my veins, and I felt as I'd been hurled into the sky to free fall. My eyes clenched shut, teeth grinding as I swallowed my instinct to cry out. I felt my body thrash against the restraints for an eternity before I collapsed into a panting heap.

"...Ashahn's... fucking... ass." I let the sharper curse out in between gasps for air. "...worse... than I... remembered."

The Operative chuckled. "And that was merely level one. Surely you wish to tell us the truth before the next wave washes over you?"

A broken chuckle was my response to that. "I know... the pattern. You're pumping... relaxants in now. Make me agreeable."

She appeared over me, tarah quivering again. "I am actually interested in that. Knowing exactly what is happening, what is to come, does that make it more or less effective?"

I coughed, clearing my throat, "Bit of both really. You... ugh. You lost the fear of the unknown waters, but... I know exactly how much pain I'm about to be in."

"Hmm. Interesting." There was the barest hint of a gesture at the edges of my vision.

It was the only warning I had before the next drugs were pumped into my tarah.

236

No amount of willpower can stop you from screaming when that happens.

I remember howling at the top of my lungs before I blacked out for several minutes. It was only when they flooded in the next section of the painkillers that I swam back to the surface, my body weakly trying to curl into a defensive ball.

"...overdid it..." I whispered.

"On purpose." My interrogator assured me. "A little variance to ruin your knowledge of what comes. What do you think?"

I thought that the relaxants were the only things stopping me from sobbing.

"Now. Perhaps you would like to tell me the truth? Who are you working for, and why did you murder that innocent pack?"

"...not innocent. No... Burned Hand.... is innocent. Killers."

There was another heavy sigh. "Let's let her drift for a few minutes, then we'll try the third wave and see how she reacts. We had to take her bond up to level four before he stopped responding, let us hope she is more reasonable."

Holde... was he really?

I didn't know.

Couldn't know.

I hurt.

"Yes sir." The Agent running the chemicals replied. "We could try the alternative level two-three combination? Or-"

A quiet knock at the door interrupted her.

The Operative staring down at me didn't bother turning. "Tell them we are not to be interrupted."

237

"Yes sir."

"Now, Riah, be reasonable. Tell us the truth, and you can live a long life on a penal colony with your pack. Surely that's better than an execution for treason?"

I licked my lips, voice cracking. "Not... a traitor."

She scowled. "We both know that you are. Make this easy on everyone and admit it."

"Not... a traitor."

"You-"

A man's voice boomed through a speaker. "Release the Agent at once, traitor."

The Operative's head whipped around, "She is-what!?"

"Silence!" A woman, the Agent, let out a pained noise before a heavy clang sounded nearby. "Release her at once or face summary execution."

Her tarah flattened at once, mouth wide open. It seemed like she tried to say several things all at once, managing nothing but a vague stutter. That lasted until four more heavy clangs brought a giant of bronze and steel into view.

And on his chest was a black diamond, surrounded by eight stars.

The Snowfall power armor was missing its heavy shoulder mount, probably to better fit indoors, but that didn't stop its wearer from casually ripping my restraints apart with his metal hands.

"Easy, Agent." The soldier of the Void Fleets spoke through his sealed helmet. "Are you cognizant?"

"Yeah." I tried to sit up, but had to abort at once. "...not mobile."

"Understood. Operative! Remove her injection patches!"

She did, hands shaking in shock and confusion. The moment they were free he slid his arms under me, effortlessly cradling me as he straightened up.

Turning on a heel, he strode out without another word, taking care not to let my head strike the doorway. On the other side more men and women in the colors of the Void Fleet moved in, cuffs and guns in hand.

So many of them were Human... their skin the color of Ashe's, their fur that same deep black.

All around I saw them. Many in standard armor, others in the uniforms of officers backed up by more Snowfall suits. Each and every one of them was cuffing, threatening, or otherwise capturing every member of Imperial Intelligence they could get their hands on.

"She came." I murmured, hearing myself let out a choking sob. "She believed us."

The soldier said nothing, carrying me out of the detention block. I let myself lay in his arms through the trip up a stairwell, and into a lift guarded by more Voiders.

When the doors opened it was to the sunlight of the main analysis room, the air filled with the controlled chaos of an ongoing operation.

"Rerth!"

If I'd had any give in me, I'd have sagged in relief to hear Holde.

"Holde." I rasped, tilting my head in time for his lips to find mine. The soldier carrying me chuckled through his speakers, but otherwise waited patiently as my bond kissed me.

He broke away slowly, reluctantly. "Are you all right?"

"Chemical interrogation." I managed to reply. "Still out of it."

"Aspects drown them all." He growled furiously. "May Ashahn flay each and every one of them... uh. Sir."

Another woman let out a deep chuckle, her rich Icar accent entirely too amused. "I've heard far worse, trust me. You must be Agent Rerth'riah, the one who found this entire nest of fanged eels."

239

The soldier turned, angling me enough to see the heiress to the entire Empire.

Void Lord Sever'amiar'delarah smiled genially, extremely long tarah lifted in interest as she looked down at me. Like many of her men she was in full power armor, the helm held by a subordinate behind her.

"Sir." I swallowed. "Apologies for not standing."

"At ease, Agent." A mechanical hand reached out, patting my shoulder with surprising tenderness. "Your old packmate is aboard my flagship. I want you there at once to rest and recover. Once you're settled, you are going to assist me in determining just how far into our rivers this rot has spread."

"Yes, Void Lord."

She nodded, patting me once more. "Good. Get her up there, and her packmates with her. Inform the Void Admiral that I will return once we have all Intelligence personnel on Altair accounted for and in custody."

"Sir." The soldier holding me replied already moving once again.

I saw Holde fall into step with him. Saw a woozy looking Jet wave off a medic to follow... then I closed my eyes, and let myself collapse into the darkness.

Knowing that when I awoke, we would find Ashe.

XXV

I nearly cried when we found the first storage crates. They were stacked in perfectly neat rows along one side of the tunnel, the floor covered in marks from the heavy carts that had moved them.

Dim lights saw us turn off the nearly dead tablet, Tasir hissing at Johanna when her excitement had her start moving too quickly, too loudly.

I think all of us had to resist the urge to open up the crates I saw labeled as containing food. To force ourselves to keep going until the tunnel brought us into a dimly lit garage. Not just part of the cave that had been converted; a fully built garage.

Our feet walked across metal rather than stone. Prefabricated walls covered up the cavern's sides, with similar construction above our heads. Pale lights hung from that ceiling, far larger ones were present but shut off. A quick count revealed four heavy carts, the exact same model I'd driven so many times, parked in a neat row.

Just beyond them was a heavy freight elevator, the lift itself open and locked down on our level. It looked like it could go either up or down. Combined with the metal flooring, I was pretty sure that the Faithful had turned the single cavern into numerous levels for their own uses.

"No cameras." Tasir murmured as we walked down a short ramp, entering the open space. "Lori?"

"I don't see any either, sir." I reported. "I can see four more side tunnels though."

"Check them, we'll look at the lift."

Nodding once, I picked up the pace, bare feet carrying me around the little vehicles. A quick look down the first tunnel proved it was just the same as the one we'd come from; long, straight, and being used for storing supplies.

Tunnels two through four all proved to be much the same, my circle of the room leaving me next to a sink set into the wall that Johanna was already guzzling from.

241

She turned a bit pink, pulling her head away from it, letting me have a turn.

Chuckling, I ducked my own head in as well, drinking straight from the faucet. I didn't care that this was definitely meant just for washing Faithful's hands free of the dust that filled the caves.

It was cold and it was plentiful.

Tasir arrived just a I was finishing, holding up a hand to forestall my report until she managed to hydrate herself as well.

"Just more storage." I told her when she was done. "Ramps are different heights... these must have been high up on the walls of the old main chamber. Probably had scaffolding or lift access in the original mines."

"Agreed." The Elder glanced between them, "What did the labels read?"

"Nearest crates all read as ammunition or dry rations." I said.

Johanna shifted her weight. "Can we...?"

I glanced at the nearest wall, at the small clock there with its blue numbers. "It's only mid-afternoon, sir. If we want to move in at night then we have some time."

The Elder's tarah rose along with her eyes, staring at the little display. "...one bag each, no more. We eat more than that we'll just make ourselves sick. You two find us something edible. Irkan? Find us guns while I check for stairs or a ladder. That lift can't be the only way in or out."

We split up again, Johanna eagerly following me to the nearest tunnel. I carefully inspected the first crate I found labeled as holding food, hesitantly tapping the release button.

I let out a breath I hadn't realized I was holding when it cracked open without any kind of alarm going off. A little tug got the cover angled up on its hinges, letting us see countless silver bags stacked in neat rows.

"Do you want Altair, or Homeworld?" I asked.

242

She shook her head, "What's the difference?"

"Sweet or spicy." I told her.

"Sweet."

I pulled out four bags of the Altair rations, handing them over before closing the crate.

"Just add water?" She asked, "That's how the fleet ones work."

"Yeah, same as ours. Come on."

Heading back to the little sink, we carefully opened the packets one at a time. Johanna followed my instructions, adding just a little bit of water to each, then carefully shaking them to get it all mixed together.

I started downing mine almost at once, tipping the bag back and squeezing bits of it between my lips. Intellectually I knew it was pretty awful. The texture was abysmal, hardly better than the gray slop we'd gotten on the barge. There was a chalky aftertaste to it as well.

But it tasted vaguely like greenfish with sweet blue sauce... it tasted like home.

Tasir arrived to take her bag, eating hers just as quickly as we were downing ours. Our Elder wasn't too dignified to scoop out the last little bits of it with the thumb on her maimed hand, licking it clean after.

"Ladder shaft over there goes up and down." She informed us when she'd finished. "That will be our way to the lower levels. I didn't risk opening it yet, but the controls read as unlocked."

I nodded, setting my empty bag aside. "Map?"

Her head shook once. "No, and we're not activating the console over there either. We're not risking anything that might set off an alarm until we can't help it."

Smart. Well, as smart as we were capable of being. We definitely shouldn't have stopped to eat, but I had no idea how long it had been since we'd had a proper meal.

More than a day with no food at all, at a minimum. Probably closer to two, maybe even three. And who knew how many days since the ambush by the river that had seen us as the sole survivors, eating what little bits of fruit and vegetables we could find on the run.

Ashahn's blood, even before then we'd been on a forced-march to try and get into position. It had probably been close to a month since we'd had a full meal, rather than just scraps.

"...you sure we can't eat more?" Johanna asked, staring longingly at the nearest of the storage tunnels.

"Yes." Tasir said flatly. "We shouldn't have even finished what we did."

She looked ready to argue the point when Irkan returned, carefully lumbering over with a small pile of guns in his strong arms.

I perked up at once when he sat them down, Khash blessing us with some more good luck. My hand reached out, pulling the nearest of them into my lap. "Kahdel Eighty-Two's.... wow. The Ix model. Wind Formation exclusives."

"That's good?" Johanna asked, carefully taking one as well. When I waved at her again, she also picked up two of the spare clips when Irkan set them aside for her.

"I don't think they'd even let conscripts look at this version." I confirmed, turning the long rifle over in my hands. Admiring the dark wood that had been worked into the metal. "Imperial-two rounds."

Tasir was less pleased, even as she picked up the Strike pistol that Irkan had retrieved for her. "This is a new model as well. Ashahn's ass, these bastards have access at every level of the technocracy."

I hefted my new weapon up a little, "On the bright side, sir. Physical proof of corruption right here, complete with identification codes worked into the stock."

"True." She turned her pistol over in her intact hand, thumb flicking a few of the buttons on the side before she grunted. "At least we're armed now. No armor back there?"

244

Irkan shook his head, "Sadly not, elder of the river sharks. This one could not find so much as a shield belt, nor grenades either. He wonders why a crate of weapons was present at all."

I rolled a shoulder, "Someone loaded the wrong crate onto the lift when they split the ammunition apart from the guns. Couldn't be bothered to haul it back to the proper level."

"And it was not noticed?" He asked.

"Even if they did, would they really care?" I waved a hand around us, "Who would make it all the way down here to find it in the first place? If they were actually concerned they'd have walled all of those tunnels off."

Tasir let out a quiet sound of agreement. "Arrogant bastards. Let's make sure they regret it."

"Agreed, sir."

She tapped a finger on the side of her pistol one more time, exhaled, and nodded. "We wait until the start of the night shift. If the Faithful are following Imperial doctrine, that'll be in six hours. Lori? Make sure Ark Fleet can point that gun in the right direction."

I glanced at Johanna in time to see her flush, a little as she admitted. "I've never used a gun in my life."

"Learn fast." Tasir told her flatly. "Irkan? You and I are going to alternate resting and staring at that lift in case it activates. If anyone comes up, we run for the ladder and start heading down."

While they got settled, and Irkan finally got to eat as well, I got Johanna up. Throwing our garbage away in a marked bin, I led her closer to the lifts, and walked her through the numerous settings on her weapon.

Honestly that made it sound more complicated than it was. The gun probably had a thousand and one features if you could link it to your armor, but without that it was just a really expensive rifle.

I showed her the safety, and made sure it stayed locked while I lectured her on never pointing it at any of us, or anyone she didn't intended to shoot.

245

After I'd told her that at least a dozen times, I walked her through reloading. Once I was sure she could manage that without getting a finger caught or breaking the weapon, I guided her through the process of aiming, using a nearby pillar as a stand in for a target.

"We'll keep it at single shot." I said, moving behind her. "Keep it against your shoulder, look down the sights. Don't try to point it at their heads or anything specific. Just at their chests. Right where that sign is on the pillar."

"Like this?"

I stepped up closer, looking over her arm to see how she was aiming the weapon. "Perfect. Can you see the ammunition counter?"

Her reply was dry, "Yeah, but it's in Caranat. Still can't read it."

"...right." I smiled, leaning down to rest my chin on her shoulder. "I don't think we have time to help you memorize the numbers. You've got sixty rounds in a magazine, so you'll have to keep track. You see the symbol on the right? When it's flashing you'll need to reload."

Johanna nodded slightly, then swallowed. "Ashe. Um. Too close."

I blinked, then realized I'd put an arm around her waist as well. And I was rather firmly pulling her against me. "Oh, sorry. Old habits."

Her weight shifted when I pulled back, both of us awkwardly clearing our throats.

"You, um, trained a lot of people like this?" She asked.

"No. Um," I coughed once, "My second pack handled most of my advanced training. Huvu... had very specific ideas about how to reward proper technique."

The other woman's cheeks colored. "Oh. Um... I'm flattered? But I still don't like you like that, Ashe."

"I don't either." I assured her, "Sorry. Habits, like I said."

"You are very touchy. I mean, you like touching people, not that you're sensitive." She said. "I'm mostly used to it, just wasn't expecting it

246

right now. Or like that. Um... if I do need to really cut loose, how do I do that?"

I stepped back in, though I was more careful of her personal space that time. "This dial. Press your thumb on it, then twist it up. The ammunition counter will turn from yellow to blue."

She tried it, frowning at it when the yellow turned to green..

"Burst fire." I provided, "Up one more. There you go."

Johanna tested flicking it back and forth a few more times, then set it back to single fire.

"Don't change that unless someone tells you." I told her firmly. "The rifle's going to be extremely hard for you to hold onto if you try to fire it full auto."

"I won't, just... in case one of them is on me."

I nodded, gently patting her shoulder. "All right. Run through reloading again."

She did, and I did it beside her. We did it several more times, until I was pretty sure that she had it down. Or as much as she could, considering we were doing it in an otherwise silent garage without anyone else shooting at us.

Not that I expected to do much better if I had to reload in combat, but I'd at least been shot at before. Shot back at the people trying to kill me. As rattled as I would be, Johanna was about to be thrown into a hurricane.

"Remember." I said once we'd finished, the pair of us sitting next to the closed hatch leading to the ladder access. "Safety on at all times. Stealth is how we get out of here."

"I remember." Johanna replied. "You don't have to keep repeating yourself."

I gave her a little smile, "You're at least half as stubborn as I am. Just have to make sure it sinks in."

"I don't think anyone's half as stubborn as you are."

247

We both chuckled, leaning back against the wall, relaxing as we digested our little meal.

I started meditating after a half hour or so, listening to the quiet hum of electricity. The soft whirring of distant vents moving air through the garage, through the caverns. Focused on those distant noises, pushing all of my fears and concerns about what was coming aside.

Two more of my checkpoints had been met, and passed. The Faithful had a base, and we had entered it. Khash had even given me his blessings for once, letting us find weapons, food, and granted us time to rest before the final plunge into the sea.

Soon enough we'd see if his merciful streak continued. If we could get through the base without raising the alarm. Find a ship capable of getting us out of here.

And get aboard it without Tasir or Irkan dying, since neither Johanna or I knew the first thing about piloting a spacecraft. Well, Johanna could probably help keep one running far better than I could, but she'd freely admitted she'd never actually flown one before.

I opened my eyes at Tasir's call, looking up at the clock that told me it was after the evening hours.

"Time to swim or drown." The Director told us. "Let's move."

XXVI

It was amazing how much having a simple rifle buoyed my spirits. I mean, considering that I still didn't have armor, or even a shield belt. We still had pretty much no chance against a trained sorcerer in a straight fight.

But the long gun in my arms helped forget about that, for a little while. Helped me feel like the conscript that I was supposed to be.

That was good, because our luck ran out quickly once we'd gotten down the ladder, creeping out into a narrow maintenance run. It was, in fact, so narrow that Irkan couldn't fit down it, forcing our first hard decision.

While there was a single door in front of us, it was completely lacking in any kind of label or icon to tell us what lay on the other side. Not about to risk it, we were all in agreement that we had to at least try the other directions to see if Khash would bless us for a second time.

Maybe we'd run right into a server room or security center. If we could take that over we'd have every chance to get a map, to keep the alarms off, and to know the location of every patrol in this facility.

"You stay here with Ark Fleet." Tasir rapped Irkan's shell with her maimed hand, "Lori and I will scout this hall and return."

I don't think either one of them was very happy about that, but they stayed in the ladder's well while we Imperials carefully moved down the narrow path.

On this side of the walls it was easier to see that this base hadn't exactly been built to code. Plenty of wires and tubes were far lower than I thought they should have been, forcing us to constantly duck to avoid running into things.

"Labels are misspelled." I whispered back to Tasir, nodding to a bit of tape wrapped around some of the wiring. "No Imperial team built this place, sir. It looks good on the outside, but it's a mess internally."

A quiet snort preceded her words, "Hundred credits says the first prisoners were the builders, and their payment for the work was being turned

249

into those things in the mountain."

It was all too easy to imagine the Faithful doing just that. "I wouldn't take that bet, sir... damn. Dead end around this corner. Just a locked exit... think the lock is on our side though. I could open it?"

"Don't risk it yet." She ordered. "Label?"

I checked around the hatch. "Hallway 3-May."

"Not what we want. We head back the other way and check that direction."

"Yes sir."

Reversing course, she took point while I followed along behind. Irkan and Johanna were disappointed when we went past them with a shake of our heads, staying in place as we left them behind once more.

Not that we were any more cheered. After a long walk picking through the hall we ended up at another door labeled Hallway 3-May. Tasir cursed under her breath for a moment, then gave me a new set of orders.

I nodded and reversed course once again.

"All three connect to the same hallway." I told our companions when I drew closer. "Johanna, you're with us. We're going to try that door and see what's on the other side. Irkan?"

"This sailor shall remain in place until he hears otherwise." He said.

"Or until you hear gunfire." I said, "Then feel free to come out shooting."

A low chuckle came from his wide frame, "The savanna need not have said that. It is obvious."

We left him chortling, slipping through the mess to catch back up with Tasir. To my vague surprise Johanna didn't have any problems keeping up, even with the gun hanging from one shoulder. If anything she seemed to be restraining the urge to tell me to stop going so slowly.

"I am." She retorted when I said as much, "Ashe, I might be helpless

250

in a jungle, but I grew up running through ship corridors even narrower than this is."

"Oh. Right." I shook my head, and tried to pick up the pace a little. "Sorry."

There was a quiet snort, both of us falling silent again until we made it to where Tasir was crouching beside the door. Pistol in her good hand, the thumb of her mangled one hovering near the door controls.

It pressed down when we arrived, the hatch sliding open without a sound, revealing a hallway with dim blue lighting.

Tasir slowly stuck her head out, pistol following her gaze as she swept it left to right. Then she glanced up to check the ceiling before pulling back. "Iriahn's fucking dick. We've got a map across the hall."

"That's good."

"There's a camera right above us."

I winced. "That's bad."

Her grunt was annoyed that I'd stated the obvious. "It's fixed to point left. If my old eyes are correct, there's a cell bloc through there. Must be where they keep their fish confined before they start cutting them."

Not at all where we wanted to be then. "Lifts? Ladders?"

She stared hard across the hall for a moment before replying. "There's a lift bank right on the other side of that door, with another maintenance ladder next to it. No way to avoid the security camera though, and the map says that those cells take up nearly the entire level."

Ashahn's blood. Really not where we wanted to be.

Johanna cleared her throat, "What about a hangar, or a garage?"

"Neither on this level." Tasir replied. "There's stairwell access at the far end, to the right. Should be a third maintenance ladder just across from that."

I nodded, "So we double back one more time, take that ladder down

251

as well. Check each level as we go until we find the right one."

Our Elder nodded, "Agreed. Let's go."

Pulling back, we went back the way we'd come. Again. Though Johanna apparently didn't feel like waiting for us that time; she moved with an easy, fluid grace through the hall.

I watched her fur ripple and bob as she ducked, bounced over pipes, and twisted to avoid getting caught on wires without so much as slowing down.

Throttling the urge to shout that she was just showing off, I followed at a far more sedate pace, Tasir right behind me. By the time we arrived Johanna had already told Irkan the plan, and he'd moved forward to be the first through the hatchway.

He opened with a cautious push of a finger, Johanna and I aiming our guns over his shoulders when it revealed the empty hall on the other side.

Irkan carefully pulled himself through the narrow hatchway, hissing something in his own tongue when his shell scraped on the metal. "...no Faithful, no cameras."

I was next out, breathing coming quicker as I checked both directions. The hallway was long but straight, with closed hatches visible in the distance on both ends. Our side didn't have any doors, apart from the recessed maintenance hatches, but the other had numerous hatches.

Sadly there wasn't a convenient map near this one. The other was probably only there because it was next to the elevators, the better to help new arrivals arriving on this floor find whatever room they were looking for.

Johanna and Tasir slipped out into the hall behind us, the Director far more cautiously than my cellmate, but at least Johanna was keeping her gun up and level.

We padded off as quietly as we could down down the corridor, Irkan and I checking each of the doors when we approached.

"Morgue Ah." He rumbled at the first one.

"...Morgue A." I whispered the second, fingers tightening around my

252

rifle.

And so it went, through six more letters of the alphabet.

I really should have expected it, but it still left me a bit rattled to walk past so many chambers devoted to storing corpses. You don't build eight morgues unless you plan on using them... and I was very, very glad that each one of those rooms was closed right now.

Reaching the closed door at the far end, Tasir was reaching for the controls when our luck ran out.

It slid open before she could touch them, revealing a member of the Faithful in plain clothes on the far side.

And right behind her was a larger group of them, the conversation dying when they realized the hall was blocked.

"What-"

I pulled the trigger before she could finish, Irkan doing the same. The three round bursts were deafening in the confined space, both of us shooting as rapidly as we could. Four of them died in those first few seconds, collapsing with holes stitched across their chests.

The last got a barrier up, turning to run as it deflected our rounds.

Tasir let out a quiet snarl, tarah flexing, and one of the man's dead companions hurtled down the hallway after him. The body was too large to deflect, taking him about the legs. He fell with a startled yelp, and Johanna finally got her safety off to shoot him in the back before he could stand.

We stood there in a panicked silence, my ears ringing with the harsh echoes of the gunfire.

Not that the pain in my ears stopped me from hearing the alarms when they began screaming. White lights began snapping to life, replacing the dim after-hours colors above us.

"Ashahn's fucking ass!" Tasir spat, "Lori! Get her rank badge and her comp!"

Obeying on reflex to her shout, I dove forward, sliding on my knees next to the first body. A quick yank ripped the icon from her uniform, a second pull getting the mesh device from her right arm.

The others were already running by the time I finished, leaving me scrambling to catch up. Johanna waited at the next door just long enough for me to arrive, then ducked through to start climbing down the ladder.

I paused just long enough to shut the hatch behind us, and to shove the wrist-comp and rank badge into my pockets. After that I was scrambling down right after her to find the others already dashing ahead again, Tasir apparently having stopped just long enough to look over this level's map.

Irkan was in the lead, following shouted directions from Tasir that were swallowed up the ringing alarms.

A member of the Faithful came stumbling out of a bathroom right in his path, and our shortest member didn't even slow down. Lowering his head, he rammed his horn into the woman's belly, twisted it free in an oddly graceful spin, and left her screaming until Tasir put a bullet in her head.

Johanna threw up somewhere around there, though she managed to keep running while she did it.

"Right!" Tasir's next shout had Irkan swerve, my longer legs finally letting me catch up as he led us down a shorter hallway. "Lori! Badge!"

I jammed a hand down, yanking it out just as we reached a sealed doorway. "Sir!"

She quickly tucked her gun under her other arm, catching it in her good hand when I tossed it. "Set!"

We all got our guns up and ready once more. Tasir nodded once, and a a wave of the badge against the security panel had it shifting from green to blue. The heavy door slid open to reveal another Trahcon in white already throwing a hand in our direction, his form mostly hidden behind a desk.

The strike slammed into Irkan, driving him back several paces, but he was too heavy to simply hurl aside.

Johanna and I returned fire, forcing him to call up his barriers before ducking.

254

Our eldest must have found a final wellspring within her soul because she snarled, clenched her fist, and more ozone filled the air when her Strike hammered his desk.

The man screamed in pain when it slammed him into the wall, something breaking with a harsh crack.

"Kill him before he immolates the room!" She barked.

I was already rushing forward, Tasir's order giving me even more reason to get in close. The Faithful had enough time to snarl at me before I finished him off, doing my best not to look at how misshapen his shoulder was.

"Done!" I shouted, swallowing down my body's own discomfort at what we'd just done. "Sir."

Tasir moved in, setting her pistol on the wood and stepping over the corpse. "Good, he didn't shut it down."

"Who was he?"

"Map on this level said it was a Commander's office." She started to reach out for the desk's controls, then hissed in frustration. As if she'd forgotten she only had one working hand. "Get over here!"

I obeyed, taking her spot and tapping the button to bring the holographic display up. "What am I looking for?"

"Cell release." The Director ordered. "We need the distraction, and at least they'll die free."

That drew a wince, but I couldn't argue either point.

"You two, shut that door!" Tasir snapped. "Let's hope they lose track of where we are long enough to pull this off."

Irkan was already shaking his head, "Blood upon our feet, elder one. There is a clear trail."

She hissed in frustration, "Then we hold the far end. Lori! Get them open!"

255

"Yes sir." I tried not to panic while my companions moved out of the room, taking up positions at the far end of the hall.

Fingers flew over the controls, poking at the various applications as fast as I could, trying to find the relevant ones. For a brief moment I really wished that Jet was here. He wasn't my favorite packmate, but he'd have already had the alarms off, security cameras working for us, and every cell in the facility open before I thought to just run a search.

"...cell controls... prison cells... cells... uh." I tried to think of another term. "What's another word for them... units? Unit controls.... units..."

Still nothing. Dammit!

"Uh..." I licked my lips, then tried the next on that surfaced in my head. "Experiments."

Experiment Containment Suites

Experiment Record System

Experiment Projections

Experiment-

I tapped the first one, trying not to grind my teeth at how they'd labeled them. "Ashahn's blood. Four hundred of them... all right, mass release..."

There was a 'purge' option that I definitely didn't want to touch. I could also open up camera views of every single cell, which made me wonder where they'd hidden the cameras on the barge. "Come on... Post-Purge Examination Protocol?"

A quick shift let me bring up the help notes for that one, some Faithful programmer kindly informing me it would open all of the cells so that the failed experimental subjects could be properly examined after the full purge was enacted.

I tapped it at once, and cursed when it demanded his override code since the Purge hadn't been used within the last hour. Leaning down, I ripped the rank badge off his chest, jamming it against the reader.

The screen flashed blue, alarms quieting to let a woman's synthesized voice speak. "Post-Purge Examination Protocol is now in effect. All Research Teams please report to your assigned Containment Blocks, all Combat Teams be prepared for any failures of the Purge system. Glory to the True Gods."

"Done!" I shouted. "I think the alarm is off too!"

"Good-left!" Tasir barked.

I jerked my head up to see Irkan and Tasir firing at someone out of sight, Johanna scrambling back when a tracer round whipped past her head.

A few seconds later, screaming, gunfire, and explosions began to make the floor rattle as the storm devoured the base.

XXVII

According to the screen in front of me, there were cell blocks on every level of the base, including this one. Which meant that, when I unlocked them all, the Faithful shooting at us soon had four hundred new problems to deal with.

At least I hoped that was what the extra gunfire and screaming was about.

"Good job Lori!" Tasir shouted over the chaos outside, "Map to the hangars! Now!"

"Yes sir!"

Doing my best to ignore the bellowing, screaming, and gunfire coming from the hallway, I closed down what I'd had open and did another search for a map of the facility. Thankfully that was a far quicker process, one not requiring I start guessing at terms.

There wasn't much good news despite that.

We were on the wrong level to get out by two floors. Once we made it down, it looked like there'd be two options; a main exit at the far end of a garage and transfer space, which would presumably let us get outside to the ships being used to conduct the Culling. There was also what might have been a secondary hangar built in beside that garage, maybe for the base's elite or something.

Biting my lip, I hesitated for just a moment before trying to get access to the security cameras again. To try and see if there was a ship in that hangar or not.

I was just pulling them up when the console went dead. "Dammit! They caught me, console's offline!"

Tasir fired off a few blind rounds around the corner, then ducked back to call. "Did you find a route?"

"Yes sir! Right turn, next stairwell down two floors!" I shouted.

258

"Either a straight run through the main garage outside to the main base, or there might be something in the Commander's Hangar!"

"We'll decide there. Move!"

Nearly tripping over the corpse still behind the desk with me, I got around it and ran to join the others.

Irkan was standing apart from them; and the brackish blood dribbling from his left arm explained why.

"A graze." He casually leaned out, firing a short burst before ducking back when someone retaliated in kind. "The plan?"

"I have one barrier left in me." Tasir jerked her head to the right, "Run. Now!"

Johanna hesitated. I didn't, running right out into the open as Tasir did the same. The old Director's face was screwed up in agony, she had to be going well past her body's limits, but the swirling energy came up around her one more time.

I ran hard down the hallway, hearing the increase in the enemy's fire when they realized we were making a break for it.

Fighting down the urge to look back, I counted my strides as I ran past a bathroom. Past another office. Past a left turn.

I swerved to the right, barely getting my gun up in time to point it at a half-shaved Naule charging me with a metal club in one of his many hands.

"Stop!"

The screech and wild swing of the club saw me jump back, pulling the trigger. It wasn't a terribly well aimed burst, taking him across a shoulder, adding howls of pain to the din.

"Please-" He came at me again with his teeth, and I put a second burst of fire into his chest. "-don't... Ashahn's blood!"

I yanked the trigger down again, barely killing another one of them as it came leaping at me, and found the entire hallway beyond filling up with the aliens rushing down from the next turn.

Johanna arrived in time to start shooting, Irkan right behind her. His shots were more accurate than hers, but even she couldn't really miss with how many there were.

"They're following!" Irkan barked, stepping up just in time to clear space for a staggering Tasir. Both of her tarah were drooping, her breath visibly ragged as she stumbled in behind.

"Move up!" I shouted over the wounded screams of our fellow prisoners, nudging Johanna with a hip. "The stairs right there!"

She nodded frantically, repeatedly yanking her rifle's trigger as she lurched for the door. It took her a kick to shove a body away, letting her haul the door open and plunge through it.

"Sir! Go!"

Tasir didn't even make it halfway before falling to a knee. Irkan put a final burst into a wounded Naule grabbing for her, dropped his rifle, and grabbed the back of her shirt in his good arm. He hauled her along while I killed two more people, following right behind them.

My last view of the hallway was that of more than a dozen dying or dead Naule, their blood covering the floor and walls, their screams still ringing.

I managed to find the lever to lock the door before more than a few hands tried to rip it open, but the sudden bursts of gunfire on the other side got me moving again.

The Faithful were catching up.

Feet hit the stairs, hands getting my rifle out of the way so that I could throw up what was left of my rations. Somehow I managed to mimic Johanna, voiding my guts on the move without losing more than a step or two.

Tasir was on her own feet again by the time we got to the ground level, Johanna hesitating at the door.

"What's on the other side?" She asked.

"Main chamber and processing." I spat some of my stomach bile out of my mouth, "Stay on the right hand wall. It'll lead us right to the ramp leading up to the secondary hangar."

Her eyes snapped to mine, "Is there something there?"

I shook my head, "No idea, but I think we can get outside from there even if there isn't."

"But-"

"Shut." Tasir rasped, "It. Run. Run and don't stop. Follow Lori. She saw the map."

Johanna swallowed, nodding once. "Okay. Ready?"

An explosion directly above us made everyone flinch. I didn't wait to hear the sound of armored feet on the stairs, simply knowing that the Faithful had just blown the door open.

"Go!" Tasir barked.

My cellmate rammed the door open with a shoulder, tearing off at a sprint without hesitating. I was right behind her, Irkan and Tasir laboring to keep up with our longer strides.

The Main Processing Chamber resembled a starport's security zone, assuming you would ever fight a battle in such a place.

Bodies lay all over the place, alarms were blaring drunkenly from shattered scanners. At least two different groups of Faithful had used sorcery to create make-shift barricades, hurling Strike spells and firing pistols at the swarm of prisoners trying to escape past them. Trying to kill them.

Said prisoners were a mix of nearly every species I knew of. Some had been shackled with modern gear, and struggled to do anything besides be cut down. The luckier had been tied up by rope or cloth, and had clearly swarmed both the Faithful and collaborators alike when the chaos had unfolded.

More prisoners were pouring out of other stairwells and ladder shafts. Few looked sane, and more than a few were visibly misshapen with cybernetics.

261

A group of them swarmed over a knot of Thondian collaborators wielding spears, they must have been trying to fight their way to a stairwell. The big aliens seemed to simply vanish as a mix of Human and Xenthan prisoners tore them apart, uncaring of how many of them were stabbed in the process.

Ashahn's blood. This was beyond madness.

I ran faster, chasing Johanna as we sprinted toward the narrow passage that was our last hope.

We vaulted over more bodies. Barely glanced at a collection of Human collaborators being gored by Mikiran prisoners when both groups made a run for the distant exit. Two more groups of the Faithful's puppets managed to get together near parked trucks, Thondians and Humans alike fighting side by side against the crazed masses.

We were nearly to our next turn when it was made clear we'd made the right decision.

"Corral the beasts!" Ice formed in my heart, feet nearly tripping when the Burned Hand's voice came over the speakers above us. *"Containment teams advance into the processing center! All other teams seal off all exits!"*

In the far distance, the dark horizon of the outdoors abruptly lit up with blue-white fire. Those few prisoners who'd made it that far were silhouetted for bare moments against those lights before falling. Their screams began to cut through the gunfire as the sorcery immolated them, the Faithful building a wall of flame to prevent anyone else from making it into the open.

"By the order of the Ascended, kill them all!"

Johanna whipped around the corner, fur swaying as I followed. The ramp was circular, clearly meant for vehicles, but it did the job of guiding us up the half-level into the Commander's Hangar.

"Mein Gott! Ashe! Look!" She gasped.

"I see it!" I called back. "Go!"

The spacecraft filling the hangar had to be a hundred yards long. Bronzed plating was covered in stylized patterns of mountains and waves, the

262

luxury pinnace's wings neatly folded in for landing.

It could have been a garbage scow and I'd have been tempted to break down crying. All that mattered was that it was sure to have an FTL drive, and the ramp was down with the hatch still open.

"Watch for anyone aboard!" We were both already running for that ramp, desperate to get aboard. "Irkan?"

"This one shall defend the ramp!" He called back. "Clear the ship!"

I nodded without looking back, Johanna and I finally slowing down when our feet hit the metal. Just being on the ship seemed to give her a sharp boost; her balance steadied, gun moving more smoothly.

"You know how to board a ship?" I asked.

"I know the drills on the other side." She replied, "Defend the bridge, defend engines, defend the hangars. Bridge first."

I nodded, taking the first step inside. "I'll lead."

The interior was just as rich as the outside. Wood paneling covered every inch, with the lights encased inside of lantern housings. Whoever had built this ship had spent an absolute fortune making it feel like a sailing ship from the homeworld.

Padding across it on bare feet, I tried to listen for movement, giving up when I realized that the chaos in the main chamber was making it up the ramp as well.

I blamed that me for not hearing the sailor until he came bursting out of a cabin with a bellow, an old fashioned sword swinging at my head.

The shout gave me enough warning to jerk my rifle up, catching the impact, letting me see a man snarling at me. His flared tarah came with the follow-up Strike that shoved me away, back slamming into the wall.

He hefted his blade up again, not seeing Johanna. Not even when she shot him in the side of the head.

"Thanks." I gasped as his corpse toppled over.

"W-welcome." She stuttered, staring at the body. At the wreckage she'd made of his skull. "Uh-"

A burst of gunfire from the ramp made us both jump, Irkan's voice a distant bellow. "Hurry!"

We got ourselves together, running for the front end of the ship. I don't know if it was his shouting and gunshots, or if it had been Johanna's, but either way another member of the Faithful was ready and waiting for us when we made it to the tiny bridge.

Johanna had gotten ahead of me again, and she took the brunt of the spell when we came through the door. It slammed her back, barely missing me, something in her arm cracking when it got caught on the doorway.

I risked a single brace of shots into the woman half-crouched behind the pilot's chair, aiming for the seat rather than her body. She let out her own howl of pain to match my friend's, bursting out from cover with one arm limp.

Ozone filled the cockpit as she called up a barrier, scrambling back, daring me to send rounds ricocheting through the critical controls.

I wasn't so panicked as to wreck our only hope of escape, and I charged right at her instead. Her back hit the far wall, a hiss escaping her before I led with the gun's barrel aimed at her chest. She managed to strengthen her barrier enough to deflect it, but wasn't ready for my full weight to follow up when I didn't slow down.

My shoulder rammed into her sternum, knocking the wind out of her when I slammed her into the wall. I think she tried to scrape together another spell, only for the butt of my rifle to slam into her jaw, breaking her concentration.

Then I shot her in the head, just like Johanna had killed the other one.

"Johanna!" I yelled.

A piteous moan was her response as she limped into the bridge, her right arm clearly broken just below her elbow. "Hurts..."

"Sit down." I waved frantically for her to come forward, "Uh... shit, you can't read any of these controls. Just sit, I'll get Tasir up here."

264

I don't know if she really heard me, but I couldn't spare the moment to check on her.

Racing back down the hall, I was nearly to the ramp when Irkan came lumbering up it.

"I need Tasir!"

"She defends the ramp." He was already moving my way, "This sailor shall pilot! Get the Eldest here, and prepare the hatches to be sealed for our departure!"

"Got it! Careful, Johanna's hurt!" I ducked into the cabin the sailor had tried to ambush me from, shaking fingers reloading my weapon. The moment Irkan was past I was back in the hall, darting down the ramp to find Tasir crouched behind a nearby cart.

Her pistol snapped off a few rounds at someone trying to come into the hangar, forcing them back.

"Sir!" I fell into a crouch beside her, adding a few covering shots of my own despite the lack of a target. "Irkan's going to get it started, we need to get you on and get the hatches sealed!"

She nodded, "Good! Help me get aboard!"

I was grabbing her arm to do just that when a tall figure came sprinting up, not hesitating when we both shot at them on reflex. Sparks flew when the rounds impacted her barrier, her rush slowing when she caught sight of us.

"*You.*" The Burned Hand snarled, stalking forward, the dress robes of a Battle-Priest swirling around her. Her eyes were locked onto Tasir. "I have had *enough* of your interference, you meddling old bitch! I will make you wish that you'd died on Alum!"

And with that threat she called up fire. The Cloak of Ashahn roaring to life around her, the living firestorm coming closer with each step she took.

With that, she brought my nightmares to life just when I'd found hope.

265

XXVIII

I froze on seeing that flame. On hearing her voice again. My finger wouldn't pull the trigger on my gun. The weapon itself began to shake wildly as the breath left my body.

"Run!" Tasir's shove sent me stumbling back. "Move!"

I staggered, making it a half dozen steps before another of the Faithful appeared from the main ramp. A tracer round snapped past me, forcing me to draw up short before I could truly make a run for the ship.

A mocking laugh came from the Burned Hand as she strolled forward. The leading edges of her spell melting the cart Tasir had been using for cover, forcing the Elder to limp back, her tarah trying to lift as if she meant to cast back.

Her flinch of pain told me there wasn't any hope of her even attempting a sorcery duel, much less winning one.

"Come." The Burned Hand called mockingly, her robes scorching, burning away to reveal armor beneath. "Use your weapons! See how much good they do you!"

I nearly did, nearly wasted my bullets into that impervious shield.

I don't know how I didn't. How I managed to get my legs moving, retreating with Tasir as we were herded away from the ship's ramp. As we were driven away from our only means of escape.

The Burned Hand took her time moving around the cart, the firestorm around her fading just enough to let me see her features when she spoke again.

"What is wrong, *Elder*?" She sneered at Tasir. "You look as if you're about to lose control, as you did when your own Agents proved their faith by turning you over to us."

Tasir bared her teeth but said nothing, leaving the Burned Hand to turn to me. "And you! Petulant little creature, I remember the irritation that you caused. Didn't you beg me to believe your false words?"

I couldn't find my voice. Couldn't reply.

"Do not worry. I shall save your tongues for last, so that you both might pray to your false gods in between bouts of scream-"

Tasir shot her once, the round skipping away when it struck the burning protection around her head. That made the false-priestess snap her head around, her snarl returning to her original target.

"Are you volunteering to die first, old fool?"

My Elder barked out a laugh, as if we weren't less than a yard away from simply being melted alive. "I know your type, bitch. You get off on torturing people that can't fight back. You need them to be weaker than you, you need them to scream."

The Burned hand scoffed. "I know your type as well. All controlling, all knowing. It is killing you to be here, to be helpless. To not know just who betrayed your pathetic little band."

"Not as much as it's going to kill you when I don't scream." Tasir sneered back. "You'll spend the rest of your miserable life knowing you couldn't break a crippled elder."

She slowed to a stop, scowling. "You're stalling for the others to escape. Devout! Go, clear the ship. Bring me the heads of all inside."

Three Faithful in full armor emerged from the ramp. Their equipment clattered as they began a run toward the ship's hatch, my heart feeling like a sinking stone in my chest. My rifle began to come up only for Tasir to drop her pistol, free hand snapping out to shove the weapon back down.

"Sir-"

"Not yet." She growled without looking away from the Burned Hand. Her hand stayed on my weapon, fingers loose.

"But-"

The deep rumble of the shuttle's power plant coming to life cut me off, a new wave of shouting from the soldiers cresting right behind it.

"Speaker! They've sealed the hatch!"

"Cut it open!" Came the furious reply. "You have power, do you not!?"

"Back." Tasir began taking slow, deep breaths, both of us retreating while the Burned Hand resumed her furious stalk. The heat of her sorcerous fire grew, the feel of it on my skin making my trembling grow worse.

"Break off from me when I say. Get home." Tasir ordered.

"Sir-"

Our executioner cackled, a hand flicking in our direction. A single tendril of flame lashed out, whipping along the Elder's arm. Her hide cloak hissed as it burned, the gray skin blackening beneath it. Tasir didn't make a sound, didn't react to the horrible burn. To the smell that nearly made me lose control.

"Her only home shall be death. As shall yours." Another flick sent a tendril at me.

I tried to be as stoic as the Director. Clenched my jaw when it curled across my belly, refusing to scream.

I couldn't stop the tears.

"The True Gods have no time for those who interfere." She spat. "There shall be no second life for you. Your only purpose, your only use shall be the way I arrange your corpses as a lesson to all unbelievers. To all those who refuse to bow."

Tasir let out a mocking scoff, still pulling me back. "Tough talk when you can't even make me flinch."

"...fine. The beast shall get to watch me break you before it is her turn." A sharp wave of her arm banished the fire around her, a Strike spell hammering me before I could even think about raising my weapon to shoot her.

It hammered me back, away from Tasir, my rifle tumbling from limp fingers when I slammed into a workbench. The blow knocked the air from my lungs, stopping me from screaming when I collapsed to the hard floor.

Shaking hands pushed me up to my knees, head rising to see Tasir staring down the Burned Hand a dozen paces away.

"Ashe'lori!" The Director barked without turning. "On your feet! It's time for you to leave!"

The Burned Hand glanced at me, rolled her eyes, then twisted at the hips to add power to the backhand she delivered to Tasir's face. The Elder staggered at the blow... then simply shook her head once to clear it, calling out once more.

"Up Lori! Now! Your Agent is waiting for your report!"

I obeyed, whispering the words. "Stubborn. Bloody stubbornness and determination. Up."

It was painful to stand up, to feel the fresh burn across my stomach moving. Cracking. The smell of it dragging out every nightmare I'd ever had.

Painful, but nothing so bad as the second lash of fire that Tasir took to a leg. A wound that should have left her howling in pain simply making her laugh, waving her mutilated hand toward the other Faithful as they scrambled back from the retracting ramp.

It slid into the hull with a clang, stopping them from breaching. Keeping Johanna and Irkan safe for a few more moments.

"Your soldiers can't seem to understand how a door works." Tasir mocked. "And yet you claim superiority?"

Above me the engines began a deeper rumble, the air turning hot as Irkan began to bring them up... and just a dozen yards away, the ramp on the other side dropped about halfway down. Just low enough that someone might have a chance of climbing onto it if they had a running start.

"As if they will go anywhere." My nightmare shook her head, calling up another lash of fire to rake down Tasir's wounded arm. Again the Elder did not flinch, did not react except to step closer, daring the other woman to do worse.

"Close the hangar!" The Burned Hand bellowed, "Close it now, while

269

I deal with this creature!"

Tasir waited until the fourth lash of fire was up, was stretching out to make her move. She lunged through it, uncaring of the flames that she'd just pushed her head through. Her working hand seized the Burned Hand's neck before the distracted woman could react, yanking her close.

"Lori! Run!"

They were the last words she said before she called on one last spell. Used up every last bit of energy she had within her soul.

I'd never seen the Wrath of Ashahn in person.

I prayed I never would again.

Tasir finally screamed as her own fire tore through her tarah, her entire body flashing out of existence within a single blink of an eye. An outline of the Elder's body remained in place for a barest moment, then the blue-white flame exploded outward, washing over the Burned Hand's howling form.

I ran for the half-lowered hatch as the Faithful shouted in alarm, as their leader writhed on the ground, her armor as blackened as her features. Her skin melting away, running down her face, body thrashing in uncontrolled agony.

Twelve yards.

Eight.

Four.

I leaped up, getting my hands on the metal, hauling myself onto it just as the gunfire began. Something tore at my left shin as it dangled, my arms burning with the strain of holding on.

Johanna's working arm grabbed at my wrist, pulling me the rest of the way up. "I have her! Go!"

The yacht trembled. Roaring engines were deafening, my left leg not working when I tried to stand. Johanna's desperate pulling had me crawl the rest of the way inside, letting her slam the hatch closed behind us.

270

"Wir müssen jetzt gehen!" She gasped. "Ashe! Tasir?"

I choked, shaking my head. "She's... she's gone. She..."

"Kommen!" Fingers yanked hard on my wrist. "Ashe! Irkan needs you! I can't read the controls to help!"

Johanna couldn't read Caranat. We... we were still escaping. I had to focus. We could still escape.

We could still tell everyone what had happened here.

"...help." Reaching up with my free hand, I slapped myself hard on the face, feeling the wetness of my tears. "Ashahn's blood... get a hold of yourself. Up."

Flexing my working leg, I managed to stand with Johanna's help. Get an arm around her neck. Hopping slowly down the hallway was painful each time my left foot struck the ground, which it did far too many times when Irkan brought the ship's hovering engines online.

We stumbled into the cockpit as the yacht's nose crept into the open air, our Mikiran pilot having shoved the chair back as far as it would go. Instead of sitting he was simply squatting before the controls, tapping them as quickly as his arms would allow.

His left arm was still bleeding, and I tried to get my leg up a bit higher just to make sure it didn't get into my new wound.

"The eldest?" He demanded without looking.

"...dead." I rasped.

His head snapped side to side, what must have been a curse in his own language escaping him. "Find the shields!"

"Get me into the seat on the right." I said.

Johanna did, quickly getting me settled. I looked over the array of controls, a sharp push of a button bringing up a control console. Glancing over it had me hit another button. "...shields coming up now. I think."

271

He grunted, pushing the throttle forward harder. "They are displayed on this one's left!"

I leaned back as best I could, looking around him. "I see it, they're up!"

"Good! Prepare the other-realm drive!"

"I don't know how-ack!" I hissed at the jab into my shoulder, "Johanna!"

"Painkillers." She said, pulling the pen back. Sure enough, a cold relief was already spreading, the agony in my stomach and leg fading away. "I've got patches too!"

"Later." I shook my head, trying to find the appropriate controls in the menu options. Trying to make sure Tasir's sacrifice wasn't in vain. "Uh... here. Starting FTL warm-up, activating the system!"

"Good." Irkan repeated, stabbing his own fingers down on other buttons. "Touch nothing else, savannas."

I nodded, Johanna clutching my seat as we stared out of the broad windows.

The Faithful's base was fully lit up in the night. Three massive barges sat in what had once been an empty landing field, what looked like a dozen shuttles parked beside them. Flashing gunfire was everywhere, the ground seemingly carpeted with still forms beneath the lights.

Here and there fires were burning. Some an honest orange and red. Most the unnatural blues of sorcery.

"...hundreds of them." Johanna whispered. "They killed hundreds of them."

The drugs didn't stop the pain in my chest. In my soul. I managed to get a hand up, finding hers. We squeezed tightly until Irkan pushed the throttle down further, pulling the nose up, turning away from the horror below to the star filled skies above.

We seemed to pick up speed, our pilot rumbling in approval as the ship ascended.

"There is one vessel still in orbit." He reported. "Another barge, it must have aborted its descent."

Johanna let out a ragged sound, "It's not a warship?"

"No." A clawed finger tapped another control. "The wings are extended. We must clear the world's shadow before we leave this realm. This sailor has shut down the ship's communications, there should be no risk of the Faithful taking control at a distance."

"...we're free?" I asked quietly.

Irkan's weight slowly settled back onto his haunches, his eyes closing.

"Yes." He rumbled softly. "This sailor believes we are."

None of us looked at one another as the last haze of Last Stop's atmosphere vanished.

As the only thing we could see through the haze of tears was the endless field of stars.

Appendix A: Imperial Intelligence Organization

Imperial Intelligence is an organization with two primary objectives; the supervision of internal security, and the protection of the Empire from foreign non-military actions.

Over the centuries it has become the primary refuge for those out of the box thinkers whose skills do not lie in military matters, or who simply do not make the cut to be assigned to a Void Fleet. This has led to it having something of a negative reputation as a 'dumping ground' for those too unskilled to make it in the armed forces.

This does them a disservice, as most Intelligence members are simply those who prefer a 'looser' means of serving the Empire, or who simply cannot abide letting things remain unknown. That such citizens are often those most comfortable operating with minimal supervision has given it a rather unique place within the Imperial framework.

Imperial DataNet Security Force

By far the largest department within Imperial Intelligence is the Imperial DataNet Security Force. As their name may suggest, their primary duty is the protection of the Imperial portion of the Galactic DataNet from hostile actors. Usually this means ensuring protection from other nations, but blocking hackers from criminal groups or overly ambitious Delne'lir also falls under their purview.

Slightly more surprising to outsiders is the fact that this department is also responsible for the physical upkeep and deployment of new FTL buoys to maintain communication through the Empire. Sub-departments handle this routine work, drafting contracts for upgraded models, and replacing those that have become worn out due to age or damage.

Every regional capital has enormous teams dedicated to monitoring and controlling traffic, while most worlds with a sufficient economic rating will have smaller teams.

As cyber-attacks from the Federation are an hourly occurrence, this department receives the most funding, manpower, and perks out of any of the Intelligence departments. This leaves their facilities as the most luxurious, and sought after, while also creating a quiet rivalry with those departments responsible for more traditional spy craft.

Contested Recon

The combat arm of Intelligence, Contested Recon controls what few warships and combat troops are directly assigned to Intelligence. As the organization itself lacks the manpower to maintain its own combat teams beyond a few elite Agent teams, the majority of these assets are on loan from the Army and Navy.

In the case of the former, these are usually conscript units that have shown some degree of promise in independent action during their early training. Their time with Contested Recon usually lasts for two or three decades, after which they will transfer to direct combat assignments or to supporting Void Fleet actions.

While most Conscripts would celebrate the chances for combat action that Contested Recon offers, the same cannot be said for the Naval crews assigned

Universally loaned Comet or Lurker vessels, Contested Recon is only ever assigned those ships capable of quiet action. As a result combat is something to be avoided at all costs. And the merits offered by Intelligence for discreet insertions and recoveries are rarely held in much esteem by the Navy at large.

Internal Observation

What passes for internal security is a shockingly lean organization by alien standards. Agents assigned to Internal Observation have a primary duty of locating and dealing with foreign agents, but also assist local security teams in investigating criminal groups that operate on a regional level.

Despite being recognized as critical, Internal Observation is often badly undermanned and underfunded. This is mostly due to the Trahcon dominated population.

Internal Agents are encouraged to have very small packs for security reasons, a restriction that makes many Trahcon chafe. Further, for every month spent traveling and seeing new sights, the Agent will spend upwards of

275

an entire year doing nothing but reading reports and compiling analysis.

Low recruitment thus forces an Agent and their packs to have to handle numerous duties at once, leading to long periods of separation that further hurt recruitment, creating a self-perpetuating loop. Many Directors and Coordinators are so short on available assets that they are forced to trade favors with one another; dispatching Agents between regions to assist on priority tasks in order to make up for their own deficits.

In recent years a dedicated effort aimed at recruiting among the alien minorities has begun to pay off, and the various Directors are hopeful that their resource shortages may be alleviated within a few decades.

Far Watch

If Internal Observation is lean and quick to accept any help it can get, then the Far Watch is truly desperate.

Acting as the foreign wing of Intelligence, the Far Watch controls those agents assigned to other nations. The bulk of these assets are in the Federation, with far smaller operations occurring in the Concordat, Near Reaches, and Far Reaches.

Their funding and ability to recruit local assets varies wildly depending upon the Empire's general outlook. During the run-up to the Near Reach campaigns they had a tremendous amount of funds available and were able to create sizable networks throughout the nations of the Reaches.

Sadly, once the general Imperial objectives were met, that funding dried up. Without it the Far Watch has retreated back into desperate improvisation, with individual Agents resorting to any tactic they can think of to gather actionable information. At their best, this can mean co-opting targets close to persons of interest or inserting mercenary assets into specific situations, operations that can result in useful data.

At their worst, Agents may find themselves holed up in bunkers, simply relaying whatever they see on the local news.

Appendix B: Imperial Intelligence Ranks

- **Asset**; Any conscript, civilian, or foreigner being paid, blackmailed, convinced to assist Intelligence on a temporary basis.
- **Supporter**: As per an Asset, but one that has either proven their loyalty or usefulness and is on long-term assignment.
- **Watcher**: The lowest official rank of an Intelligence officer, automatically given to members of an Agent's pack, and to graduates of an Imperial Academy who took the Intelligence program.
- **Analyst**: Second level officer, given to a Watcher who has been acknowledged to master a specialization.
- **Agent**: Second level officer, most often the pack-leader or most experienced member of a pack within intelligence. This is the first rank given independent assignments or command of specified projects.
- **Operative**: Third level officer, typically in operational command of four to eight Agents, depending upon the region in question.
- **Observer**: Designation for a senior-level Operative, but otherwise their duties are largely identical
- **Coordinator**: The highest level of 'field' officer, Coordinators are senior Observers responsible for overseeing projects deemed critical by their superior officers.
- **Director**: Head of a given system's Intelligence team within the Empire, or a sub-region in colonial or foreign stations.
- **Regional Lead**: Head of intelligence within a region of the Empire. In the Far Watch, they will be responsible for command of an entire nation-state or sector.
- **Oasis Commander**: One degree higher than a regional observer, Oasis Commanders make up the command staff of Intelligence as a whole. They determine the budgets for each department, and appoint one of their member as the Head of Observation.
- **Head of Observation**: Appointed by the Oasis Commanders, the Head of Observation is less the 'leader' of Intelligence as a whole, and more the designated liaison to the Torlah, Supreme Command, and Imperial Circle.

www.ingramcontent.com/pod-product-compliance
Lightning Source LLC
Chambersburg PA
CBHW031425200626
46814CB00016B/2164